THE
BLUSH FACTOR

Praise for Gun Brooke's Fiction

Fierce Overture

"Gun Brooke creates memorable characters, and Noelle and Helena are no exception. Each woman is "more than meets the eye" as each exhibits depth, fears, and longings. And the sexual tension between them is real, hot, and raw."—*Just About Write*

Coffee Sonata

"In *Coffee Sonata*, the lives of these four women become intertwined. In forming friendships and love, closets and disabilities are discussed, along with differences in age and backgrounds. Love and friendship are areas filled with complexity and nuances. Brooke takes her time to savor the complexities while her main characters savor their excellent cups of coffee. If you enjoy a good love story, a great setting, and wonderful characters, look for Coffee Sonata at your favorite gay and lesbian bookstore."
—*Family & Friends Magazine*

Sheridan's Fate

"Sheridan's fire and Lark's warm embers are enough to make this book sizzle. Brooke, however, has gone beyond the wonderful emotional explorations of these characters to tell the story of those who, for various reasons, become differently-abled. Whether it is a bullet, an illness, or a problem at birth, many women and men find themselves in Sheridan's situation. Her courage and Lark's gentleness and determination send this romance into a 'must read.'"—*Just About Write*

Course of Action

"Brooke's words capture the intensity of their growing relationship. Her prose throughout the book is breathtaking and heart-stopping. Where have you been hiding, Gun Brooke? I, for one, would like to see more romances from this author."—*Independent Gay Writer*

September Canvas

"In this character-driven story, trust is earned and secrets are uncovered. Deanna and Faythe are fully fleshed out and prove to the reader each has much depth, talent, wit and problem-solving abilities. *September Canvas* is a good read with a thoroughly satisfying conclusion."—*Just About Write*

The Supreme Constellations Series

"*Protector of the Realm* has it all; sabotage, corruption, erotic love and exhilarating space fights. Gun Brooke's second novel is forceful with a winning combination of solid characters and a brilliant plot. The book exemplifies her growth as an inventive storyteller and is [sure] to garner multiple awards in the coming year."—*Just About Write*

"Brooke is an amazing author, and has written in other genres. Never have I read a book where I started at the top of the page and don't know what will happen two paragraphs later. She keeps the excitement going, and the pages turning."—*MegaScene*

Visit us at www.boldstrokesbooks.com

By the Author

Course of Action

Coffee Sonata

Sheridan's Fate

September Canvas

Fierce Overture

Speed Demons

Change Horizons

The Blush Factor

The Supreme Constellations series:

Protector of the Realm

Rebel's Quest

Warrior's Valor

Pirate's Fortune

THE
BLUSH FACTOR

by

Gun Brooke

2014

THE BLUSH FACTOR

ISBN 13: 978-1-60282-985-5

THIS TRADE PAPERBACK ORIGINAL IS PUBLISHED BY
BOLD STROKES BOOKS, INC.
P.O. BOX 249
VALLEY FALLS, NY 12185

FIRST EDITION: FEBRUARY 2014

CREDITS

EDITOR: SHELLEY THRASHER
PRODUCTION DESIGN: SUSAN RAMUNDO
COVER ART BY GUN BROOKE
COVER DESIGN BY SHERI (GRAPHICARTIST2020@HOTMAIL.COM)

Acknowledgments

This story means so much to me. Of course, all my stories are special to me in their own right, but this one lived with me a long time before I wrote it, and I thought about the characters afterward, more than usual. I have a certain affinity for May-December pairings—not sure why—and this is very much the case in this romance. Age is not an issue, unless when it is, if you understand what I mean. Love knows no numbers, but reality checks can be harsh, and when two people have such different outlooks on life, and different statuses as a whole, love has to be really strong to smooth out the grooves.

I've been blessed by being surrounded by several people who help me smooth things out on a professional level. Len Barot aka Radclyffe, who appears ready to take a chance even on my more unorthodox ideas, sometimes. You are absolutely great, and I hope you know how much your faith in me means to me.

Dr. Shelley Thrasher, my editor for twelve novels now... where did all the years go and all the books come from? You are my safety net, my teacher, and my friend.

Everyone associated with helping me make this novel the best possible—Sheri, Stacia, Cindy, Lori, Sandy, et al—you are amazing and I appreciate all of your hard work.

As always, I have people around me who are invaluable when it comes to helping me by reading through my manuscript before I send it in to BSB.

Laura, Texas—you had a total understanding of these characters and, like me, especially adored Stacey. Maggie, Stockholm—your interest in my writing combined with the best of friendships was inspiring. Sami, South Africa—my friend and longtime first reader, your comments added their own flavor. Eden, Arizona—meticulously, you helped me find foolish grammar mistakes and strange wordings. All four of you—thank you for rescuing me from embarrassing mistakes and for offering your opinion and encouragement.

My family and close friends, what would I do without you? You always express your pride in my writing, and when it comes to Elon, without your never-ending love, your support and the way you cook, I would not fare very well. My kids, Malin and Henrik, you always show your joy when each new book is published, and that gives everything that special magical dimension. My brother Ove and his Monica, my son-in-in law Pentti, my extended family in the USA, Joanne, Carol, and Francis—you all express your support on a continual basis.

Last, but perhaps most important of all, you, my beloved readers. I love every note, Facebook greeting, Twitter, Tumblr, and e-mail you send me. If I can provide some entertainment and/or escapism for you, that's a truly humbling feeling. Thank you from the bottom of my heart.

Dedication

For Malin and Henrik
My brave children

For Alexandra and Angelica
My wonderful granddaughters

CHAPTER ONE

Something about this young woman made it impossible
for Eleanor to merely close her laptop and stop watching.
Eleanor noticed the nearly transparent hazel eyes immediately. A
charming band of freckles danced across her nose, which, together
with her full, soft, pink mouth, gave her an aura of innocence. Her
blinding smile, wide and guilelessly open, pulled Eleanor in. She
called herself "Blush," and this girl seemed to know everything
about makeup, hair, and skin products—anything related to
beauty. Blush acted so natural in front of the camera, whether
at her vanity or in any other room in her home. Her voice was
melodious and her laughter contagious.

Eleanor had found this woman's channel on YouTube while
searching for the beauty gurus that had the most subscribers. With
more than 350,000 subscribers and millions upon millions of hits
on her more than five hundred clips, Blush was among the most
successful. Young girls and women couldn't seem to get enough
of her advice, her reviews, or her tutorials. Eleanor snorted. She
was no different. This was the third evening in a row she'd sat for
hours, thinking she would click on just one more link, watch one
more clip of this fresh-faced young woman. So she did, like an
addict.

Blush's intro played and her now-familiar face came into
view. Her hair in a ponytail and with no makeup on, she seemed to

be wearing only a bathrobe, which made Eleanor swallow twice. Frowning, she tried to focus on what Blush was saying.

"Hello, you wonderful people," Blush said, waving. "It's been a whole week, I know, and I'm sorry. Real life entered and I had to…deal with stuff." A shadow flickered across her features but was gone so fast Eleanor knew she would be replaying the clip later to see if she'd imagined it.

"Today I thought I'd show you how you can look better for less. I know we all love the expensive brands, but hey, most of us can't afford them. I can't, normally. Some of the high-end brands send me samples and new products to test, but you know my rule: if I didn't buy it, it's not going on my channel. I usually end up giving those items away to charity. The sealed ones, that is." She shrugged, a funny little jerking movement of her left shoulder. "I built this channel by earning your trust, guys, and I'm not going to ruin that by being greedy. So, here's my idea for a nice look for work that can easily morph into a nighttime look if you don't have time to go home and change."

Blush expertly put on a neutral makeup, using brands Eleanor had never heard of, as she didn't buy her makeup at the pharmacy or the local grocery store. No matter what she used, Blush looked stunning. She chatted about everything and anything while she applied her makeup, giggling when she made a mistake with the liquid eyeliner, but then turned that into a lesson in itself, showing how to remove and reapply.

Once she was done, Blush leaned closer to the camera, turning her head every which way to show off the result. "There, you see? Isn't that color gorgeous? Remember, this goes with most eye colors, especially green and brown, of course, but anyone can rock this look." Smiling broadly, she suddenly looked off camera. "Yes. I'm recording. Yes, I'll be done soon. Go back to bed, honey."

Eleanor sat up, frowning. Was that a husband? A boyfriend?

"Sorry, guys. My sister needs my help, so I'd better wrap this up. I'll be uploading a new clip tomorrow that I shot today when I got some new things in the mail. I know you love those haul videos." She smiled broadly and there it was again, that shadow that slipped across her features without warning. "If you have questions or want to request videos, you can write me via the YouTube messaging service. If you have a professional issue or question, feel free to use my business e-mail below. Night-night!" Blush waved again, and the screen went black for a second before the YouTube default setting appeared.

Eleanor had a lot to think about. She copied Blush's e-mail address into her contacts, knowing she needed to approach this young woman. Inheriting an old makeup company that had been waning for almost thirty years, mismanaged by none other than her father, Eleanor needed an innovative approach to turning around its fortunes. Social media had been a revelation, and she'd joined Facebook, Twitter, Tumblr, and YouTube using a pseudonym. Now that she was about to contact Blush, she'd have one of her assistants use the company e-mail. In the meantime, she'd keep researching what young women, and men, for that matter, thought of modern beauty products.

She finally closed her laptop, rose from the large armchair by the window, and padded over to her bed. It was way past midnight, and she had several meetings lined up before lunch the next day. As she climbed into the king-size bed and settled against the down pillows, she closed her eyes, completely exhausted. Even so, hazel eyes and a smiling pink mouth appeared in her mind. The perfect complexion, the quick, tapered fingertips that applied makeup with sure strokes, and the voice...

Eleanor huffed impatiently and rolled onto her side. "I need to sleep." The laughing young woman only nodded at her in her mind and stuck her tongue out to the side as she painted a perfectly winged eye line. "Oh, God. I must be going mad." Eleanor tugged yet another down pillow close and gave in to whatever her mind was set on displaying. She knew better than to fight it. Sleep would come eventually.

❖

"My head hurts today." Stacey showed up in her pink flannel pajamas, holding her left temple. "I still gotta be in school. Mr. Geller is posting the final result of the auditions."

"And you want to be Elphaba." Addie Garr looked affectionately at her younger sister. She remembered with both terror and nostalgia being a junior in high school. "Do you know any of the ones auditioning for Glinda?" The glee club was producing *Wicked—the Musical* for spring, and five girls, her sister among them, were in the running to play Elphaba. The fact that her head hurt again was worrisome though.

"Yes, one of them. Charlene is in my French class. She's really good. I think she'll get it, unless Mr. Geller is suddenly tone deaf."

"Has he shown any such tendencies?" Addie poured herself some coffee and then pulled some extra-strength Tylenol from a cabinet. "Here. Take two. If we nip it in the bud, you can still make it today."

"Ugh. I hate swallowing pills, but I don't have any choice, do I?" Stacey made a disgusted face and swallowed the capsules. "Yuck."

Addie checked the calendar. Stacey needed surgery as soon as possible, and she still had no idea how to come up with enough money for the rehab. Medicaid paid for the basic care, but the doctor had emphasized how vital it was for Stacey to have a topnotch physical therapist. Not just once a week at the clinic, but every single day during the first weeks. If not, she would in all likelihood miss out on most of her junior year and definitely wouldn't be playing Elphaba in *Wicked*.

Addie's stomach hurt at the thought of it all, and she still hadn't told Stacey the cold facts. She'd been running a virtual persuasion campaign directed at her bank contact to get a loan, even if she didn't have any collateral or equity. Miracles could still happen, couldn't they?

"I'll just grab a banana now and get something more at school later, okay?" Stacey said as she put on her jacket. "If I go now, I can ride with Maureen and her mom. The school bus sucks when my head hurts."

"I know, honey. Thank Mrs. Henderson properly."

"Yeah, yeah. Always do, sis." Stacey gave her a hug as she passed her on her way to grab her backpack. "Good luck with today's makeup session. Any new pervs sending you stuff?"

"You brat. And no. Well, I haven't checked my mail since noon yesterday. So who knows? I promise I'll let you know when you get home."

"I'll text you when I know about the part."

"Can't wait!" Addie waved as Stacey walked out the door and down the narrow path to the curb, where an SUV had just pulled up. She watched through the window as Stacey climbed in and hugged her friend Maureen. They'd known each other since they were four.

Opening her e-mails, she was once again very glad she had a great filter system. It was wonderful to get what Stacey called "Addie's fan mail," and she tried to answer most of it, but she usually had to resort to some automatic-response version. No way could she write hundreds of individual e-mails every day. She still thought it was totally surreal that she received e-mails from total strangers who felt they knew her.

She shifted her gaze to the folder where anything business-related ended up. Three new e-mails. She clicked on the folder, hoping it wasn't the usual "endorse our product and we'll send you all the mascara you'll ever need" kind of e-mail.

The first two e-mails were just that, and Addie sighed deeply as she clicked on the third. It was from the president of a company, Face Exquisite. Addie frowned, tapping her lower lip. The name of the company was familiar. A quick search via Google confirmed that it was a makeup brand. It used to be highly regarded, but most people now thought of it as a brand for older women, loyal customers stuck in a rut, who wouldn't change brand regardless.

What could Face Exquisite want from her? Addie made it perfectly clear that she was mainly about the affordable drugstore brands and such. Sipping her coffee, she began to read.

Dear Ms. "Blush,"

My name is Eleanor Ashcroft, President of Face Exquisite and also of the Ashcroft Group, a conglomerate of companies located all over the Eastern Seaboard. I have a business proposal for you.

I am not asking you to endorse any products, but rather to consult with us and help us bring forward new, exciting beauty products under the Face Exquisite label. As you might be aware, being self-employed as a consultant is financially beneficial and would allow you to keep up the excellent work on your YouTube channel.

If this proposal interests you, please call my assistant to set up an appointment. If you are located far from New York, we would be happy to cover any expenses you might have to fly here.

You will find all the details you need to contact us below.

Yours sincerely,
Eleanor Ashcroft

Back on Google, Addie instantly found the information about Eleanor Ashcroft she wanted. The woman was not only stunningly beautiful, but she was also extraordinarily wealthy. The official photo of her on the Ashcroft Group's website showed a woman of indeterminate age, perhaps her forties. Short blond hair, kept in a stylish, wavy hairdo, barely touched her earlobes. Perfectly groomed eyebrows framed clear gray eyes. Her face, with its high cheekbones and slightly square jawline, suggested strength of character.

Skimming through the short biography on the official site, which really didn't say a lot other than that Ms. Ashcroft was single and very successful, Addie then turned to other, more gossipy sites. There she read that Eleanor Ashcroft was infamous for being a direct, no-nonsense, and not always very well-liked woman. She knew what she wanted and made sure she obtained her goal, whether in business or otherwise. What this "otherwise" entailed wasn't quite clear, but perhaps the powerful businesswoman was used to landing the man she wanted for the moment as well. Maybe a barracuda both in and out of bed? Could Addie see herself being associated with someone like that?

She reread the e-mail and kept returning to the sentence that spoke of their potential collaboration being financially beneficial. Was this the answer to her prayers? Was this Stacey's chance to get the rehab she'd need?

As a barista at Starbucks, Addie didn't make enough to support them and keep the house, but the extra income from the ads on her YouTube channel filled in the gaps unless something unforeseen happened. Their father's life insurance had been enough until Stacey became ill. It was a blessing that it had made it possible for them to keep the house after the accident. As usual, the thought of her parents made Addie's stomach tremble. She pushed the images to the back of her mind.

Addie checked her watch. She was on the late shift today. No matter what, she needed to keep her annoying weasel of a boss happy until she found something else. Impulsively, she pulled the keyboard closer and began typing.

Dear Ms. Ashcroft,

My name is Addison Garr, but you know me as "Blush." Thank you for writing me with your suggestion. As you might realize, I get a lot of e-mail from viewers and quite a few suggestions from makeup companies that want my endorsement, which I'm hesitant to give—unless I found and paid for the product myself.

I admit you have caught my attention with your e-mail, though, and I will be calling your assistant—Ms. Fuller, was it?— to see if we can find a date that works for both of us.

I live in Newark, so I'm just across the Hudson. No airline ticket required.

Looking forward to meeting you, Ms. Ashcroft!

Yours sincerely,
Addison Garr a.k.a. Blush

CHAPTER TWO

Addison cursed the train as it slowed down and came to a halt again. Glancing at her watch, she realized if this kept up, she'd be late despite having given herself plenty of time to make her meeting. Desperate to call the restaurant, she checked her cell and cursed the nonexistent bars of the connectivity indicator. Eleanor Ashcroft was probably entering Aquavit, a posh, very trendy Scandinavian restaurant, at this very moment. If she thought Addison had stood her up, she'd be pissed off big-time and retract her offer in a flash. The thought of missing out on the opportunity to make some real money made her nauseous. She hadn't yet told Stacey about this new development, as she didn't want her to be heartbroken if it didn't pan out.

True to her nature, Addison had researched Eleanor Ashcroft and her company further and had actually come across a few clips of her on YouTube. One clip showed her giving the commencement speech at Harvard Business School two years ago. The woman was charismatic, in an intimidating sort of way. She exercised considerable charm while addressing the graduates, but also nailed them with icy gray eyes, as if challenging them. She hadn't said, "If you don't live up to your potential, I'll blacklist you in the business world," but that was what Addison took away from her speech. What would it be like to be the sole recipient of that laser-like focus? Addison shuddered. Unless the train remained stuck forever on the damn track, she'd find out soon.

❖

Eleanor checked her Rolex and frowned. Addison Garr was almost fifteen minutes late. She wasn't sure why she wasn't adhering to her usual rule: wait ten minutes and, if the person guilty of tardiness had still not shown up, leave. Tapping her glass of mineral water with perfectly manicured blunt nails, she glanced out over the restaurant patrons.

Hasty steps made Eleanor turn her head toward the entrance. Addison hurried toward her, her long auburn hair fluttering freely around an expertly made-up face. Of course.

"Ms. Ashcroft? Oh, God, I'm so sorry. The train ran into some problems and just *stopped*, and I didn't even have a chance to jump off and run here. I swear I left Newark on time. I'm usually never late." Addison stood next to the table, fidgeting with the shoulder strap of her pale-tan purse. The faux leather had cracks along the creases and clearly wasn't new. She was dressed in black leggings and a long dark-green knitted top, its large neckline slightly off her right shoulder.

"Have a seat, Ms. Garr." Eleanor gestured at the chair across from her. "I took the liberty of ordering something for both of us to be served upon your arrival." She watched as Addison hurriedly sat down after folding her jacket over the backrest. "I normally don't wait if someone is late, but I'm also aware of this city's unreliable transportation system."

"Thank you for being so understanding. And please, call me Addie. Everybody does."

"By all means. I'm Eleanor." She raised an eyebrow deliberately, knowing full well the effect this had on people. "Nobody calls me Ellie."

"Ever?" Addison smiled shyly, but she didn't seem intimidated, which was a surprise.

"Ever."

A waiter arrived with their salads, which gave Eleanor a chance to observe Addison as she communicated with the young man. Her smile was kind, but not flirtatious. She was obviously polite and well brought up, and even though the young man fawned over her, Addison seemed more interested in the food.

"This looks wonderful," Addison said to Eleanor. She pushed her fork through a piece of apple, dipped it in the dressing, and put it in her mouth, actually whimpering as she chewed it. "Apple, blue cheese…and this vinaigrette…mmm." She smiled. "Awesome."

Eleanor had dined at Aquavit many times and, she admitted, become somewhat jaded by the fantastic food, though she still enjoyed it, of course. Watching the young woman across the table, clearly in a blissful state over a mere salad, she wondered if she'd ever been that young and impressionable. She was pretty sure she'd never been that unknowingly sensual.

"First time at Aquavit, I presume?" Eleanor began eating her own salad. The melding of flavors was exquisite, and she nearly hummed too.

"Oh, for sure. I've heard about this place, though. I mean, even Obama comes here. Slightly out of my price range, to be blunt." Addison looked with some sorrow at the quickly disappearing salad.

"Don't worry. This is a two-course meal." Eleanor felt her mouth curl into a smile against her will.

"I admit I'm famished. Too busy today to eat anything. Just a mug of coffee this morning and that was it. You'd imagine I'd be sick of coffee by now, but really, who can get sick of the best hot beverage known to mankind?" Addison quieted, her flawless forehead furrowing. "Unless you're more of a tea person?"

"I dislike tea." Eleanor couldn't remember anyone daring to talk to her like this young woman did. Why wasn't she intimidated? Nervous, yes, but not scared and panicky.

"Me too." Smiling more broadly now, Addison showed more of her YouTube persona, Blush, with each passing moment.

"Why do you call yourself Blush?"

"When I decided to create my own channel, Stacey insisted that it needed a really cool and catchy name. We made list after list, even going so far as to create an Excel document and matching up words. Eventually Stacey came up with The Blush Factor. It covers so much. Blush as in makeup, blush as in how flustered I was at being on camera.

"The word 'factor' hints at the old makeup brand, Max Factor, which I used to buy all the time before they stopped selling it in the U.S. And from that, I chose Blush as my nickname because I don't want people to know my real name. Plenty of weirdoes out there."

"And Stacey is?"

"Stacey is my younger sister. She lives with me."

"Younger, you say? How much younger?"

"She's a junior in high school." Snapping her head up, Addison looked alarmed. "Is that going to be an issue? I mean, my having responsibilities and such?"

Blinking, Eleanor was taken aback by the panic in Addison's eyes. "I don't see why. Do you foresee a problem?"

"No. No, not at all." Addison smiled weakly. "It's just… some employers do when they learn of someone my age caring for a teenage girl."

"I wouldn't be your employer. I'd be your client." Eleanor leaned back when she'd finished her salad, and immediately the attentive waiter was there to remove her plate. Addison had finished hers, and he smiled warmly at the young woman as he cleared her plate as well.

Addison returned the smile, then turned her attention back at Eleanor. "That's true." She seemed to ponder this while sipping her water. "I did a bit of research. I wasn't aware that Face Exquisite belonged to your conglomerate."

"It doesn't. It's an independent company that used to belong to a relative of mine. I inherited it and found it needed a complete overhaul. Admittedly, the beauty industry isn't something I've had cause to look into before, which means I need to surround myself with the right people."

"And you really think I can do this? From watching some of my YouTube vids?" Addison seemed astonished.

"All of them." Eleanor cursed herself for admitting to that. At least she hadn't revealed how many times she'd seen some of them. "I wanted to determine for myself the reason behind your success. Having so many subscribers and that many hits—it's not commonplace."

"God, I have to pinch myself every day. I mean, I'm just a regular girl from Newark, serving coffee as my day job."

"Serving coffee?" Eleanor had raised her glass to sip her water but halted halfway to her lips.

"I'm a barista at Starbucks in NewPark Mall."

"I was under the impression you did The Blush Factor full time." Eleanor was seething. A barista? Heads were going to roll in her research department.

The waiter returned with their main course, Penobscot chicken breast, and seemed to notice the deteriorating mood. He murmured, "Enjoy your dinner, ladies," and left quickly.

"I've thought about quitting Starbucks, but I need the money and the insurance. If it had been just me, fine, but I have Stacey. I can't risk not being able to provide for her." Her shoulders slumping now, Addison pushed the food around listlessly. "You seem disappointed."

Eleanor regarded Addison and saw her close her eyes hard for a second before sitting up and squaring her shoulders. This impressed her most of all. Addison seemed sure Eleanor was retracting the offer and was trying to not look devastated.

"I'm not. Just taken aback, a feeling that every single person working for me can testify doesn't sit well with me." Eleanor motioned toward Addison's plate. "Eat while it's hot. I think you'll enjoy it."

"So, you're still interested in using me. I mean, my expertise?" Addison cut off a piece of the chicken and placed a piece of butternut squash on top before placing it in her mouth. Her full lips closed around the bite and she hummed as she chewed.

"Yes."

Addison swallowed quickly. "Oh, good." The relief was obvious as she lit up. "I suppose you'll have to tell me what you want from me. Need. Advice for new makeup? Insight into what's current? Trends? An evaluation of existing lines?"

"That's a good start." Eleanor put down her utensils. "I take it you've heard of Face Exquisite. Have you ever used any of its products?"

"Eh...no." Addison shrugged apologetically. "They're too pricey for me, and, to be honest, they're not made with women my age in mind. I mean, I remember my grandma using stuff like that. Even my mom thought it was, uh, meant for the older generations."

Eleanor wanted to strangle her father. When he took over the company, Face Exquisite had been the preferred brand among models, actresses, and celebrities. How the hell had he been able to run it into the ground to such a degree that even women her generation and older thought it was a brand for senior citizens?

"I mean, nothing wrong with that," Addison said contritely, "if that's what you're going for. Some people only trust one brand and stick with it all their lives. But if you want to expand the demographic for your products, you have a tough journey ahead."

"And you know this because...?" Eleanor was aware her voice had sunk to a very frosty octave.

"Because I know makeup. I know the women and girls who buy it." Addison had answered calmly and then finished her entree. "Surely you realize this, or you wouldn't waste your time on a beauty guru from Newark."

Addison had guts. Eleanor wasn't sure how it had happened, but she seemed to have stumbled upon one of the few people she didn't automatically intimidate. Sure, if she tried, she could probably scare the living daylights out of the girl, but Addison's direct and open glance showed promise.

"Very well. Do you have an attorney?"

"Um, in a manner of speaking. My friend's older brother is a lawyer, and he helped me when I started earning money from YouTube."

"Then I suggest you bring him with you when you come to my offices next week to sign your contract."

"Okay. The only thing I know about contracts is never to sign anything without reading it first."

Eleanor had to smile. "That's the cardinal rule. If you get back to me in a few days with information on your fees, I can have my attorney work it in. That way we save time. I want to get this show on the road as soon as possible."

"Fees. Okay." Addison nodded, then brightened. "I look forward to this. I love makeup, as you might have guessed." She laughed, sounding a little breathless.

The sound of Addison's nervous laughter, paired with the enthusiasm she radiated, sent a pleasant shiver through Eleanor. She couldn't fathom what it was about this woman young enough to be her daughter that made her respond like this. Whatever it was, she needed to get a grip before it got in the way of business.

As Eleanor took care of the bill after texting her driver, she harnessed that rebellious part of herself that found Addison utterly charming. Instead she put on her game face, slamming it in place with a force that actually hurt. This was about saving Priscilla's company, about undoing what Eleanor's father had done to his only sister. She couldn't let any odd, unwelcome attraction get in the way of that. As she said a stern good-bye to Addison, she could tell the other woman sensed the difference.

"Thank you for lunch, Eleanor. See you next week." Addison shook her hand and blinked as her smile was left unreciprocated.

Eleanor strode out of Aquavit and found where her driver was idling. Getting in the car, she took a deep breath.

"The office." The driver pulled into traffic just as Addison stepped out of the restaurant. She was on the phone with someone, smiling widely and gesturing descriptively in the air, as if the person on the other end of the conversation could actually see her. Her long hair fanned out in the wind as she skipped along the sidewalk a few steps. The New Yorkers just walked on by as if they saw nothing odd about anyone jumping for joy.

No. Eleanor pressed her lips together. She had to remember, no matter how lovely this woman was, Eleanor Ashcroft did not let anything get in the way of business.

CHAPTER THREE

W ell?" Stacey's dark-chocolate curls bounced around her face as she leaped into the hallway. "What did she say? Was she as scary as the papers make her out to be? I saw a clip of her and she's stunning, isn't she?"

Addison had to laugh at her antics. Ever since Stacey had found out she was going to play Elphaba, her energy levels had spiked. She sang around the house until Addison had to bribe her to be quiet when she was shooting her makeup vids.

"She was...quite extraordinary. I don't think she's scary. At least she wasn't today, but she's very no-nonsense. I can see how she might intimidate people. No way I'd ever go into a meeting with her unprepared."

"And is she as hot as in those pictures from the *Forbes* article?"

"What *Forbes* article?" Addison hung up her jacket. "What are you talking about?"

"I did what you did. Googled her. I found an interview they did last year. Here, come see, and you have to tell me *everything*." She dragged Addison toward her room.

Addison's heart filled with joy at the happiness in Stacey's eyes. Stacey had spent so much time clutching her head in utter agony that seeing her this excited was amazing. "I was late, so I was really nervous. I thought she'd string me up or something, but as it turned out, she was kind of cool. Demanding, yes, but that's to be expected. I think I pissed her off at one point, but for some reason she decided to overlook that. Didn't seem like her usual MO, but—"

"She must really want you." Stacey brought a second chair to the desk. "Keep talking. I'll pull up the pictures."

"Well, toward the end, she became kind of frosty, for some reason. Not sure what that was about, but I'm going to take Peter with me to negotiate fees, hours, that sort of thing. If the time commitment is more than thirty hours per week, I'll have to cut back my hours at Starbucks."

"Quit."

"What?"

"You heard me, sis. Quit." Stacey turned and smiled broadly. "This is your chance to do what you love. Between the consulting and what you earn from YouTube, it'll be enough to make a living for us."

"Not only that. I'll be able to get that physical therapist Dr. Reimer talked about. You won't miss out on most of your junior year."

Stacey stopped typing. "Really?" Her voice was suddenly small, like a child's. "I really have been worried for...I know it's ridiculous and I should think about the academic part first, but I've been so worried I'd miss out on playing Elphaba."

Fighting back tears at Stacey's hopeful expression, Addison put an arm around her. "Honey, I understand. I really do. I couldn't carry a tune if my life depended on it, but if I could, and if I burned for music like I do for my channel, I would have freaked out too."

"So she's going to pay you well enough to do this?" Stacey sucked her cheeks in, a telltale sign she was close to crying.

"Yes. So, come on. Where are those pics?" Distracting Stacey, Addison motioned toward the screen.

"Oh, yeah. Here. She's a looker!"

Addison merely stared. These were professional photos and the camera *loved* Eleanor Ashcroft. The first photo showed Eleanor dressed in a soft blue-gray pantsuit and a white silk blouse. She was smiling faintly but didn't look very friendly. More of a shark smile, really. In the second picture, she wore a dark-maroon skirt suit, the jacket unbuttoned and showing off a deeply cut, cream wrap-around blouse. She was half-sitting against an antique desk with one leg bent; the way the pose showed off her legs and Louboutin pumps was insanely sexy.

Realizing where her mind was going, Addison reeled herself in. She couldn't go into this business deal thinking her future client was sexy and attractive. That's when Stacey clicked the third and last picture. Here Eleanor was outside, leaning against a black BMW, the driver's door open as if she was just about to say good-bye and leave. Her sleeveless, form-fitted, red dress hugged her without being tight, and her red sandals matched it perfectly.

"Holy smoke." Addison blinked and kept looking.

"Need a drool bucket, sis?" Stacey said in a fake angelic voice. "You can't sit around with your tongue hanging out while you're in meetings with her."

"I'm not drooling and my tongue is where it's supposed to be."

"I could say something really crude, but I won't." Stacey laughed. "All jokes aside, Addie, you're staring at her like she's prime real estate or something."

"Oh, you're so funny. Not."

Stacey stuck her tongue out and then looked back at the screen. "She's amazing, and I'm not a lesbian. She's totally hot."

"Just because I'm a lesbian doesn't mean I find all types of women hot." Addison sighed.

"I know that!" Stacey punched her shoulder lightly. "And you know that I know."

"I do."

"So?"

"What?" Addison understood what Stacey was asking but wasn't sure she could, or would, answer it truthfully.

"Oh, come on. I've never seen you act or look this way when it comes to any woman. She triggers something. Tell me I'm lying."

"You're…you're not lying." Covering her eyes with her hand, Addison moaned. "She's really something, in more ways than one. I was already aware that she was stunning." She lowered her hand and looked at the photo of Eleanor again. "Then I stumble into that restaurant, all winded, sweaty, and *late*, and she's sitting there. Calm, cool, rather acerbic, and gorgeous. I swear her eyes were like sparkling icicles. She was only wearing very light makeup, very classy."

"Trust you to notice that."

"Brat."

"So, go on."

Addison squinted and tilted her head. "I should just drop this. Erase it from my mind and be totally professional. I'm going to advise her company. I'm sure I won't be working anywhere near her, really, but I should still make sure I regard her only as a client."

"Uh-huh. Sure. That'll work." Stacey snorted. "You have no idea you just licked your lips, do you?"

"What? I didn't."

"Did too. Like this." Stacey licked her own lips slowly and with an exaggeratedly blissful roll of her eyes.

"Oh, you awful brat!" Digging her fingertips into Stacey's side, Addison tickled her. "Take that back."

Squealing with laughter, Stacey tried to escape the sisterly punishment, but Addison had found the secret spot that would render her sister helpless with laughter and continued to tickle her.

"I give up. I give up."

Addison chortled and stopped the tickle attack. "See what happens to liars?"

"I may have exaggerated, but the licking-lips part wasn't a lie." Stacey swiftly moved out of reach. "You did do that."

Somehow, this time Addison believed her. "God. I'm screwed if I let the least bit of this…this, whatever, instant crush, show."

"I could be really crude now, but that would only get me grounded, so I won't—ah!" Diving out of her room, Stacey hurried into the bathroom and locked the door. "I was kidding, I was kidding!" She laughed so hard she could barely speak.

Addison couldn't keep from chuckling. Stacey was a bit of a rascal, that much was true, but to see her have a really good day was worth everything. She tapped on the door. "Don't think you're safe forever. You still have to help with dinner, and you never know when I'll get my revenge."

"Oh, yes, I do. As soon as you start cooking, your revenge begins."

Addison guffawed at Stacey's quick wit. Her lack of skill in the kitchen was legendary, but at least she hadn't poisoned anyone yet. "Oh, please. I'll have mercy on you and make spaghetti and meat sauce. That stuff you like. From a can?"

"Oh, thank the Lord." Stacey opened the door and suddenly Addison found herself wrapped up in a fierce hug. "Thank you."

"No need to go overboard. It's just pasta with canned meat sauce." Addison patted Stacey's back. "Isn't it?"

"Yeah. That and the fact that you're taking this step, this amazing leap into the unknown. I know you're doing it for me. I mean, you would've had to launch a career since so many subscribers and viewers love you, but...it's because of me that you're doing it now."

"Hey, don't worry, honey. I'm excited about this opportunity. Yes, I confess I'd work in the sewers if it meant getting you the best physical therapist, but now I get to work with what I love. It's not exactly a sacrifice on my part, Stace."

"Perhaps. In a way I think it is." Stacey began to pull Addison toward the kitchen. "You're quitting a steady job, albeit not your dream job exactly, to go into business on your own with all it brings with it. I'm glad Peter will be able to help you. Just let the poor guy down easy, okay? He's totally into you."

"What?" Addison turned around so fast she nearly smacked her head on the pantry door she'd just opened. "Peter? You're joking."

"Uh-uh. He looks like a pitiful St. Bernard whenever he and Janet come over. Haven't you ever wondered why he hangs with the two of you? He's hoping he'll be the one who makes you switch teams."

"Oh, God." Closing her eyes, Addison rested weakly against the pantry door for a moment. "Well, no matter, I'll just keep things very professional—"

"And where have I heard this before? Hmm? Oh, yeah, in my room a few minutes ago when someone told me she'd be very professional when *she* has the hots for her new client. I see a trend here."

"And I see a teenager who'll be cooking the rest of the week if she doesn't quit the smart-ass routine." Narrowing her eyes deliberately, Addison gave Stacey her best glare before she pulled out the pasta, smiling at Stacey's yelp.

"All right, all right. I won't mention anything about professionalism, crushes, team changes, or smoking-hot middle-aged women. Nuh-uh."

Addison tried to stay stern, but as usual, Stacey made her giggle as if she were still a teenager herself. Clutching the spaghetti, she laughed helplessly as she held onto the counter. Stacey joined in, actually ending up sitting on the floor holding her stomach and wiping at tears of laughter.

"Brat," Addison managed, and began filling a large pot with water. "I don't know where I went wrong with you."

"See, even that's your fault," Stacey pointed out helpfully. A few moments later, her face grew serious and she came up to hold her around the waist. "Actually, you're pretty awesome, Addie." She pressed her forehead against Addison's shoulders. "Eleanor Ashcroft better realize that and treat you accordingly, or she'll have to deal with me."

Addison closed her eyes briefly. Stacey wasn't joking.

CHAPTER FOUR

Riding the elevator up to the twenty-first floor of the Ashton Group's building, Addison found herself tapping her foot and fiddling with the shoulder strap of her messenger bag. Her other hand opened and closed repeatedly until she willed it to relax.

This was ridiculous. All the legal stuff was ironed out, thanks to Peter, who'd accompanied her when she met with the marketing manager and personnel manager. She was going to work full-time with Face Exquisite and combine this position with managing her YouTube channel. No doubt, she'd have a lot of long days, which she worried about. Once Stacey had her surgery, Addison would feel torn, but earning what was for her an unfathomable amount of money made it worth every effort. It didn't compare to her job as a barista, not by a long shot, and she could now take care of Stacey's needs.

When she arrived at the top floor, one of the senior assistants she'd met before stood waiting for her by the elevator. Immaculately dressed in a light-gray skirt suit that made Addison worry she might have dressed completely wrong, the woman guided her through a maze of brightly lit corridors. Addison wasn't underdressed, but she didn't own any power suits or formal office outfits. Instead, she wore a dress made of green linen. Over it, an off-white bolero cardigan and a black, short blazer helped keep her warm.

"They're waiting for you, Ms. Garr." Susan, the assistant who had met Addison, opened a door and motioned for her to step inside.

"Thanks." Addison smiled politely at Susan and entered the conference room. Four individuals sat around the oval conference table and, to her surprise, Eleanor Ashcroft sat at the head of the table, focusing on her cell phone. The last time Addison was here, Eleanor had been out of town on some last-minute business, and for some reason Addison hadn't expected her to be at her first meeting with the CEO and different managers at Face Exquisite.

"Welcome, Addison." Eleanor stood and rounded the table, her hand extended. "Have a seat. Do you know everybody?"

"Only Ms. Leighton. Hello again." Addison nodded at the marketing manager, shaking her hand. Vanessa Leighton was Eleanor's age and just as elegant, if not as stunning.

"This is Keith Berger, Face Exquisite's chemical engineer."

A sparse man in his late fifties remained standing as he greeted her. He seemed skeptical as he regarded her through stark, black-framed glasses. "My pleasure, Ms. Garr."

"Please, call me Addie."

He nodded briskly and sat down.

The last person to greet Addison was a woman closer to her own age. "I'm Linda West, the coordinator and your go-to person whenever you need to contact anyone." Her slightly overbearing tone made Addison pause and take note. Clearly this Linda regarded her position as important.

"Thank you, Linda. Good to know," Addison said amicably, and took her seat on Eleanor's right. She thought she saw Linda narrow her eyes and wondered if sitting on the head honcho's right was indicative of anything.

"You will soon get to know the entire team we're putting together to revive Face Exquisite." Eleanor pulled out some documents from her briefcase. "Everybody here has had the opportunity to peruse your YouTube channel. Vanessa, I believe you had some ideas?"

"Yes, Eleanor. I do." Vanessa turned to Addison. "As popular as your channel is, I still believe you can do a lot to streamline it and make it more professional."

What? Addison laced her trembling fingers together and listened to the accomplished woman speak as she tried to figure out why her channel was on the agenda. "Go on."

"I commend you on the quality of your videos. Not bad since they're done from your home. Quite good for an amateur. Still, it's clear we need to move you to a studio and—"

"No." Addison smiled gently and shook her head. "That won't work."

"If it's a matter of cost—"

"It's not. Well, it would be, if I thought it was a good idea. I'm sorry, Ms. Leighton, but it's not. My channel remains the way it is, until I decide it needs to change. I'm here to be your consultant, ma'am. Not the other way around." She wasn't sure if it was wise to call Vanessa "ma'am" or to take a stand so early into the meeting. Inside she was trembling, fearing that Eleanor would tear up the contract and leave her with no way of paying for Stacey's rehab.

"Surely you can understand that we need to streamline your channel and make it the best it can be in order to promote our brand." Vanessa's lips thinned. "Eleanor?"

"I think you're starting at the wrong end," Addison said quickly, fearing Eleanor might kill the whole project. "My channel is growing with each passing week. I don't need advice or streamlining—at least, not yet. But *your* company and *your* brand are in dire need of CPR. If we're going to do something about that, we need to determine what's not working. I've been going over all the products Eleanor sent me, and I know why they're not selling."

"By all means." Eleanor motioned for Addison to continue.

"But Eleanor…" Vanessa shrugged as Eleanor slowly shook her head. "Fine."

"Let's start with your lipsticks. The colors are dated. The formula is drying and has a tendency to leave your lips chapped and looking patchy. And they smell. I mean, that old-fashioned chemical-lipstick smell that I remember from my grandmother's lipsticks."

"I see. Go on." Eleanor placed her elbows on the table.

"Your mascaras are equally dated. Hasn't anyone researched what all the other brands are doing with the brush alone? While applying it I tried every technique I've picked up over the years, and I still ended up with spider legs."

"Excuse me?" Eleanor's eyebrows went up. "Spider legs?"

"A term used when your mascara clumps the eyelashes together several at a time. Makes it look like you have five thick strands instead of tons of defined, long, voluminous strands. You need a great formula and an even better brush."

"That can be done. Continue."

"Okay. Eye shadows. Not entirely a fail, but the color range needs expanding. Some were too powdery and others not pigmented enough, but throughout your entire line of products, I see one major flaw that you need to address." Addison let her eyes deliberately meet those of everyone else, making sure they were paying attention. "I researched your way of producing the makeup and face products, and it saddened, but didn't entirely surprise me to find that not only you, but also your suppliers, all test the products on animals."

"So do a lot of the big companies!" Vanessa sat up straight. "It's necessary to ensure—"

"It's not!" Addison tapped the folder in front of her. "You can get even better results by testing on people. Volunteers. And what's more, making the entire brand cruelty free is a selling point in itself."

"You have a point, but it's a large undertaking to change the entire chain of production." Eleanor looked down at her notes. "I assume you will have a verdict on all our products once you get through them all?"

"Yes. I really gave the ones I tested the benefit of the doubt, but just as you have a brand to change, to save—I have a channel to maintain that has taken me four years to build. My viewers regard me as a truthful, unbiased source of information. As it stands right now, I can't review a single one of the products in a favorable light as none of them are cruelty free. Nor could I afford them—yet."

"What?" Eleanor's eyes narrowed into thin slits. "Your job as our consultant, according to your contract, is to work with us to make Face Exquisite visible to your viewers."

"As soon as I can give my honest opinion in a positive way, when all the criteria are fulfilled, I will do so. And as you know, I don't review any products that I haven't bought myself. Peter made sure that's in my contract as well." Trying not to let on how Eleanor's icy glare made her tremble inside, Addison refused to be intimidated. "After I took a position on this issue last year, after educating myself on the matter, I don't buy any brands that aren't cruelty free."

"Even if we decided on the spot to go along with this unrealistic and romantic idea of cruelty-free manufacturing methods, it will take time. Time we don't have." Linda spoke curtly. "It's one thing to have a wish list for a brand, but another matter to execute it. Your inexperience when it comes to business endeavors evidently makes that hard for you to understand, Ms. Garr."

"I may not have a college degree in economics, but I can add and subtract, Ms. West." Addison curled her toes to keep her legs from shaking. "Your company has been on a downhill slide for the last twenty-some years. It's not up to me to judge, but no money has gone into research or product development. I don't have to examine any books to tell you that. It's like time has stood still. Makeup is like…like toothpaste and toothbrushes. Haven't you seen how they're coming up every season with new high-tech stuff for both the brushes and the paste? The competition is fierce—for them and for the makeup industry." She turned her full attention to Eleanor and had to swallow at how intently the woman was gazing at her. Perhaps she was risking everything, but this was why she'd been contracted.

"So this is your advice?" Eleanor spoke slowly, her voice even. "I can understand the reasoning behind modernizing the products to suit today's market, but this company doesn't have a large budget due to the inaction of the previous management. In fact, it's a miracle this company isn't bankrupt by now."

"We have a steady customer base that has always used Face Exquisite," Vanessa said defensively. "They trust our products, and I'm afraid we might lose them if we adopt all the changes Ms. Garr suggests."

Addison couldn't understand Vanessa's reasoning. Were they so dead set on catering to the older demographic that they were prepared to disregard everyone under sixty? She couldn't say that out loud, of course, but perhaps her point of view was clearly visible on her face, because Keith straightened in his chair.

"Creating better formulas and better products in general won't make us lose customers." He tapped his fingertip against his computer tablet. "As for the cruelty-free aspect, I'm not so sure. I don't think enough people care for it for such an endeavor to be financially sound."

"That's what I'm thinking," Eleanor said. She glanced quickly at Addison. "I'll need to see this broken down in numbers before I make a decision. Surely you can see the reality of this, Addison?"

"I'm starting to feel I'm the only one here doing that." Addison leaned back and crossed her legs. "The feedback I get all points in the same direction. A majority of my subscribers claim they want cruelty-free, preferably vegan, products."

"Vegan?" Keith gaped. "What the hell? Nobody's going to eat the damn eye shadow!"

Addison wanted to slap her own forehead in sheer frustration. How could they be so clueless? Were they pulling her leg perhaps? Was it a test to see how she would approach them if they pretended to be total morons?

"Addison, I want you to work with Keith to create some samples of a few key products. I want them made in two versions: the traditional way and according to your ideal specifications.

While they're working on the products, I want Vanessa to run the numbers, which is ultimately what it comes down to, to keep the company alive." She let her gaze meet all of theirs, one at a time. "And make no mistake—that is my goal here. To return this company to its former glory." Zeroing in on Addison, she added, "Find me in my office when you're done for today."

Eleanor stood and left. Addison studied her surreptitiously as she made her way around the table, moving with such grace and economy and, yes, with total femininity.

The rest of the meeting consisted of Keith and Addison working out a schedule that suited them both. Vanessa and Linda added a few meetings, and their tones convinced Addison they wouldn't be easy to deal with. Why did the two women seem so hostile and overbearing? Was it because of her, or because Eleanor had brought someone in from outside the company? Telling herself she could put up with a lot as long as she made the money Stacey needed, Addison finally politely wished everyone a good day and headed to find Eleanor's office. Just as she was closing the door behind her, she heard Vanessa's acidic voice.

"Can anyone tell me why Eleanor didn't simply hire an agency with brand expertise?"

Cringing at the malicious tone, Addison lengthened her stride as she walked toward the foyer to locate Susan. No way was she going to stumble around this maze of corridors unaided, especially as she knew Eleanor hated to be kept waiting.

CHAPTER FIVE

Eleanor glanced up from her laptop as the intercom buzzed and pressed the large red button. "Yes."

"Ms. Garr to see you, Ms. Ashcroft." Susan spoke in her usual efficient manner.

"Show her in."

The intercom clicked, and then the door opened and Susan motioned for Addison to enter. It was quite enlightening to watch Addison's reaction to Eleanor's office. Her eyes grew bigger and her mouth fell open as she came to a full stop, gazing out the panoramic windows. Perhaps the young woman had never seen this particular view this way before?

Overlooking a large portion of midtown and in the distance the famous skyscrapers, the view was astonishing. As a child, while visiting her father in this very office, Eleanor had been intrigued by the view and had stood there for hours sometimes, her nose pressed to the glass. She had firmly believed he ruled the world, that the miniature people down there below them were his minions. The sad thing was that Kenneth Ashcroft had completely bought into the idea of how far his power stretched. He may have resided in this ivory tower and wielded his power ruthlessly, but for Eleanor, he fell from grace the day he betrayed his sister. It had given Eleanor immense pleasure to dethrone her father.

"Have a seat." Eleanor pointed at one of the visitors' chairs.

Addison sat down, perched at the edge of the seat. She looked tense and something glimmered in her eyes, a shadow or a glimpse of pain.

"Are you satisfied with the arrangement you discussed with the team today?" Eleanor leaned forward on her elbows, interlacing her fingers.

Addison's smile looked polite at best. "Parts of it, yes."

"What do you mean?" Surprised at her own annoyance at whoever said something to erase this young woman's spark of innate joy, Eleanor frowned.

"To be honest, how well did you explore the idea of bringing me in on this project with Face Exquisite's staff? I think they expected someone within the industry, someone with extensive business experience, I mean." Her hazel eyes so open and honest, Addison looked a little tired.

"We have a great deal of business experience readily available. I need someone who knows makeup, who understands our future customers and what they're willing to pay for. If anyone—and I mean *anyone*—at Face Exquisite doesn't understand this, I'm sure they'll realize they'd be happier somewhere else." It was rather amusing to watch Addison follow her reasoning. Eleanor prevented a broad grin from appearing when the young woman looked completely aghast.

"Oh, God. You can't just fire someone for not liking my presence. I mean, I'm the new kid on the block here. They…I mean, you just can't." Pale now, she looked imploringly at Eleanor.

Clearly, Addison knew an enormous amount about makeup and very little about the cutthroat world of business. "If they stand in the way of what's best for the company and don't work as a team according to the guidelines I've set, I most certainly can. Face Exquisite is my company. I own eighty percent of the shares, and I will do what it takes to bring it back to its former glory. It was seriously mismanaged before."

"By your father," Addison said, and nodded.

Eleanor flinched and tried to hide her reaction. "You've done your research."

"Yes." Addison sounded apologetic. "I risk a lot by giving up my day job to do this full-time instead. I needed to find out everything I could. Peter, my lawyer, helped me, but Stacey and I did most of the research online."

"Ah, yes. Your sister."

Addison looked surprised. "You remember."

"Why wouldn't I? You were so concerned I'd see the fact that you have private, personal responsibilities as some sort of issue."

"Yeah." Looking flustered now, Addison actually squirmed a little in her seat. "I can't tell you how much this assignment means to Stacey and me."

"Well. I imagine consulting pays better than working as a barista. Nothing against that profession, not at all. Baristas help keep me sane."

"You're right. The money's not good. I mean, I had been there long enough to have basic insurance for us, but this way, I can set money aside for when...when we need it."

It was obvious Addison meant to say something else, but Eleanor didn't push. Soon enough she'd find out what she might be hiding. Her mind brushed against the question of why she would bother in the first place, but she didn't venture too far into this realm. She was curious about the woman who would be instrumental in saving Priscilla's company. Of course she was. She couldn't let anything, or anyone, fail. Eleanor hastily changed the subject. "I need you to attend a cocktail party this Friday."

"Friday?" Addison quickly pulled up her phone and ran her fingertips over the screen. "Sorry. I can't."

"If you examine your contract, you'll see that you are obligated to participate in events that showcase our products and our company." Eleanor gazed sternly at Addison, making sure she infused into her eyes the force that was known to make even the most hardened people shiver. "Networking at the occasional function is part of our agreement."

"I understand." Oddly enough, her practiced glare didn't seem to affect Addison. "My sister is going to a party, something she's been looking forward to for months, and I have to make sure she gets there and back safely."

"I'm sure you can arrange for the parent of one her of her friends to drive her."

"You don't understand. I have to be there to accompany her on the subway." Addison shrugged. "I have to sit this one out, Eleanor. I'm sorry."

Not at all pleased, Eleanor rapped her fingernails against the cherrywood desktop. Reluctantly, she had to concede that even if this hurdle annoyed her, she admired Addison's loyalty to her sister. The only time she'd been on the receiving end of unconditional love was when she'd spent time with her Aunt Priscilla as a young girl. Her father had expressed nothing but callousness most of her life, and her mother had been absent, emotionally and physically, for as long as she could remember.

She slowed her fingers as she thought of a compromise. "What if I arrange safe transport for your sister? Just give me the address and the time this party starts and ends."

It was interesting to see how Addison actually gaped at this suggestion. Eleanor couldn't fathom why this suggestion would cause such a response but found it rather refreshing. Most of the people around her lived lives where such arrangements were commonplace, but perhaps that wasn't the case in Newark.

"It's that important I attend?" Addison straightened in her chair, her eyes narrowing.

"Yes. I've arranged for you to network with several other makeup experts. Quite a few of them are looking at diversifying and expanding. I want you to put your ear to the ground and listen to the buzz, then go online and compare what you pick up to what the beauty bloggers are saying."

"And Stacey will have a ride to the party?"

"Yes."

Addison gazed out the window, clearly mulling the possibility over. Eleanor knew what her answer would be before she turned and said, "All right then. Thank you for realizing that Stacey is my number-one priority." She sighed and slumped back against the backrest. "I know it's probably not very business savvy to express that, but it's the truth." Eleanor thought she could detect fatigue on Addison's face no matter how perfectly her makeup was applied.

"Perhaps not, but I appreciate honesty."

"All right. Thank you." Addison pulled her bag toward her and stood. "Unless you have anything else you need to discuss with me, I'll be going. I have two new clips to post to YouTube. I thought I'd film the 'big announcement' one about my new assignment and have it ready for when you think it's time for me to post it."

It was rather ridiculous to feel close to giddy at the thought of new clips appearing on The Blush Factor. Ever since they had spoken in the restaurant, Addison had posted only once a week. To have access to two new ones was going to make coming home to her vast penthouse condo a little less...lonely. Angry at feeling vulnerable in the presence of the one person who'd managed to penetrate her carefully constructed walls for the first time in a long time, Eleanor merely nodded briskly. "By all means. My assistant will have the drivers contact you on Thursday, midday, at the latest."

"Drivers?" Addison stopped and turned so fast she had to hold on to the backrest of the visitors' chair. "Drivers, plural?"

"Of course. You need a ride to the function."

"Oh. No, no. Not necessary, Eleanor. I'll just take the train. I'm used to it."

"I'm sure you are." Eleanor wrinkled her nose slightly at the thought of being crowded by complete strangers while dressed in a cocktail dress. "How many times have you ridden the train dressed in a designer outfit?"

Addison looked affronted. "Designer dress? I'm sorry, but I don't have enough money to get my hands on one of those. But I do have a dress that'll be great for the occasion. It's from Forever 21."

Eleanor blinked. "Forever 21. Can't say I've ever frequented that chain."

"You're hardly their intended demographic." Addison's expression shifted and now she had the gall to look amused.

Too old. "Really?" Eleanor's frosty tone would have sent her assistants into exile in Canada.

"Uh-huh. Off the rack. Not elegant enough."

Eleanor wondered if Addison knew how many points she'd scored by not playing the age card. "You may be right. And still you maintain you have a dress that's appropriate."

"I do. Besides, where would I get a designer dress?" Addison's hair flowed down her left shoulder as she tilted her head. Her beauty was mind-boggling and enough to make Eleanor cross her legs, a reaction she couldn't remember ever having experienced before.

"I would have supplied you with a selection, of course. I'm your client, but you also represent Face Exquisite. It's strictly for business."

"I realize *that*. What else would it be?" Little cheeky devils glittered in Addison's eyes.

"Exactly." Eleanor thought quickly. "Would you mind texting me a photo of yourself in this dress?" She held up her hand as Addison's face darkened. "Listen. I don't distrust your taste or your ability to choose an outfit, but a lot rides on your making a good first impression."

"Oh, all right. I can do you one better. If you give me your Skype nickname I can show you on my webcam." Addison smiled, and again the perplexing sparkles appeared among the translucent hazel.

Eleanor was as close to speechless as she ever got. This woman wasn't like anyone she'd ever come across, either privately or professionally. Why wasn't she responding to her foolproof means of intimidation? "Very well," she heard herself say, pulling a notepad closer. She wrote down her Skype username. "What's your handle so I know to accept your call?"

"Blushaddict. One word."

"Figures," Eleanor muttered, and handed over the note. "I'll be home after nine pm."

"See you then." Addison took the paper and glanced at it. "'Valkyrie.' Cool."

Eleanor shrugged, determined not to look as flustered as she felt. "It's the one I use on my private laptop."

"Okay." Addison tucked the note into her briefcase. "See you tonight then, sort of."

"Well. Yes." Eleanor sat motionless as Addison waved with that little flick of her fingertips that she'd done once before and left.

Had she just made a huge mistake, giving Addison her private Skype username? Normally she used the company premium version while conducting business, but it didn't seem appropriate to watch Addison display outfits on the company machine. Her laptop at home wasn't on the company intranet. Instead it was connected to the Internet via an air card. Eleanor wasn't quite sure if she was protecting herself or Addison with these security measures, but she trusted her gut feeling that it was the smart thing to do.

❖

Addison placed two dresses on her bed. She had forgotten about the midnight-blue cocktail dress her friend Katie had outgrown when she couldn't shake the extra pounds after her pregnancy. It was a lovely dress, by Calvin Klein, no less. Perhaps Eleanor would deem it more suitable for Friday.

"So when's this runway show starting?" Stacey poked her head in. "Should I bring popcorn?"

"Hey, you're not going to be here. You're still not done with that essay." Addison shook her head, looking her best stern self. "I can do without your smart-ass comments."

"Ah, such language, Ms. Garr. Are you sure that's appropriate with the rich and famous of Manhattan? I'm sure they kiss the air around each other's cheeks and go, 'Oh, dah'ling, it's been ages since we played polo.'"

"Please." Addison had to laugh at Stacey's antics. "All the more reason for you to do your homework in your room and let me do my thing here."

"And show off the schexy dresses for schexy Eleanor."

"That's it. Go get smarter. If possible." Addison pushed Stacey out through her door. "And no silly pranks. Remember, this is important."

"Yeah, yeah, I'm only kidding." Stacey pouted. "Where's your sense of humor?"

"Oh, I have a sense of humor, but I can't be all giggly when I talk to my first big client via Skype. She's going to see me, and I'm going to have to try to not look like a total dork in these dresses—not to mention the shoes."

Quickly growing serious, Stacey gave Addison a quick hug. "Don't be like that. She's the one who's lucky to have you save that company of hers. You look freaking awesome in both those dresses, and I for one think it's great that you finally get some use out of them. When was the last time you went clubbing?"

Like never? Addison tried to remember. Her days consisted of making coffee drinks, filming for YouTube, taking care of Stacey, and doing housework. Clubbing? As if. "Thank you for the compliments, sweetie-girl."

Stacey tugged the ends of Addison's ponytail, something she did when she was emotional and didn't want to show her feelings too blatantly. She disappeared into her room and soon the sound of One Republic hammered against the door.

Checking the clock on the wall above her desk, Addison saw she had only five minutes to get ready. Hurrying, she put on the black Forever 21 dress. She added a hammered-silver cuff bracelet but didn't want to look "too much," so she left the matching necklace in the box.

At one minute to nine, the familiar tones of Skype ringing made Addison jump in her desk chair. Her fingers were ice cold as she clicked to answer. Feeling bold, she let her laptop connect with the webcam on directly.

Eleanor came into view and she'd clearly just gotten home. She was standing a few feet from her computer, pulling off a mustard-colored trench coat. Tossing it on a—was that a bed? Were they both in their respective bedrooms? Addison swallowed. "Hello, Eleanor."

"Good evening, Addison. Is that the dress you intend to wear?" Eleanor came closer and sat down in front of the computer, tilting her head. "You have to stand up and back off a bit."

"I found one more that I forgot I had, if you don't think this one's good enough." Addison felt clumsy and was grateful she hadn't thought to put on heels as well. She was wearing a bra under the dress, but her only black one that worked with the thin fabric was rather flimsy. Suddenly very aware of how her breasts swayed as she shifted and stood, she chewed on the inside of her cheek to keep from thinking about it too much.

"Farther back," Eleanor said, and folded her hands under her chin. "Turn."

This was totally awkward. Addison knew she wasn't model material; she was too short and too curvy for that. She glanced at the full-length mirror at the other end of the room. The dress was cinched in at the right place, giving her more of an hourglass figure.

"So?" Addison placed her hands on her hips and met Eleanor's gaze.

"Not too bad. I trust the material isn't too cheap looking?"

"No. I don't think so. Look." Addison stepped close to the webcam and tugged at the fabric at her shoulder to get the camera to focus on it. "See? It has very subtle flowers, woven in with some silky thread."

Eleanor coughed. "Um. Yes. I see."

Addison glanced at the monitor, where she saw her own picture in a smaller version in the corner. When she realized she'd more or less pressed her entire décolleté into the camera to show off the fabric, she backed up so quickly she nearly toppled over. "Oops."

"Careful, now." Eleanor didn't look offended, and why would she be? They were both women. It's not like Eleanor was an ogling guy or something. Quickly disregarding the fact that had the roles been reversed, Addison would have been the one doing the ogling, she scooped up the blue dress. "I'll go change into the other. Be right back." She dove into her bathroom, where she spent the first ten seconds thudding her forehead against the mirror.

"I'm such an idiot!" Hissing at herself, she finally changed dresses. The blue dress wasn't as thin when it came to the fabric, but it was decidedly shorter. Not so much that she looked indecent, or at least she didn't think so, but schexy, to quote Stacey. Holding her breath, she returned to her bedroom.

Eleanor tried to calm down her speeding pulse. Addison's impulsive nature and the way she was used to being on camera were obvious. When she'd walked up to the computer and bent forward to show off the fabric, Eleanor had gotten more of a view of satin-skinned cleavage than she bargained for. Flawless in high-definition, Addison's chest had been far too close and made Eleanor's throat dry up and her heart pound with painful contractions.

Now the door at the far end of Addison's bedroom opened and she emerged in a dark-blue dress that simply stole the last breath Eleanor had counted on keeping. Short, but not sleazy, it hugged every beautiful curve of Addison's body. It was as if it were tailor made for her, and even if this dress meant trouble—because Addison would have to fight both men and women to keep them off her—Eleanor knew this was the one.

Addison pivoted slowly, her hands raised. "What do you think?"

"I think…that's it."

"Really?" Addison's mouth fell open. "It's kind of short."

"Are you uncomfortable with that?"

"No, well, not really. It's rather forgiving. Stretchy. I think I'll be okay. I have black pumps to wear with—"

"No. I have to object. This dress needs a statement when it comes to the shoes. You need some in the same color. Give Susan your size and I'll have some sent over." She could tell Addison was about to disagree; her hands were back on those curvaceous hips. Eleanor held up her right hand, forestalling the words. "Non-negotiable. If you wear this with the wrong shoes, it'll cheapen it. It's a designer dress, right?"

"Calvin Klein," Addison said, her voice barely more than a murmur.

"I rest my case." Eleanor waved her hand dismissively. "You'll have several pairs to choose from. I'll make sure my personal shopper delivers them in time for you to get used to them."

Addison sat down with a thud on the bed. "Personal shopper?" she asked weakly.

"Yes. A very efficient use of my time, not having to browse through stores when Yvette does it ten times as fast and knows just what I want." Eleanor checked her watch. "It's getting late. I have work to do and I'm sure you do too." She hesitated for a moment, feeling rather silly. "Did you post the new video to your channel?"

"Yup," Addison said, and came over to the desk, looking a little more relaxed. "It should be ready to be viewed now. It's actually a hair tutorial and a mini haul of affordable makeup from Walmart and Target."

Eleanor enjoyed those types of videos, as she got to view Addison and see her personality shine through. Like now, she realized. Now that Addison didn't act so self-conscious, the sparkle was back in her eyes and her smile was bright enough to light up half of Newark.

"Well. If I have time, I'll watch it later." Eleanor knew she was such a fraud. She had several important dossiers to go through and contracts to read, but she'd watch Addison's video first.

"Oh, great. Well, I suppose I'll run into you at the cocktail party?"

"Yes. Good night." Eleanor clicked the red button and closed the video call. With embarrassing eagerness, she clicked over to The Blush Factor's YouTube channel and then hovered with the cursor over the link to the newest video. She wasn't ready to analyze why she was like a trembling schoolgirl at the prospect of having a few minutes more of Addison, but she would have to sooner rather than later.

Now that she knew more about Addison and would be seeing her on a regular basis at Face Exquisite, she needed to get this...this damn *infatuation* under control. Watching Addison parade in sexy cocktail dresses certainly hadn't helped. Despite her reasoning, Eleanor clicked on the link and pushed back as Addison came into view. Dressed in a soft-looking blue cardigan set, her auburn hair flowing down across her left shoulder, she smiled and waved with that familiar flick of the fingertips again.

"Hello, everybody. You like the Rita Hayworth waves? You can easily make them with a flat iron. Yes, a flat iron, I'm not joking." Addison giggled. "All you have to remember is to use some heat-protective spray in your hair to protect it..."

The clip lasted fifteen minutes, and when Eleanor refreshed the web browser, she saw that more than 175,000 people had viewed Addison's tutorial and haul. She couldn't say she was surprised. Whatever quality Addison possessed to generate such interest, clearly it worked on middle-aged business tycoons as well.

A small voice in the back of her mind insisted that this interest could very well be her undoing.

CHAPTER SIX

A limo? A freaking limo?" Stacey's voice cracked as she glanced behind the woman at the door. "What—I mean, did your Eleanor arrange this?" She turned to Addison.

"First of all, she's not *my* Eleanor, but yes, so it would seem." Addison shook her head as she greeted the woman waiting patiently to be acknowledged. "I'm so sorry. Forgive our less than sophisticated squealing. I'm Addison. This is my sister, Stacey."

"I'm Gina Gallo, Gallo's Limo Service," the compact brunette said. She wore her hair in a ponytail under her chauffeur's cap, and her black uniform was flawless. "The Ashcroft Group has an account with us, and I'm to drive Ms. Stacey Garr to a party at a locale in Midtown. I'll wait for her until midnight, or if she wants to go home sooner, and also stay with her if nobody is home."

"God, you're a babysitter too?" Stacey clearly was torn between awe and outrage.

"So it would seem."

"No offense, but I can't let a stranger into our home to 'babysit' Stacey, even if it's a nice idea."

"I'm not a stranger, per se. I'm the president of Gallo's Limo Service, and Ms. Ashcroft has known my family and me for more than a decade. You can verify this if you need to." Gina looked friendly and calm. "In about an hour, Piotr, one of my employees, will arrive to drive you to the function, Ms. Garr. He will pick up Ms. Ashcroft on the way also."

"Ah. I see." Addison really didn't, but she had to concede that Eleanor had thought of everything.

"Very well. Do you have my cell number in case you need to get ahold of me?" Addison looked pointedly at Gina, who nodded.

"I have that and, of course, Ms. Ashcroft's details."

"Okay, sweetie-girl." Addison hugged Stacey quickly. "You have your medication?" she whispered in her ear.

"Yeah, yeah. You asked me twice already."

"And you know—"

"If I need to, I'll go home early. I know that too."

Stacey meant what she said. If she got one of her migraines, she wouldn't be able to tolerate the sound levels of a party full of teenagers. "Good. Now go have fun. You look fantastic."

"Thanks." Going a little pink, Stacey motioned toward the white limousine. "Guess I should at least try the bar in this thing."

"She's kidding," Addison said to Gina, who flinched. "Aren't you, Stace?"

"Of course I am. I don't drink."

"That's a relief," Gina said, and began walking toward curb.

Addison watched as Stacey stepped inside the vehicle and grinned as she heard yet another squeal from Stacey. "Whoa, there are freaking *stars* on the ceiling!"

Gina pulled out into the street, and even if Addison couldn't see Stacey through the tinted windows, she stood in the open doorway until the limousine was out of sight. She sighed deeply, feeling happy for her sister but also strangely unnerved. This wasn't the first party Addison had ever attended, but it was the first time she'd gone to such a huge event. The fact that it was held in Manhattan wasn't making it easier. "At least I'll be in the same area, more or less," she murmured to herself.

She closed the door and walked inside. She'd already put on her makeup but had to dry her hair and get dressed before the next Gallo limo arrived.

❖

Eleanor adjusted the spaghetti straps of her black Chanel cocktail dress. As it was cut just above the knees, she was grateful for having youthful skin, not to mention the means to indulge in massages and facials. Though not very vain, she knew attractive looks were part of being successful in business, which was even truer for women. She sprayed her hair once more to lock the perfect waves in place. With little patience for having stylists and makeup artists poke and prod her, Eleanor had learned to perfect her signature look by herself. She had also picked up several tips from Addison via YouTube, and she wondered briefly what it would be like to have the young woman do her makeup. She pressed a hand to her midsection and forced the thought away. Checking the time, she donned her black faux-mink fur coat. Reaching to her hips, it gave her a nice silhouette.

The elevator down to the foyer played experimental jazz as usual, clearly meant to sound classy, but Eleanor thought it was ridiculously snobbish. Making a mental note to have Susan file a complaint, she stepped out to the foyer. The doorman held the door for her.

"I believe your car is here, Ms. Ashcroft." He smiled, which made his white mustache curl. A former homicide detective, he had worked as a guard and doorman for as long as Eleanor had lived in the penthouse.

"Thank you, Bernard." Eleanor nodded in passing.

Outside, the wind had picked up and the streetlight swayed above her. The chauffeur, a young man with white-blond hair, held the door open. Cursing under her breath, Eleanor hurriedly stepped inside before the wind completely destroyed her hair.

"Good evening," Addison said softly from the other end of the backseat. "Looks like we're in for a storm."

"Addison." Eleanor let her gaze travel from the rich, auburn hair that billowed around Addison's shoulders. The Calvin Klein dress looked even more spectacular as Addison was sitting down, thus making the hemline ride up and display more of those shapely thighs. She was wearing a simple dark-gray wool coat, making

Eleanor wish she'd thought to ask about that. She glanced down at Addison's feet and was pleased to see blue four-inch Jimmy Choo pumps.

"Do I pass inspection?" Addison tilted her head and her shiny hair slipped forward over her left shoulder, a pose with which Eleanor was already only too familiar.

"Of course." Eleanor settled in, enjoying the heated seat.

"You, on the other hand, look amazing. It's just—" Addison broke off and colored faintly. She gestured at Eleanor's hair. "The wind…"

"What?" Eleanor heard herself bark in that low growl that normally sent her minions scurrying.

Not Addison. Instead, she opened her clutch purse and pulled out a compact. Opening it, she handed it to Eleanor. "Look. Want me to fix it?"

Eleanor checked her appearance and frowned when she saw how the wind had wreaked havoc with her hair. Clearly the hair spray she'd used before she left her penthouse hadn't had time to set before she stepped outside. "Damn," she muttered. "Yes. Thank you."

"Okay." Pulling out a mini hair spray of a different brand and the tiniest hairbrush Eleanor had ever seen, Addison scooted closer.

"You have to lean in a bit, or I might end up on your lap." Addison chuckled, a nervous sound, but her hands were steady as she angled Eleanor's head. "Like so. Yes."

Addison's fingers worked quickly as she rearranged the errant tresses, and all Eleanor could do was focus on her breathing. She really wanted to close her eyes, to avoid the visual impression of the beautiful creature sitting so close. She could smell Addison's perfume, discreet and mixed with something else, something decidedly more innocent. Baby oil? Baby shampoo? The vision of Addison was certainly not innocent. In an attempt to avoid looking straight at her, Eleanor let her glance sweep past Addison's neck, down to her chest. The plunging décolleté was enough to make her tremble. What the hell was going on? In all her forty-nine years, Eleanor couldn't remember ever before having this type of physical reaction to another woman.

Yes, she worked in a business normally dominated by men in dark suits. At her level, women were still not well represented. As she closed her eyes, her mind leaped between different memories of different female friends and colleagues, some of them perhaps even more physically beautiful than Addison. None of the images elicited any reaction whatsoever. Not one. She opened her eyes and found Addison closer than she had been just moments ago. Eleanor tightened her abdominal muscles so as not to lean in closer to inhale more of that sensational mix of scents.

"There. Much better. I like it when you fix your bangs like this. It shows off your eyebrows, which in turn makes you look even younger."

"Even younger?" Eleanor echoed, and her words seemed to color Addison's cheeks again.

"Yeah. Well, you look impossibly young, Eleanor. Surely you realize that."

"I—I didn't. Um. Thank you." Eleanor raised the compact mirror and scrutinized her appearance. Her hair looked bigger and, well, *fluffier*, than normal, but Addison was correct. She did look rejuvenated. Handing back the mirror, she nodded and glanced out the tinted side window. "We're almost there."

"Good timing then." Addison smiled broadly, but her grip on her clutch made her knuckles go white.

Realizing Addison was deeply anxious, in fact she looked ready to bolt, Eleanor placed her hand on top of one of the tight fists. "You'll be fine," she said in a low voice, meaning it.

"Thank you." Addison turned her hand around and clasped Eleanor's tightly for a few moments.

"Here goes, then." Eleanor watched the door open and their chauffeur extend a hand to her. She gracefully stepped outside with a practiced maneuver. Before the chauffeur could do so, Eleanor turned around and reached for Addison's hand. She wasn't sure what compelled her to do this, and she knew it wouldn't go unnoticed as the photographers' cameras went off as if they were celebrating the Fourth of July.

"Who's the girl, Ms. Ashcroft?" several voices called out.

"That your girlfriend, Eleanor?"

"Look this way, pretty lady!"

"Oh, my God." Addison stood rigid next to Eleanor, holding on tight to her hand. "What the hell are they doing?"

"Smile." Eleanor knew she sounded gruff, but it seemed to work. Addison did smile, broadly and blindingly. If the cameras had rattled before, they were now going off in an ear-deafening cacophony.

"Gorgeous, darling!" some paparazzo close to them yelled. "Closer together. Closer!"

"Let's go." Eleanor moved her hand and placed it at the small of Addison's back, hoping she would follow without falling on her face. This was baptism by fire, and if she failed this, Addison's involvement with Face Exquisite might come to an end.

"Oh! Look. Look! Blush! It's Blush!" a shrill girl's voice called out. "I swear it's her. Blush! I love your vids."

Eleanor turned to find the origin of the voice behind the unexpected words. Just behind the band of paparazzi she spotted a group of adolescent girls, maybe high-school juniors or seniors. The two closest girls were jumping up and down while holding hands, calling out, "Blush," over and over.

"Holy crap." Addison gasped at Eleanor's side, stepping closer to her. "They know me?"

"You have half a million followers. Don't tell me you've never been recognized in public?"

"I haven't. I look different when I'm not all made up. Plain."

Eleanor nearly guffawed at that last remark. Plain? Addison? Not likely. "Time for you to step out of your shell then." She nudged Addison toward the girls. "Go on. Sign some autographs." This would definitely get the photographers' attention. Standing back at first, she watched Addison walk toward the girls, broad smile in place but with slightly faltering steps. For reasons not quite clear to herself, she took two quick steps forward and once again placed her hand on the small of Addison's back.

❖

Addison slowed her steps, feeling dizzy. Facing the photographers and these screaming girls, most of them Stacey's age, was too much, too soon. Then, that hand. Eleanor's presence radiating through her hand against her back. She sighed in relief and felt her smile turn genuine.

"Hi there. You enjoy the YouTube videos?" Addison paid no attention to the paparazzi going nuts around her. She saw the adoration in these girls' eyes and suddenly they were all Stacey.

"Oh, yeah. We watch you, all of us. I bought all that Revlon stuff you recommended." A tall African-American girl held out a small writing pad. "Can I have your autograph?"

Hesitating, Addison accepted the item and took a deep breath as she signed The Blush Factor across the page, making sure "Blush" was underlined. So far she hadn't shared her real name on YouTube or any of the other social media.

It was beyond surreal, but after a few moments, Addison had signed at least twenty autographs, some of them to people she was pretty sure had no idea who Blush was.

"Time to go." Eleanor guided her back to the red carpet and they entered the hotel. Inside, their coats magically disappeared into the hands of Eleanor's assistant Susan. They rode in the elevator with two men and one woman. It seemed odd and perhaps she was imagining it, but it looked like they were careful not to meet Eleanor's gaze and gave her and Addison a wide berth.

The room where the cocktail party was being held was enormous. Addison had never seen so many people dressed so well in one place. She was now grateful that she'd remembered she had the Calvin Klein dress. Had she arrived in the Forever 21 dress, she would've felt even more out of place. Ridiculous, but true.

"Come, let me introduce you to some people." Eleanor guided her by placing her hand on her back for the third time. Her skin tingled under the dress, making her shiver. This was so wrong on so many levels. Eleanor was being accommodating and making sure her foray into the world of business went well. She could *not* allow her body to respond to the innocent touches like this. Eleanor was bound to notice and, God, that'd be horribly embarrassing.

They stopped next to a group of people, and the way they scattered into a circle around her and Eleanor was rather interesting. Eleanor introduced her. They were all working in different companies that had one thing in common: they belonged to the Ashcroft Group. Eleanor was their ultimate boss.

"Addison Garr?" one of the women, Kit Nielsen, said, and frowned. "From which branch?"

"Oh, you didn't realize." Eleanor's silky voice was like the purr of a tigress. "Addison doesn't work for me. In fact, I'm her client. She's an independent contractor with whom I will be working closely to breathe new life into one of my companies. Addison will be most instrumental and will serve as our connection with the public. All of our products will originate from her. I promise, next time you see her, you'll know exactly who she is."

She would be *what*? What did Eleanor mean by the products originating from her? Would she have her okay *all* Face Exquisites products? Glancing at Eleanor, she saw the pleased expression that reminded her of Mr. K., the cat her parents gave her when she turned eight. He would sport that exact expression when he caught a bird or a mouse. Addison almost expected Eleanor to spit a feather elegantly from the corner of her mouth. Snorting softly, Addison tried to control herself.

The hand on her back jumped a little, barely noticeably, but enough for Addison to arrange her features into something blank.

"Let's go find a waiter. I want some champagne." Eleanor merely started walking, clearly so sure people would move out of the way she didn't slow down.

Addison followed her, missing the hand and actually feeling a little cold now that it was gone again. A waiter approached and Eleanor snatched two champagne flutes. Handing one to Addison, she raised hers, smiling faintly. "Here's to fame."

"Fame?" Addison frowned. What kind of toast was that? "I'm not in this for fame. You're going to be really disappointed if that's what you expect from me. If that is *all* you expect?" She didn't raise her glass. Instead she twirled the tall stem between her fingers.

"Then to what would you toast?" Eleanor pressed her lips together.

"Oh, that depends on who I'm with. Right now, in this particular situation, I'd merely say thank you."

Eleanor blinked. "Thank you. To me? What for?"

"Thank you for taking me with you so I could start this new journey. Thank you for making it possible for me to meet those girls outside. Thank you for making it possible for Stacey to attend her party." Addison raised her glass for each sentence and then finally took a sip. The champagne wasn't what she expected. Not sweet, not very bubbly, and even a little bitter. "This really is real champagne?" she asked, wrinkling her nose.

Eleanor laughed, a low, discreet chuckle, but it sounded genuine. Rare. "No, this is some cheap knockoff. Rather pitiful of the hosts to save on champagne when they're entertaining every single one of the movers and shakers of the Manhattan corporate world."

"I'm kind of glad this wasn't it. I suppose I may have a romantic view of what champagne should be like, but this certainly isn't it."

"At the first appropriate opportunity, I'll treat you to real champagne." Eleanor's eyes softened for a fraction of a moment. "All right?"

"It's a date." Addison wanted to kick herself for her choice of words, especially as Eleanor's pupils grew, darkening her eyes. "Um. I mean, it's a deal. Yeah."

"All right then. Now, let's work the room. Pay attention and memorize names. You might even get some business cards. You should give them yours—what?" Eleanor stopped in mid-stride.

"You will think I'm a moron, but I don't have any hardcopy business cards."

"How's that even possible? Everybody has—"

"No. Not everybody. Remember, I conduct my business online. I have digital business cards. So much easier to share, store, and look up."

"Really."

"Yes. If anyone wants my business card, I can send them one with a tap on my smartphone. Surely you do that too?" Addison couldn't believe that a powerful businesswoman like Eleanor wasn't using the latest technology.

"I don't trust technology the way you do." Tension increased around Eleanor's perfect pink lips. "Perhaps a generational thing."

"Nah, I don't think so. Just different habits." Addison did her best to defuse the sudden unease between them.

Eleanor stood quietly for a moment, and then she turned and walked toward yet another group of people. Addison could only surmise that she wanted her to follow, so she did. It occurred to her during the rest of the evening that people generally didn't approach Eleanor. She was the one who initiated contact. They parted around her as if she were the queen and the rest of them her loyal subjects.

As for loyal, Addison wasn't so sure about that point of the analogy. She had seen a range of emotions in the faces of the people around them. Greed, envy, anger, reluctant admiration, but rarely devotion or loyalty. Were they all afraid of her? Yes, she was intimidating, that was true, but *afraid*? What did they think she would do? Fire them on the spot? Run them out of Manhattan? Have them shot at dawn?

Eventually, and now Addison's feet were aching so badly, she was ready to walk barefoot all the way to Newark, Eleanor signaled to Susan to bring their coats.

"Time to go before you fall over." Eleanor glanced down at Addison's shoes. "Make sure you walk often in the other pairs I sent over. You'll be expected to attend functions on a regular basis. We can't have you limping and holding on to the walls for support."

Addison let go of the table she'd been stealthily leaning against. "Sorry. I'm a bit sore."

"I bet you are. Susan should have the car pulled up. Let's go."

Thank you, Unnamed Deity. Addison managed to walk without falling or limping only to more or less dive into the limousine. She pushed off her pumps immediately and pulled her feet up on the seat while moaning out loud. "Oh, damn. I can't wait to dip them in some icy saline."

"Icy saline? Your feet?"

"A trick I learned from someone else on YouTube. It hurts at first, but then it really soothes the feet. I used it when I was on my feet forty-eight hours a while ago." Quickly changing the subject, as she didn't want to think about the time Stacey had been so sick with migraines she had to be hospitalized, Addison shifted sideways and massaged the ball of her right foot. "Ow."

Eleanor cleared her throat and seemed to have lost her train of thought. Addison followed her gaze and realized that while she'd pulled her feet up, the short dress had ridden up and showed her right thigh almost to the edge of her lace panties. Trying to move casually, she lowered her foot off the seat and tugged at her dress. Her cheeks warmed and she didn't know what to say.

Why was Eleanor even looking at her that way? If it had been any of the few girls Addison had dated, such a look would have been easy to decipher. Such looks meant there was a definite attraction. Someone giving you such a heated glance meant she had the hots for you, one way or another. But this was Eleanor Ashcroft and she wasn't a lesbian. She was a middle-aged, straight, accomplished magnate, whose only interest in Addison was purely business.

Addison straightened and met Eleanor's gaze head-on. And totally lost her breath. Something was amiss. Or at least strange as hell. Eleanor's gaze burned through her clothes as they traveled from her face, down her dress, along her legs, and slowly back up again.

The car came to a stop, sending a jolt through Addison.

"Good night," Eleanor said, and slipped out of the limo before the driver had the chance to open the door. She hurried toward the entrance where a bear of a man opened the door for her.

Addison closed her eyes after checking the time on her phone. Stacey should be home and in bed. She had to have some time to herself to try to figure out exactly what the hell had happened just now. The vehicle pulled out into the busy Friday-night traffic.

Addison couldn't wait to get home.

CHAPTER SEVEN

Eleanor stopped inside her front door, slamming it shut with her back. What the hell was going on? What must Addison be thinking of her? Her mouth dry, she tossed her coat on a chair in the living room and her clutch on the coffee table. Pouring herself a Four Roses bourbon, she grimaced at the way it burned and soothed at the same time. Normally she settled for a single glass of red wine, but that wouldn't be enough on an evening like this.

She poured one more shot of bourbon and took it with her to the bedroom, where she removed her cocktail dress. Moving more out of habit than real concern for the designer dress, she hung it carefully on a hanger in her walk-in closet. After returning to the bedroom, she caught her reflection in the full-length, triple mirror. She stopped, staring at herself. She wished she could see herself with Addison's eyes. Or perhaps not. To a young woman in her mid-twenties, someone close to fifty was old. Not just old, but boring-old, no doubt.

Trying to take stock objectively, Eleanor scanned one area of her body after another. Legs. Yes, not bad. Pilates did wonders for keeping them toned. No major cellulite. Hips, curvy. Waist, not as narrow as it used to be, but smaller than her hips. That was all right. Chest...She unhooked her bra. Her breasts were the only thing she'd had fixed a few years ago. No implants, but she'd had them raised just enough so as not to look droopy. So, breasts were all right. Skin. Soft and smooth. Eleanor chuckled; showing off her parts like this didn't reveal the entire truth. It was when you put all the pieces of her together and paired the whole with her persona that things got interesting. Addison had seen some of the reactions she induced in the people they'd encountered. Not very encouraging when combined with being twice Addison's age.

"Fuck. I'm not making any sense!" Eleanor headed into the bathroom and ran the shower. She removed her lingerie and rolled off her stockings before stepping under the hot spray of water. Moaning, she closed her eyes as she washed the hair spray and makeup off.

That turned out to be a mistake. As soon as she closed her eyes, a vision of Addison appeared behind her eyelids. Her long, auburn hair hung over her left shoulder, as usual, and she was dressed in that sinfully sensuous dress. It had ridden up like earlier, but this time on both legs. Addison's skin glimmered like pale satin. She was massaging her foot, and with every flick of her wrist, blue lace flickered between her strong thighs.

"No, no. No." Desperate for something to distract her, Eleanor pressed her forehead against a cool tile. "No." Why were these images, these thoughts, haunting her? She rinsed off and wrapped a soft terry-cloth robe around her shivering body.

Hurrying into her bedroom, she was ready to climb into the king-size bed when she heard a popping sound. Listening intently, she heard it again; it came from her desk. Her laptop. She logged in to get past her screen saver and saw that Skype was active. Immediately, she spotted Addison's nickname. "Blushaddict is online."

Not sure what possessed her, Eleanor took the laptop with her to bed and typed a message.

Valkyrie: Is your sister home safe and sound?

Nothing happened for a couple of minutes, but then Eleanor could see the pen-symbol move, an indicator that Addison was typing.

> *Blushaddict:* Yes. She had a great time. The limo was the coolest part, according to her.
> *Valkyrie:* Excellent.

Another minute-long silence.

> *Valkyrie:* Well. Good night, then.
> *Blushaddict:* Wait. Please? I'm sorry if I embarrassed you in the car.

Eleanor stared at the screen. *She* was sorry? She typed quickly before she started editing herself.

> *Valkyrie:* I'm the one who should apologize. I'm sorry too.
> *Blushaddict:* No, I didn't mean to flaunt myself like that. I'm not used to such short dresses.
> *Valkyrie:* You did nothing of the kind.

Several moments went by.

> *Blushaddict:* Can we talk? I mean do a video call? Or you might have had enough of me for one night.
> *Blushaddict:* Oh, God, I can't believe I just wrote that.

Eleanor thought fast. She was in a modest bathrobe, completely free of markup, but this was just a brief video conference, wasn't it?

Her heart pounded as she clicked on the button that dialed Addison's computer. As soon as Addison's webcam had focused, Eleanor knew she was in trouble.

"Hello," Addison said, and pulled her laptop closer on what had to be her bed. She was dressed in what most likely was her night attire: a formerly black, now charcoal-gray sleeveless T-shirt that reached her hip bone and light-blue flannel pajama pants. "Thanks. I was a little uneasy as we left things a bit weird."

"I'm sure I don't know what you're talking about." Eleanor curled up on the large white chaise lounge.

"So you're saying I imagined you more or less fleeing from the car?" Addison raised an eyebrow as she put her chin in her hand.

"I did nothing of the sort. Were you expecting some mindless chitchat or to be invited for a nightcap?" Inwardly wincing at her tone, Eleanor expected Addison to hang up on her instantly.

Instead, Addison looked at her thoughtfully for a few moments before speaking. "You know I wasn't. I think you're trying to make me angry, or even upset, so I won't dare question you again."

This was unheard of. Of all the people she stared down on a daily basis, the only one who dared stand up to her was this...this *girl*. Still, there was nothing girly about the way Addison looked at her now. Yes, she was young, but something in her eyes and the way she carried herself showed the kind of maturity that only developed from experiencing hardship one way or the other. "And so you persist." Eleanor ran a tired hand across her forehead. "Why do you need to know something so personal?"

"Because I felt it was my fault. That I did something that made you embarrassed or uncomfortable. I didn't want you to think I was, you know, coming on to you or something."

Eleanor tried to inhale, but her respiratory system was clearly failing. "What—what are you talking about?" She stared at the vision of Addison, her long hair spreading all over the pillows around her, the neckline of the old T-shirt hanging sideways, showing off the upper part of her right breast.

"Maybe I should've told you. I mean, before we signed the contracts and all, but I honestly didn't think it would have any sort of impact." She pushed impatiently at some errant hair tresses.

"What are you talking about now?" Bone tired suddenly, Eleanor gave in and carried the laptop over to her bed. She pulled back the down duvet and slipped inside, still in her robe.

"Um. Eh. You're going to bed. It's late." Suddenly their roles were reversed and Addison was the one being evasive.

"I'm tired and, yes, it's getting late. Speaking of that, did your sister enjoy herself?"

"She did. I found a note when I got home. Everything was a hit, from the limo to the dancing." Smiling softly, Addison looked so beautiful. "Gina was promptly invited to be one of the chaperones instead of me. She was 'the coolest one there,' according to Stacey."

"Excellent. I knew you wouldn't send your sister off to be supervised by just anyone. Gina Gallo is a friend of my family and she did it as a favor."

"That was really thoughtful of you, Eleanor. I can't say how much I appreciate that. She's all I have." It was as if Addison had curled up around the laptop. She was closer, and clearly her camera was amazing.

Eleanor could see everything in perfect high-definition. Suddenly self-conscious, she remembered she wasn't wearing any makeup at all. She no doubt looked her age and then some. "She's lucky to have such a caring sister."

Looking softer now, Addison only smiled. "I'm the lucky one. She's a great kid, and she never gives me any trouble like some of her friends at school do to their parents. I guess our bond is strong in a special way. I'm not her mother. I never will be. I'm her parent in the sense that I provide for her and love her to bits, but I'm not her mom."

Eleanor wanted to reach out and pat Addison's hand, which wasn't her usual response. She rarely engaged in private conversations, and never with anyone she worked with. Still, Addison's voice was mesmerizing and Eleanor found herself genuinely interested. "I understand. Perhaps that's why she's not as inclined to rebel."

Addison smiled, looking happily surprised. "Yeah, could well be." She pulled her lower lip in between her teeth, hesitating. "Eleanor. I didn't mean to totally flash you."

"You didn't." Eleanor pressed her lips together. Her stomach clenched, as did her thighs when her mind recalled the heated pictures of long, naked legs.

"I know you were ill at ease. Since we're going to work together, we can't have this between us. Sooner or later you're going to find out…about me. I figured I might as well tell you up front."

"Tell me what?" She could hardly breathe. What was Addison planning to say? Whatever it was, it was clear that Addison thought it would have a major impact. She narrowed her eyes. Was Addison teary-eyed? What was going on? "No matter what it is, just say it. It's late. I don't have time for any drama."

"I'm a lesbian." Addison's eyes grew huge and she kept blinking.

Eleanor stared at the woman she couldn't get out of her mind. "Is that all?" She struggled to sound matter of fact.

"Yes." Her voice weak, Addison dragged a hand through her long locks. "And I wasn't coming on to you. Not deliberately."

Not deliberately? Eleanor crossed her legs underneath her robe. What did that mean? Was Addison attracted to her? That was utterly ridiculous. She'd gone over in her mind every single reason why she was too old. And it was a moot point. No matter whether Addison was a lesbian, the young woman was lovely and kind, and could get any woman she wanted, no doubt.

"Your sexual orientation is of no consequence to this project." Eleanor waved her hand dismissively. "I didn't notice anything untoward tonight—"

"Then why did you practically run from the limo?"

Damn it, Addison was too persistent for her own good. "I was…I *am* tired."

Addison slumped onto her pillows and the laptop shifted, angling the camera to zoom in on her face further. Her chin trembled, and Eleanor knew more was going on than she'd first thought.

"Addison. You didn't offend me. I admit I was taken aback by my reaction to—to you. I didn't want you to notice. Not to embarrass *you*." It pained her to admit as much, but the vulnerable image of Addison was more than she could take. This was so unlike her; she refused to acknowledge just how much.

"Really?" Addison looked up, tugging a pink blanket closer. "I'm not good at this coming-out part. Never was."

"I realize it may be uncomfortable, but this is the twenty-first century. Surely we've come a long way."

Addison looked up and wiped her cheeks hastily. "Yeah. You'd think so. I'm blessed with a bunch of friends who've always accepted me. Stacey knows and she's cool with it." Her lips tensed again. "But my coming-out at nineteen killed my parents."

❖

Addison couldn't believe she'd just blurted out her biggest source of pain, and her shame, just like that. What was it about Eleanor that simply triggered this…this candor, in her? Normally she went through her days pushing these dark thoughts away while taking care of Stacey, filming her videos, and being the ever service-minded barista.

"What do you mean, Addison?"

Oh, no. Eleanor's voice had softened. Only marginally, but it was obvious to her. "Seven years ago, when I was nineteen, I came out to my parents. Let's just say they hated the idea of having a gay daughter. They argued with each other, casting blame, and tried to prevent me from hanging with any of my friends. They believed that one of my female friends must have turned me gay. Then, only a few days after my big announcement, they were driving home from visiting some friends. They called me on Dad's cell phone while I was babysitting Stacey. She was ten at the time. Mom was very upset with Dad and they kept arguing in the car.

I tried to distract them, make them stop…make them listen. Dad yelled at me to be quiet, that I'd said enough for quite a while—and then the phone went dead." Addison wiped at her eyes again. "As did they. They drove right up on the train tracks. Something was wrong with the crossing arms. Police said they probably never saw the freight train that plowed right into the station wagon."

"And you've lived with the guilt since then," Eleanor said quietly.

"Only in my head. I've never said anything to Stacey. I can't risk her…hating me."

Eleanor's hand passed the camera lens and Addison realized she was touching the screen. "Don't pity me. I can't take that right now."

"I don't do pity." Eleanor sounded her usual stern self, but her eyes glimmered suspiciously. "I find it unproductive and a waste of time."

Eleanor moved her hand and Addison wondered what part of the screen she was touching. Or what part of *her* Eleanor was touching…if she was doing that at all. She glanced at the smaller screen showing herself next to the image of Eleanor. The T-shirt covered most of her, but it had slipped sideways a bit, showing a bit of cleavage at the bottom of the screen. Blushing profusely, Addison wondered if that was what Eleanor was tracing with her fingers, back and forth.

"I do not, however, condone bigotry or intolerance. I may have a reputation for not having any patience for fools, and this is true. But you need not fear any repercussions for confiding in me regarding your sexual preference." Eleanor swallowed hard. "And while we're being confessional in the middle of the night, I should do you the same courtesy."

Addison licked her dry lips, and Eleanor followed the tip of her tongue's journey quite openly. "Yes?" Addison urged her softly.

"I did react in a completely unusual manner when faced with your beauty. I apologize, as it was inappropriate and uncalled for." Eleanor pulled back her hand and clenched her fist.

"That's why you ran," Addison whispered.

"Very astute observation. It's getting way too late now. Enjoy your weekend. I'll see you on Monday. Good night." The image of Eleanor flickered once and then disappeared.

Moaning, Addison pulled a pillow into her arms. Fuck. This was going to be a hell of a weekend after such confessions. "Oh!" Closing her eyes, she pulled the image of Eleanor's hungry stare from her memory. So, she hadn't imagined it after all.

Holy smokes.

CHAPTER EIGHT

A ddison rubbed her tired eyes. She'd been looking at swatches of color until she was dizzy and didn't feel much closer to a solution. She had a strong feeling this wasn't the way to go about this. What was more, she suspected that Keith, the chemist, and Linda, the "go-to person," as she'd introduced herself at their first meeting four weeks ago, had suggested this project to get her out of the way. Suddenly angry because these people were wasting Eleanor's money by not utilizing her time properly, she jumped up.

Shoving the swatches into her tote bag, she left the desolate conference room. This floor of the Face Exquisite's domain was hardly in use, which only strengthened her feeling that she was being deliberately ostracized. Did her presence really threaten Keith and Linda that much? Shaking her head at this ridiculous idea, she took the stairs to the floor above. This was where the head honchos of the company had their offices, with Linda as the spider in the web as Eleanor's XO while the company underwent serious restructuring.

Addison marched up to the bleached-blond young woman who worked as Linda's assistant.

"Hi again, Christa," Addison said, and smiled politely. Christa was the type of girl who made her teeth hurt. She was all for being nonjudgmental, but this woman gave beautiful, model-like women a bad name. Christa was disdainful and contemptuous; why she'd chosen to work in a service profession was anybody's guess. "I need to see Linda."

"Oh, well, I don't know. Let me check if she's available this week."

"This week?" Flames of annoyance licked the inside of Addison's belly and rose through her throat. "Are you telling me it's impossible for Linda, who referred to herself as my 'go-to person,' to give me ten minutes of her time this week?"

Christa blanched. "Um. Just let me—let me check." She typed away at her computer. "I'm sorry, Ms. Garr, I don't see any—"

"Fine. Fine!" Furious now, Addison whipped out her cell phone and dialed Eleanor's office at the Ashcroft Group. Pretty sure Susan wouldn't give her the runaround, she tapped her foot impatiently. This didn't help alleviate her jitters at the idea of hearing Eleanor's voice for the first time in three weeks. She'd been on an extended business trip in Europe, which had given Addison ample time to get antsy about their last Skype conversation.

Susan's friendly voice interrupted her thoughts. "The Ashcroft Group, Eleanor Ashcroft's office."

"Susan, hi, this is Addison Garr—"

"Addison! Wonderful. Ms. Ashcroft and I were just talking about you. She's been away, as you know, and between you and me, you were the first topic on the agenda when she arrived this morning."

I was? Addison coughed to clear the sudden lump from her windpipe. "Hmm. Really. I've run into a snag, Susan. I really need ten minutes of her time."

"Of course." Susan sounded as if she was smiling. "I'll put her on right now."

"Oh. Wow. Thank you." She felt totally unprepared, not only for the fact that she'd already been the topic of Eleanor's conversation on her first day back, but also that Eleanor was ready to take her call instantly.

"Addison? Everything all right?"

"No." Angry at herself for not being able to pull herself together and stabilize her voice, Addison took a deep breath. "You need to know that you're paying me to sit on my ass and look at swatches. For several days now. They're wasting my time and your money. I still get paid, but this wasn't what I signed up for."

"I'm on my way. Meet me at that little Italian place on the corner across the street in fifteen minutes."

"Oh. Okay." Addison blinked as she stared at her now-disconnected cell phone. She redirected her attention to Christa, who she guessed had been listening in and would report every single word she overheard to Linda. Fortunately Christa had heard only Addison's part of the conversation. "Well, as Linda doesn't have time to try to save this company according to Ms. Ashcroft's specifications, I'm out of here."

"Oh, but—"

"Later, Christa." *Go back to that nail filing you're so good at.* Addison hurried out the large glass doors and into the elevator.

Outside, the sun was making vehicles sparkle, and surely people were smiling more than they did last week. Or was it her mindset, the knowledge that she was going to see Eleanor in just a few minutes? She crossed the busy street, merely grinning at a cursing cabby who ended up smiling back at her out of sheer surprise, no doubt. The restaurant, which turned out to be a very small, intimate place, had just seen the last of the lunchtime mob, it seemed. A waiter was cleaning one of the corner tables when Addison stepped inside, requesting lunch for two.

"Oh, I'm sorry. We have no table available, ma'am," the maître d' said with a condescending smirk. "Usually, lunch here is booked in—"

"I see my favorite table is available, Rodolfo." Eleanor's voice sounded from behind. "Very kind of you to not give it away to just anyone, but this is my *associate*, Ms. Garr. I expect you to treat her like you do me in the future. Like family."

Addison forcefully closed her mouth as her jaw threatened to land somewhere around her feet. Had Eleanor said family? Today was shaping up to be surreal.

The maître d' certainly looked like he agreed. "Ms. Ashcroft. I had no idea. Please, this way." He guided them to a corner table cleverly tucked behind a wall of tall green plants, obscuring them from any of the other patrons. "Dora will be with you shortly to take your order."

"Thank you," Addison muttered.

Dora, the waitress, appeared instantly. They both ordered mineral water and accepted the menus. Addison opened hers but hardly looked at it. "I'm having a rather interesting day, Eleanor. How about you?"

Eleanor placed her elbows on her open menu and tilted her head while resting her chin against laced fingers. "Do tell."

"Let me ask you something first. What kind of reports are you getting from Linda and Keith?"

"From Keith, nothing. Everything goes through Linda. She's my eyes and ears at Face Exquisite."

"Are you telling me she's acting with your complete approval?" Her mood plummeting, Addison wondered if she'd misinterpreted Eleanor's eagerness to see her.

"Yes." Eleanor drew out the one-syllable word, not sounding entirely sure. "As you may know, I've been visiting six of our European headquarters and one in Dubai. I've received e-mails from Linda from which I gathered that you were struggling to get a handle on some of the basic ideas."

"What?" It was possible to see red when infuriated after all. Probably the blood pressure skyrocketing. Addison gripped the edge of the table, which kept her from slamming her fists into the linen-clad surface. "Let me guess. Linda mentioned nothing about my daily attempts to get the ball rolling. Nor did she write one single sentence about the three times my meetings with Keith have been interrupted by her, or by him. Yes, I've been having some issues with the swatches, that's true, but mainly because that's *all* I've been doing. I've stared at those freaking things so much, they could all be purple and green polka dot, and I'd still pick them just to get on with things." Addison gasped for air, feeling her lungs constrict. "I still get paid for my hours, but they're wasting your money by wasting my time. What's this Linda up to? Am I that much of a threat to her position at Face Exquisite?"

Eleanor's face didn't give anything away as she listened to Addison. She blinked slowly and Addison sensed that this movement was indicative of anger, studiously harnessed until unleashed. "Linda has worked for the Ashcroft Group for several years and for Face Exquisite ever since I took over. I've never had reason to doubt her allegiance or honesty."

That was that. So much for the dream of making this work, of doing what was best for Stacey. Addison's stomach clenched, and of course the waiter chose that moment to return to take their orders. Nauseous now from sheer disappointment, and from something else, a heartache stemming from something she couldn't decipher, Addison shook her head. "I'm sorry. I'm not hungry." She snapped the menu closed and handed it back to Dora. "Let me just pay for the mineral water..." She dug into her purse, looking for her wallet.

"Stop." Eleanor's voice made Addison jump and glance up, her eyes stinging. "Don't jump to conclusions." She turned to the waitress. "Give the menu back to Ms. Garr. There. I recommend the chicken parmesan or the salmon ravioli, but anything on their lunch menu is very good."

Addison saw something new in Eleanor's eyes, something hard as well as unforgiving. The question was, toward whom was it directed? Her stomach was still reacting like it normally did when she was anxious, but she ended up ordering the ravioli anyway. Dora thanked them, gathered the menus, and left. Addison sipped her water as she waited for Eleanor to continue.

"Just a moment." Eleanor pulled up her cell phone and pressed a button once. "This is Eleanor Ashcroft. Get me Linda. Now." A small frown appeared between perfect eyebrows. "Now." Her voice, so gentle before, was back to sounding lethal. "Linda. Hello. Yes, I'm back. I'm having lunch with Addison Garr."

Oh, God. Addison closed her eyes briefly as she pictured what tale Linda might be spinning.

"Why have you not made yourself available to Ms. Garr as we agreed?" Eleanor listened for ten seconds. "Your view on this is noted, but I really couldn't care less. This is not your area of expertise. You're the liaison between the Ashcroft Group and Face Exquisite. You're a facilitator. Addison is the expert on what is current, what signifies high quality, and most important, she's my personal choice. You've been a great asset to my company until now, which is the only reason I'm prepared to give you one more chance to do this right. I expect you to follow my directions tomorrow, or you may pack your bags and leave without the favorable letter of recommendation your tenure would generally garner. I don't have to go into detail how that will affect you in any future endeavor in Manhattan, hmm?" She listened again. "I thought so. No. Don't say that to me. You should direct any apologies to Ms. Garr." Tilting her head again, Eleanor sucked her lower lip in between her teeth. "And while we're on the subject of employment? Fire Christa Mueller and find an assistant who isn't a complete disaster. I do not appreciate the way she has performed."

Addison nearly dropped her glass. Eleanor had just told Linda off in no uncertain terms. Not only that, she'd made sure Linda knew her future employment with Eleanor's companies depended on how well she handled herself from now on. And Christa was out. Wow. Addison jerked as Dora placed plates of steaming food before them.

"Surely your appetite is back by now?" Eleanor speared a piece of chicken and looked pointedly at Addison's plate.

"Um. Yeah. Yes." She wasn't so sure about that, but at least now she could breathe. Relaxing against the backrest of the booth, she chewed the first forkful of her ravioli while studying Eleanor closely. For the first time today, she spotted signs of fatigue. "Oh, God. Here you come home after that marathon headquarters-hopping and I give you more grief. I'm sorry." Addison lowered her fork and took Eleanor's free hand before giving herself time to consider this bold move. "This has got to be the last thing you needed."

"Actually, Face Exquisite is more of a priority than any of the headquarters right now. I only went because it'd been planned for so long. I don't have to tell you how cutthroat corporate business in the U.S. can be. As for what I need? Sitting here, relaxing—finally—is just what I need." She glanced down at their joined hands. "It's nice to see you again, Addison."

Her face heated quickly when she realized she was still holding Eleanor's hand. She let go and fiddled with her knife. "Likewise. I mean, I'm glad you're back."

"I've kept up with your makeup videos," Eleanor said, and then to Addison's amazement, her cheekbones colored a faint pink.

"You have? That's great. I hope you found them to be of the caliber necessary for a representative of Face Exquisite."

"Yes. Absolutely." Eleanor pushed some penne pasta around her plate. "I learned a lot about lipsticks I didn't know. Especially about long-lasting ones that don't smear."

Addison crossed her ankles and pulled her feet in under her chair. The idea of Eleanor and smearing lipsticks was hot. Too hot for a conversation over lunch. "Glad it was useful," she murmured.

"Oh, it was." Eleanor's eyes scorched her as they homed in on her face, then traveled down to her hands and up again. "We need to discuss work-related details further, but I have a meeting in thirty minutes and I'd rather just have my lunch and some coffee. Will you be home this evening and available on Skype?"

Nothing was wrong with her heart. It beat just fine between her lungs. "Sure. Eight? Eight thirty?"

"Eight thirty." Eleanor nodded and methodically ate about half of the food on her plate.

Addison's appetite hadn't returned, but the crushing weight that had pressed her to the ground moments earlier had lifted somewhat, and she took a few bites so as not to give away just how Eleanor affected her. She still couldn't fathom how she'd held Eleanor's hand. Feeling guilty for wearing the jet-lagged woman out completely, she'd been prepared to take the blame even for things that weren't her fault.

Soon, Eleanor asked for the check, and when Addison began looking for her wallet again, Eleanor shocked her by stopping her with a hand on her arm. "This is on me." Her stern voice didn't allow for objections.

"Only if you let me buy you lunch next time." Groaning inwardly at her habit of speaking before thinking, Addison pressed her tongue hard to the roof of her mouth.

"By all means." Eleanor signed the receipt and then stood, donning her coat. "I'll see you later."

"Yeah." Hesitating only briefly, Addison placed a hand on Eleanor's arm as she was passing. "Thank you," she said softly. "For listening and for believing me."

"Addison, you don't possess much of a poker face. I knew you were telling me the truth." She placed her hand on top of Addison's, which was still on Eleanor's arm. "Don't change."

Addison couldn't think of a single sensible thing to say to that. The way Eleanor's voice had sunk an octave when she said "Don't change" was enough to render her mute, obviously.

"Until later." Eleanor left the restaurant, escorted the last few steps by Rodolfo, who was almost tripping over his own feet to reach the door and hold it open. He still stood there when Addison passed, clearly not sure in which category she belonged.

"Don't worry. No hard feelings," Addison said, enjoying his confusion a little too much as she stepped outside. The sun was still shining, people were still smiling. All in all, that was a pretty promising sign.

CHAPTER NINE

Eleanor sat down at her desk in the study and made sure she had enough lights on to avoid looking like a washed-out ghost on Skype. She checked the time. Eight forty-five p.m. Damn, she was late. She booted up her laptop and watched Skype load, and then she frowned. Addison wasn't online. Of course, why should she wait around? No doubt Addison's life was busy as it was, juggling a new job, her YouTube channel, and taking care of her sister.

The disappointment wasn't surprising in itself, but the *level* of it was disconcerting. She hungered for the sight of those sparkling hazel eyes and, oh God, that smile. When Addison looked at her, smiled, and tilted her head just so, it was as if nothing else mattered.

Annoyed at herself for this obvious weakness, she was just about to slam the laptop lid shut when the familiar signal announced someone's presence. Glancing at the chat window she saw Addison's nickname highlighted. *Finally.* Before Eleanor had time to react, a message appeared.

> *Blushaddict:* God, I'm sorry I'm so late, Eleanor. Are you still there?
> *Valkyrie:* I am.
> *Blushaddict:* Can you forgive me? I had an...Oh, damn. I'm ringing you.

The Skype signal rang from the laptop and Eleanor stared at the last line from Addison. Something was wrong. She clicked the green receiver icon to accept the call.

"What's going on?" Eleanor studied Addison's tousled appearance with growing concern. Her hair was in wild disarray, and she was dressed in a camouflage tank top with one shoulder strap half off her shoulder. "What happened?"

"We're okay now. I mean, we'll be fine. I was making dinner and I heard Stacey getting sick. I…It was a bad one. She's in bed now, sleeping, but I—" Addison wiped at her eyes. "And time got away from me and, and…" She stopped talking and slumped back in her chair, her eyes vacant as she stared at something beyond the screen.

"Addison. Please. What's wrong with Stacey?"

"I can handle it." Addison's lips were thin now, tense, as if she was willing them not to tremble. "I've handled it for years. This is just another…this is…" She hid her face in shaking hands.

"Addison." Feeling helpless as she watched Addison's distress, Eleanor reached out to touch the screen. Something had to be really bad for her to break down like this. "Will you tell me what's wrong?"

Addison rubbed her cheeks and then pushed away the strands that clung to her damp temples. "No, no. That's all right. Nothing I can't handle, I promise. Let's get down to business. That's why you're here. I mean there." She smiled self-deprecatingly. "You know what I mean." Addison breathed deeply and suddenly she stood, and the swaying image indicated she was carrying the laptop with her.

Eleanor's mouth fell open. Did Addison have any idea of the view she presented as she pressed the laptop against her, her breasts more or less resting on the keyboard? Her tank top had slid down farther, and the expanse of creamy skin filled the screen.

Eleanor refused to allow the groan building up inside her to escape. How had this young woman pushed past all her defenses? Not to mention wreaked havoc with her libido in a way she'd never experienced before?

Finally the swaying image settled as Addison sat down. Or lay down, as it were. Eleanor sighed inwardly as Addison got comfortable with the laptop clearly resting on her stomach. Her face, earlier so wracked with pain, now clearly showed her attempts at being stoic and pulling herself together.

"I'm sorry. I just couldn't take a minute more on that chair. I have to get a new one. It's killing my back." Addison snorted mirthlessly. "So where were we? Yes. Business. I have an idea how to announce my involvement with Face—"

"Wait. I want to hear this. I really do." Eleanor raised her hand. "But you have me worried. What's going on with Stacey? Please tell me. I promise, it's off the record and it goes no further." Eleanor couldn't remember ever having to beg someone to confide in her. Usually, she extricated herself from such situations very quickly, not very interested in heart-to-hearts. No wonder she was fumbling her way through this conversation.

Addison's lower lip quivered. "Really? I mean, it's hardly anything that impacts our business arrangement, and I know you're all about business. That's the reason we...we..."

"Addison," Eleanor said sternly. "You should know by now that I never say anything I don't mean, and if I say I want to hear about what is the matter with your sister, then that's what I mean, all right?"

"Oh. Right. Hmm. Okay." Addison spoke in the choppy way Eleanor had come to associate with her feeling unsure.

"I'm not forcing you, or, perhaps I am in a sense, but I really am interested. I've never seen you this unhinged."

"Unhinged? Oh, boy. I guess I look a mess." Appearing self-conscious now, Addison patted down her wild hair. "Stacey has a cerebral aneurysm. Until recently it's been chemically maintained. Now, a neurological team is seeing her and has decided she needs surgery soon. A lot of days you wouldn't know by looking at her that anything's wrong. Then on other days, like today, she's throwing up and her head hurts." Addison looked up at the ceiling for a moment, blinking rapidly as the rest of her words came out staccato, her voice harsh. "And every time I fear, you know, that this is it. This is when the fucking thing bursts and she—she bleeds out right in front of me. She's seventeen. Seventeen!" Addison was now looking pleadingly at Eleanor with swollen eyes.

"I'm so sorry, Addison." Eleanor felt completely helpless and inadequate, feelings she despised. "I can understand how worried you must be. Stacey has the best sister possible to help her through this."

"Help her. Yes. Or maybe no? I guess I feel I'm buckling under the pressure a lot lately." Addison gave her one-shoulder shrug. "I miss my parents. I mean, I miss them all the time, but lately I've missed having someone to share this situation with. Just *someone*."

"Share it with me. Isn't that what you're already doing?" Suddenly eager to show Addison she meant what she said, Eleanor leaned closer to the webcam. "Talk to me about it. Don't buckle, as you say. You're not alone. We're engaged in a business endeavor together, something we're both very interested in. Why not take advantage of our situation in other ways as well? You need a sounding board, and a shoulder, at times, and I..." She faltered, her stomach fluttering at the thought of being so up front with Addison. To offer herself like this, not her money, not just the business deal, but also herself and her time, was almost making her dizzy. "I enjoy our conversations, regardless of the topic."

"You do?" Addison's full lips formed a perfect "O." "Really? I mean, I love chatting and stuff, but you must be the busiest person in New York. You won't always have time for me and my worries." She was frowning now.

"Listen." Cursing the fact that she wasn't physically present and couldn't at least take Addison's hand, Eleanor rubbed her temple. Though afraid that her next words might make Addison feel uncomfortable, she still needed to be honest. "To be blunt, I wasn't doing so well during my trip. Business-wise it was a success and I accomplished my goals. Why you were on my mind so much, I don't know. It was completely unexpected, and the more

I fought them, the more resilient these images of you became. I'm not quite sure what's going on with us, or me, rather, but if I can help you—and Stacey—in any way, I wish you'd allow it."

"Our contract has helped me pay for the best care and also for the PT and care after the surgery. I don't need more money."

Clenching her hands out of sight, Eleanor knew Addison didn't understand. "I'm not talking about money, exactly," she said quietly. If that was all Addison thought she was able to contribute, a whole new world of pain would open for Eleanor.

Addison glanced up, suddenly wincing. "Oh, God. That's not what you meant, was it? I'm an idiot. You're right. I could use a, what did you call it, a sounding board? Someone who...cares?" Her cheekbones turned a faint pink. "And I absolutely love talking to you. Here or face to face." She looked flustered and covered her eyes for a moment. "I'm really not that shallow."

"I know." A tiny glow of relief in her chest made it easier to breathe. Eleanor tried for an encouraging smile. "Feel any better?"

"Oh, Eleanor." Addison pushed the laptop off her and set it down on the bed. Curling up on her pillow, she pulled a blanket over her shoulder. "I'm exhausted."

"Why don't you go to sleep?"

"I can't sleep for too long." Addison yawned, covering her mouth. "I have to check on Stace."

"Leave Skype on, then. I'll wake you in an hour or so." Eleanor could see how Addison relaxed at her words. "I'll mute the microphone so I can work without disturbing you."

"Okay. Thank you, Ellie."

Eleanor's heart twitched painfully at the shortened version of her name. Normally she'd correct such an attempt, but Addison had spoken unfiltered, and the nickname had sounded oddly right. Familiar.

"Go to sleep. I'll be right here." Eleanor muted the microphone and kept a small window of Addison's sleeping form in the upper corner of her laptop screen.

Deciding to follow Addison's example and crawl into bed, Eleanor sighed deeply at the thought of the two documents she needed to peruse. She'd been honest with Addison. The business trip had been harder than it should have been, since sleep had eluded her. She'd tried to relax, even going so far as counting damn sheep, but more often than not, she ended up where she really didn't want to be. She was aware of how desperate and pathetic her addiction to Addison's YouTube channel made her seem. The only relief was that nobody else knew just how much she craved listening to Addison's melodious voice and watching her animated expressions as she shared what was going on in her life with her viewers.

Now, when Eleanor was getting to know Addison and learn about her private circumstances, she realized Addison wasn't sharing very many details with her viewers, even if it would seem so. She never disclosed where she lived or what she did, or used to do, for a living. The comment section below the video clips always held personal questions, but Addison only answered the ones dealing with beauty-related issues.

A few of the comments were quite hateful. At first, Eleanor had been appalled and outraged at the horrible words people hurled at Addison. Some complained about her looks, others about the brands she spoke of. Lewd comments were usually flagged right away and removed, but then there were the ones that really upset Eleanor, the ones that suggested Addison was nothing more than a bought-and-paid-for makeup monger. Addison's integrity was above reproach in her eyes, which made her realize just how carefully they'd have to work when introducing Face Exquisite via her channel.

Now Eleanor didn't even try to read the documents. She knew she wouldn't be able to focus. Instead she checked her e-mail for update alerts, and yes, there it was. A new update to The Blush Factor channel. Double-clicking on the link, Eleanor waited impatiently as Addison's intro ran its course. Addison came into view and Eleanor had to chuckle. Auburn hair wrapped around big blue curlers adorned Addison's head, which made her look extraterrestrial.

"Hello, my friends." Addison wore pajamas and a fleece robe. "I have an important meeting tomorrow, so I need to look my best. And no, I'm not going to try to sleep on these things. I'm not that desperate. I am, however, going to show you a trick when you know you'd rather sleep in than do hair at six a.m."

Eleanor didn't really care about the clever advice, but she listened to Addison's voice with the same eagerness a starving man would regard a T-bone steak. She let her eyes roam over the clean, fresh face of the young woman. Addison was stunningly beautiful when she had applied her beloved beauty products so expertly, but like this, so close to the camera and with her face devoid of makeup, she was gorgeous. Her ethereal features suggested she might be frail, but Eleanor this knew wasn't true. Addison was strong and resilient. Capable of raising her younger sister alone and still finding the time and energy to produce this video channel all on her own. Nothing in her demeanor suggested how she struggled, coping with Stacey's illness and the uncertainty of the outcome of her sister's surgery.

Glancing at the serene Addison sleeping in the live feed in the corner of her screen, Eleanor knew without a doubt her life had changed. Long before she met Addison, she'd been pulled in by her personable nature and easy-on-the-eyes appearance. Now that she knew how wonderful this young woman was in real life, Eleanor realized she was in trouble. No matter if this was some midlife crisis, or merely hormonally induced, she was going to have to get a proper grip on herself. All she should do was be there for Addison when she needed her, make sure Stacey got the medical treatment she required, and work on Face Exquisite's resurrection. Anything else remotely personal, *intimate*, she would need to push back to the dark corners of her mind. Addison didn't need her to confuse matters.

The YouTube video ended with Addison looking absolutely gorgeous, of course, her hair in perfect waves, her makeup impeccable, and her smile blazing through the screen. Eleanor grabbed one of the pillows on her bed and hugged it close, moaning at the sight. How the hell was she going to pull this off when she wanted with her entire being, body and soul, to get in a cab, go over to Addison's house, and hold her tight?

Impatient with herself, Eleanor sat up abruptly and tossed the pillow across the room with a growl. She tugged her laptop onto her legs, her grip harsh as she pulled up her documents. Glowering at them, she knew whoever wrote them would probably faint at the sight of all the red corrections in the margin. No doubt they'd complain that she was impossible to please, but she didn't care. She had less than one hour to work off this frustration before she woke up Addison. Someone had to suffer for all this pent-up anguish, and it sure as hell wasn't going to be the young woman sleeping under her guard.

❖

"Addison. It's been an hour. Time to check on Stacey."

"What? Stacey? Oh!" Addison nearly tipped her laptop over as she sat up, trying to find the source of that sonorous voice. "Eleanor?"

"Right here." Eleanor chuckled. "Watching you wake up is so informative."

"Huh?" Addison pushed her wild hair from her face and stared at the screen where Eleanor was studying her while clearly lying on her own bed.

"Are you always this disoriented?"

"Only when I can't find who's talking. Disembodied voices do that to me." Addison covered her face for a moment. "Ugh, thank you for letting me sleep. I feel a bit out of it still."

"No wonder. You've had quite the evening. Why don't you go check on your sister, and I'll be here when you get back. I'm still working on this dismal attempt at an analysis."

"Oh, wow. Sounds like someone is in for a rude awakening when they get it back."

"Exactly."

Addison quickly tiptoed into Stacey's room where she slept so hard, she didn't even stir when Addison checked her pulse and felt her forehead. No fever. Strong, even pulse. Still worried, Addison tickled the soles of Stacey's feet and sighed in relief when she grimaced and pulled her legs up.

Returning to her bedroom after a detour to the bathroom to brush her teeth and put on an oversized T-shirt, Addison stopped as Eleanor gasped.

"What?" Addison had no idea what was up.

"Oh, God." Eleanor pressed her fingertips to her lips. "You're trying to keep me from focusing on my work, is that it?"

"Why would I do that? And how?" Addison crawled into bed, pulling back the covers.

"How's Stacey?" Eleanor tugged at her long necklace, her eyes roaming over Addison's body.

"Sleeping. She's okay, thanks." Addison pulled up the duvet and reached for the laptop. "Thank you. For being here."

"You're welcome. I didn't do much. I was here working anyway." Eleanor waved dismissively.

"You did more than that. You know you did." Addison ran her fingertip along Eleanor's cheek on the screen. "If you only knew how it felt to have someone here…sort of. Who cares."

"Oh, Addison." It looked like Eleanor placed her hand on the screen as well. "I would've liked to be there in person. I would've liked to hold you." She spoke so quietly, the microphone barely caught her words. "I hate to see you distressed."

"I don't like it much either." Addison tried for some humor. "I would've loved for you to be here. To be able to talk to you face to face. You know."

"I know." Her eyes so soft now, they nearly looked blue, Eleanor sighed. "It's getting late. You should go back to sleep."

"Yeah." Addison didn't want to turn off Skype and lose sight of the woman she couldn't get enough of. She could look at Eleanor forever, memorize every one of her features: the high cheekbones, strong jaw, pale-pink lips, and, oh dear God, those expressive eyes. She confessed to herself that she also wanted to run her fingers through the short, wavy hair. It looked like it would be silky, and she could imagine it curling around her fingers and pulling her in. "Um, may I ask a favor?"

Eleanor nodded briefly, a tiny frown on her forehead.

"Can we keep Skype on just a bit longer? You can turn it off if I start snoring." She pulled her right shoulder up in a quick shrug. "If that's okay."

Eleanor smiled. "If you want. Sure."

"Thank you." Addison curled up and grabbed one of the pillows to hold against her. "Night."

"Good night, Addison."

Not sure where her courage came from, Addison pressed her fingertips against her lips and then the screen. Closing her eyes, she listened to the faint sound of Eleanor typing and using the touchpad on her laptop. It was oddly reassuring, and in only minutes she went back to sleep.

CHAPTER TEN

Addison stepped inside and dropped the grocery bags on the hallway floor. Bone tired, she rubbed her neck. Spending a whole day editing video clips sure did a number on her trapezius muscles. Carrying cartons of milk and orange juice three blocks from the grocery store wasn't exactly relaxing them either. Truthfully, she'd been this tense for two days, ever since Stacey had her bad migraine attack.

She hung her jacket up and frowned at the sight of Stacey's jacket and schoolbag sitting on the floor. Was it really too much to ask of her to use one of the hooks? They were right there. Muttering, Addison hung up the black leather jacket she'd worked so much overtime to be able to buy for Stacey's seventeenth birthday.

She walked down the hallway and found Stacey's door closed. Knocking, she frowned when she didn't get a reply. "Stacey?" She opened it and found her curled up, silently hugging a large pillow. "You all right, honey? Is it your head?" Forgetting her annoyance, she rounded the bed. Stacey's face was streaked with tears and smudged mascara, and her chocolate hair lay in wet tresses against her cheeks.

"No. Head's fine." Stacey spoke in a low, scratchy voice. "I'm terrific, but clearly I'm not Elphaba."

"What? What do you mean?" Addison pulled her into her arms. "I thought it was decided."

"It was. *Was*." Stacey freed herself and pulled her legs up, hugging her knees. "Until my so-called friend Christine went to the director and explained that I wasn't fit to sing since I was having surgery and might have permanent fucking brain damage afterward."

Stiffening, Addison clenched her teeth so hard, she was prepared to hear them shatter before she was able to relax them enough to speak. "She did what?" she murmured. Her tone broke through Stacey's sadness, and she flinched.

"Oh, God. That voice means you're going to kill someone. I know it."

"She went to the director and this person *listened* to such garbage?" She couldn't remain seated. "I want you to give me the director's phone number. This. Instant."

"Addison. Please. Don't blow a fuse at him."

"Oh, trust me, my fuses are blown." Addison pulled out her cell phone. "Well?"

"All right, all right. Geez." Stacey grabbed a binder from the shelf above her desk, browsing through it with trembling fingers. "Here. That one. Mr. Hiller."

"Okay." Addison dialed as she left the room and walked into her own bedroom, closing the door. She wasn't going to murder this man over the phone in Stacey's presence. He might also ask hard questions that she wasn't prepared to answer in front of her.

"Hello?" a male voice said, sounding slightly out of breath.

"Mr. Hiller?" Addison sat down on her bed, hugging a pillow tight.

"Yes?"

"I'm Addison Garr, Stacey Garr's sister. I just came home and found my sister crying, completely heartbroken."

"Ms. Garr. I'm sorry. I'm on my way to a faculty meeting—"

"I don't care. Why did you take the part of Elphaba away from Stacey?"

"Because it was in her best interest, Ms. Garr. Her medical condition alone—"

"Her medical condition? You don't know anything about that." Tapping her foot now, Addison fought to remain calm.

"Of course not in great detail, but I learned from one of the other students that Stacey hadn't explained her situation fully, and neither I nor the school can assume responsibility for her safety."

"What the hell are you talking about? It's a school play. Not *Survivor* on an uninhabited island."

"It's a school play where Elphaba will swing from the rafters in a harness, Ms. Garr. If Stacey gets ill or her condition deteriorates, she could fall down or, worse, her aneurism could burst. It wasn't an easy decision to make. I know how happy Stacey was to be cast as Elphaba." He sounded sincere, even distraught. "I wish I could do something, I really do, Ms. Garr. Stacey's voice was the best by far, and her stage presence is amazing. When her health is restored, I think I can guarantee she will be cast in the next musical in her senior year. It would be a crime not to."

Addison gave a muted sob, muffling it against the pillow. She hadn't known about Elphaba swinging from any rafters. "I apologize for yelling at you," she said. She could hardly speak, her voice was so husky. "I understand, Mr. Hiller." She did. The school would be held accountable if anything happened to Stacey while rehearsing or performing. The truth was, until Stacey's aneurism was dealt with, she was a ticking time bomb. She couldn't blame Stacey for sticking her head in the sand and pretending everything was fine. She'd been doing the same thing. "I'll talk to her. I'm not sure she'll understand, at least not right away, as this was her dream part."

"If it's any consolation for her, tell her that friends of mine will be attending the dress rehearsal. I don't know if you've heard of Chicory Ariose. They're a pretty famous all-female group."

"No, I don't think so. Stacey might have, though. She's the one with the music talent at our house."

"Anyway, two of them, Eryn and Mike, have been friends of mine since I lived in East Key. I was so excited about this year's cast, including Stacey, I asked them if they'd come listen. When they come, I'm going to insist they hear my original Elphaba sing. Would you please let Stacey know that?"

Addison changed her initial opinion of Mr. Hiller completely. "Thank you. I really appreciate your honesty and that you're looking out for my sister. She's been through a lot over the years and it's still tough going, as you can imagine."

"Anytime, Ms. Garr. And please, when it's time for Stacey's surgery, do keep us in the loop."

"I will. Thanks for taking the time to explain." Addison said good-bye and disconnected the call. Sighing, she rubbed her temple. She felt so bad for Stacey. Feeling her pain and disappointment, she wanted to ease her sister's heartache.

Just as she was about to get up and go back to Stacey, her phone buzzed, notifying her of a text message.

How is Stacey doing?
E.

How could one text message infuse more oxygen into the air? Addison smiled and held the phone harder. Tapping the screen she typed in her reply.

Her head is better. Major disappointment here today re: school musical. Lost her part. Going to try to cheer her up now.
Addie

Tucking the phone into the pocket of her hoodie so she'd feel it vibrate, Addison thought of how Eleanor had watched over her as she slept, completely drained, two evenings ago. The way they'd interacted after Addison woke up still made her blush. Weak at the knees, she recalled Eleanor's voice calling her name, waking her via Skype.

She stopped her mind from going there and hurried back to Stacey, who now sat listlessly at her desk, staring down at her homework without moving.

"Sweetie-girl, listen." Addison pulled up a pink-and-blue stool to sit next to her. "You won't be playing Elphaba, that's true." She explained about liability and how it worked, but she could tell this didn't help lift Stacey's mood at all. "Have you heard of Chicory Ariose?" Addison stroked Stacey's back.

"What? Chicory…? Oh, yeah, the improv jazz and blues group. I have, yes. Mainly because they've done several songs with Noelle Laurent." Stacey looked interested for the first time since Addison came home. "Why?"

"Mr. Hiller was actually quite heartbroken to lose you as Elphaba. He said you were a shoo-in next year when they do the musical your senior year. And"—she held up a hand when Stacey's eyes darkened again—"and this year, at dress rehearsal, two members of Chicory Ariose are going to be present. Mr. Hiller hoped you'd be available to sing even if you can't play Elphaba."

"Wait. Run that by me again." Stacey sat up straight. "Mr. Hiller knows someone in Chicory Ariose and thinks they should hear me sing? Me? Really?" A smile broke through, and even if her eyes were red and swollen, that smile illuminated her entire face.

"Really. I believe he called them Eryn and Mike."

"Mike? Oh yeah, the drummer is a girl, but her name is Mike. I think she's the one who's with the opera singer. You know, the one who lost her sight?"

Addison gaped. "Vivian Harding? Even I've heard of her."

"And Eryn, the other one Mr. Hiller mentioned, is married to a woman also. Can't remember her name, but she's super rich. Perhaps your Eleanor knows her."

"She's not *my* Eleanor." Addison's cheeks warmed. "Don't keep saying that. Someone might overhear you one day and that could mean trouble."

"Only if it was remotely true or if—oh, God, you're blushing!" Stacey's eyes grew huge. "You're totally blushing and that can only mean one thing. Something happened."

"What on earth are you talking about?" Annoyed now, and also a little bit relieved that Stacey wasn't crying anymore, Addison put her hands on her hips.

"Last time we talked about Eleanor Ashcroft, you were all hung up on her not listening to you and how those yoyos at Face Exquisite were undermining you. And now...you blush when I mention her. When I call her *yours*." Stacey mimicked Addison's stance. "And what's this? You only go 'oh, I'm your big sister so don't give me that' on me when I'm close to figuring something out. Honestly. Like taking candy from a baby."

The girl was too clever for her own good, Addison thought darkly, and glowered at her. Yet a part of her wanted to cheer since this was enough distraction to keep Stacey smiling. "Eleanor and I—"

"See? Exhibit A, 'Eleanor and I,'" Stacey said, sticking her index finger in the air.

"Shut up. Eleanor and I have Skyped a few times, mainly about business, but also that evening a few nights ago when you were so sick, remember? She's been really nice and understanding. I actually got a text from her asking about you just now. See?" Pulling her cell phone from her pocket, she handed it to Stacey.

Stacey tapped the screen a few times, and then her eyebrows seemed to fly off her face. "Um. Addie? You sure you mean *this* particular text?"

"What do you mean?" Taking the phone back, Addison scanned the messages. She saw the one she'd replied to and then discovered another one from Eleanor she'd missed while focusing on Stacey.

I wish I could be there for you. I keep thinking about our chats. I missed you last night. Tonight at 8? I hope that will help me sleep.
E.

Crap. And of course Stacey had to see that one.

"She missed you? I thought you work together?" Stacey looked more confused than teasing at the moment.

"We do, but mainly at a distance. She's very hands on, really—" Her face on fire after that stupid comment, Addison forged ahead. "I mainly work with her representative in another building and the head chemist right now. I told you that. We're coming up with new products. And she didn't *miss* me. She missed me as I didn't make it to the chat last night."

"Ha. I think I'm right and you're wrong. As for the makeup, yeah, I remember. Cruelty free against cruel ones." Stacey tilted her head. "So since you two aren't working together in the same place, she *misses* you. That's awesome." Stacey winked.

"It's not what it sounds like. You're forgetting something, Stace. Eleanor isn't a lesbian."

"We talked about that already. According to the tabloids, she hasn't been in a long-term relationship for years. Hardly ever, as far as I've found out. I know you didn't want me to, but I've researched her some more since you're so gone on her."

"Gone on her? Oh, my God, Stace. I find her attractive, but that's all. She *is* attractive. I'd think so even if I was straight." Covering her face with both hands, Addison peeked at Stacey between her fingers.

"Which proves my point. You're totally obsessed with her." Looking proud of her own powers of deduction, Stacey ticked off more arguments on her fingers. "So, no long-term boyfriend for Eleanor. She's very private and she's a workaholic. Even if she's not aware of why she's hot for you—"

"Stacey!" Shocked and amused at the same time, Addison thumped Stacey's shoulder. "Not another word. You're impossible." And she was too close to the truth. Eleanor had confessed to being confused about Addison. Surely that's what Eleanor meant when she'd said, "I found myself thinking of you far more than what's logical, or prudent, for that matter." That said, Addison was still terrified of reading anything more into what Eleanor was saying. She'd met straight women who were curious and eager to experiment, only to decide they were really very straight once they'd satisfied their curiosity.

Having fallen for that once, she'd put it right up there on her list of stuff she didn't care to do again. If that happened with Eleanor, it would break her heart. It was much better to keep her distance and just enjoy the fact that Eleanor seemed to like her, as well as her efforts at work.

"You feeling better?" Addison slid a hand underneath Stacey's hair and cupped the back of her neck.

"Yeah. A little. Mr. Hiller's idea that I should perform for half of Chicory Ariose isn't bad. Makes it hard to stay mad at him."

"And you'll get a part next year." Addison smiled encouragingly.

"Seems far away, but that's cool." Stacey sighed and looked at her desk. "Better get on with my French homework. How one language can have so many exceptions to rules in its grammar is beyond me."

"I know. I remember tearing out tons of hair when I took French."

"And your French still didn't stick, did it?" Stacey stuck her tongue out and grinned.

"Behave, or dinner will—shoot!" Remembering the groceries sitting on the hallway floor, with ice cream melting all over the place, no doubt, Addison sprang to her feet. "Do your homework and I'll start dinner, okay?"

"Okay." Stacey sat motionless for a moment before suddenly hugging Addison tight. "Thanks. You're the best," she whispered.

"Oh, sweetie-girl." She hugged Stacey back. "Love you."

"Love you too."

As she walked out to the abandoned groceries, Addison answered Eleanor's text.

Thank you. Crisis averted, I think. Looking forward to 8 pm.
Addie

The response came just as she dumped the groceries on the kitchen table.

Good. See you then. If there is anything I can do for
Stacey, you must tell me.
E.

This wasn't the first time Eleanor had offered to help with Stacey. What could Eleanor possibly get out of caring for a girl she'd never met? Perhaps she was merely a caring person despite her boardroom-barracuda reputation? To be honest, Addison hadn't seen any of the barracuda personality directed toward her. Yes, Eleanor had dealt harshly and methodically with those on her staff that weren't doing their jobs to her satisfaction. That was true. Still, Eleanor seemed to really care about her. Addison wanted to believe in Eleanor's good intentions and the attraction she had all but confessed to, but how could she possibly lower her guard when she knew so little about her?

Putting away the groceries, Addison tried to push away the thoughts of what it would be like to give in to her desire when it came to Eleanor. What if she came on to Eleanor and she realized being with a woman wasn't her thing? Eleanor could be totally repelled, which would crush Addison once and for all.

Addison didn't understand how she could be so certain, but she was. When it came to Eleanor, she would have to be very careful, but a small voice in the back of her head snickered insistently, "Too late!"

CHAPTER ELEVEN

Eleanor regarded the text on her cell phone with equal parts trepidation and excitement.

I know we said we'd chat at the usual time. How about having dinner with Stacey and me instead? It's pasta night.

She couldn't get over how fast her nerves kicked in as soon as anything new developed that involved Addison. After three weeks of Skyping, at least once every other evening, she'd grown almost addicted to hearing that clear voice. They spoke of work mainly, that was a given, but before they logged off, personal topics would creep in, and Eleanor had confided things to Addison that she would be loath to tell anyone else. Nothing mind-blowing, merely little personal things that were special in a humble way.

Addison seemed to grasp this point. She never made a big deal about what Eleanor told her, but she listened intently, her head tilted and her big eyes narrow and completely focused.

Last night, Addison had asked her about how she came to inherit Face Exquisite. Even if Eleanor had held back, she hadn't bitten Addison's head off, which she would've done with anyone else that dared raise the subject. The thought of what her father did to her beloved Aunt Priscilla was still an open wound. What if more touchy subjects ended up on the agenda when she went to Addison's house?

She'd considered coming up with an excuse, but so much pulled her toward Addison. She wasn't fooling herself regarding just how much she wanted to see her. She was also curious to meet Stacey. At least she hoped she wouldn't come across as too obvious once she was actually there. She had accepted via yet another text, and now it was time to get ready.

Staring at the rows of clothes in her walk-in closet, she groaned. What the hell did someone wear to an informal dinner in Newark? She hadn't been to anything informal in ages. Business dinners, luncheons, banquets, lonely dinners in hotel rooms, and fancy dinners in restaurants—these she could easily dress for. How pathetic it was for her a mere family-type dinner to stump her. Eleanor tried to envision what Addison would be wearing. Jeans. Yes, denim, for sure. Stacey too. Did she even have any jeans? She walked over to where she kept her leisurewear. Ignoring the workout clothes, she found not just one, but three pairs of Levi's hanging to the far left. Checking the size, she nodded absentmindedly. That would do. Now, what to wear with the jeans so she wouldn't look like she was trying too hard. She snorted. As hard as she actually was.

She decided on a tailored, white button-down shirt, which she decided not to tuck into the jeans. A necklace she remembered Addison expressing admiration for and her new Hublot man's watch completed the outfit nicely. The owner of the store had tried to talk her into buying the one-million-dollar watch, but even if she could afford it, she would never splurge on such a ridiculously expensive item. She did love watches though, and the Classic Fusion on her arm was a masterpiece.

Donning black ankle boots and a black leather jacket, Eleanor grabbed her purse and a bottle of cabernet sauvignon, and left her penthouse. Downstairs, one of the doormen had pulled up her Maserati Coupé. The black car hummed to life under her hands as she turned it out into the early evening Manhattan traffic. She used voice command to enter Addison's address into her GPS system and soon was crossing the Hudson. For a moment it seemed she was leaving everything old and familiar behind and moving toward something entirely new.

After fifteen minutes, Eleanor turned into a homey street, a place where children played on the sidewalks, rode their bicycles, and no doubt went trick-or-treating to all the neighbors in the fall. She pulled over by a light-blue house boasting a large porch with a white railing.

Grabbing the bottle and her purse, she stepped out of the car and inhaled the crisp air. Could the air really be that different between Newark and Manhattan? It would seem so. The garden path was made of traditional flagstones and the lawn well kept. Was Addison into gardening as well, or perhaps Stacey? Somehow Eleanor doubted the latter.

To her surprise, the door was half open, and Eleanor stood indecisively just outside as she heard voices.

"You can't go, Stacey. You know that," Addison called out from inside the house.

"Everybody else is. It's not like I'll be doing anything dangerous."

"I'm not signing the consent form." Addison sounded sorrowful. "You have to realize—"

"I don't have to realize anything. No Elphaba. Okay. But everyone's going on this trip!"

"Everyone doesn't have surgery coming up in less than two weeks, Stace."

Eleanor had raised her hand to knock on the doorframe when a young girl backed up toward the doorway, gesturing wildly with her arms to someone inside the house. "Just so you know, I hate this. I *hate* you!"

"Really?" Eleanor said from where she stood less than a foot behind the girl. "I'm crushed."

Pivoting, the girl who had to be Stacey Garr stared at her with big brown eyes. "Oh, God, Eleanor. Ms. Ashcroft. I didn't mean you. I'm so sorry!" She held up her hands, palms forward. "I'm so, so sorry."

"From where I stand, I think that apology might be better directed toward your sister?" Eleanor tilted her head, clearly seeing the family resemblance even if Stacey's hair and eyes were darker and she was also taller than Addison.

"What? Oh. You heard it all, didn't you?" Stacey slumped against the wall. "Please, come inside. If you haven't changed your mind because of me."

"It takes more than that to deter me." Eleanor hid a smile and stepped inside. Stacey closed the door behind her.

"Eleanor's here. Oops, I mean, Ms. Ashcroft."

"Already? I mean, she is? You mean, inside?" Addison came through a door to the right, wearing a blue apron that said MESSY BUT CUTE! Her eyes grew big at the sight of Eleanor. "You're here!" She checked her watch. "But—oh, God, it's seven already? Fu—I mean, darn it."

"Hello, Addison." Eleanor looked back and forth between the two sisters. "I think I can guess why you lost track of time."

"You can?" Addison glanced at Stacey. "Oh, no. Don't tell me you overheard that."

"Part of it, yes."

"Welcome to the family yelling contest." Wiping her hands on the apron, Addison smiled broadly. Her hair was tied back in a high ponytail and she wore minimal makeup, which made her look so young and fresh, Eleanor's heart ached. *So unattainable.*

"Stacey?" Eleanor said, looking pointedly at the younger of the Garr sisters.

"Um, yeah. Uh, sis? I'm sorry I yelled at you." She sighed. "You know I don't hate you. I love you. I'm just so disappointed."

Eleanor could tell that Stacey was close to tears and decided to intervene. "When is this trip you can't go on?" Eleanor handed the bottle of wine to Addison. "I hope you like this."

"Thank you." Addison glanced at the label. "Wow. I'm sure I'll love it. It'll go great with the pasta, even if my food won't do it justice. Stace, Eleanor asked you something."

"Oh, yeah. It's on Tuesday of next week. We're...I mean they're going to an indoor waterpark and then dining out in

Connecticut. A whole day of fun stuff. I really shouldn't have been such a bitch to you. Oops, sorry again, Ms. Ashcroft."

"Do call me Eleanor, Stacey."

"Well, I knew all along, I think, that it'd be too much for me. Especially as I can go into surgery pretty much any day after next week. The sooner the better, Dr. Reimer said."

"I could actually use your help that day, if it's all right with your sister," Eleanor said as she removed her jacket and gave it to Stacey to hang up.

"Really? Doing what?" Stacey's face lit up. "I'd do anything rather than sit in school and be bored out of my mind. Lick stamps. Empty bins. Anything."

Eleanor chuckled. "What I have in mind should be a little more challenging and fun than licking stamps." For some reason, Eleanor's gaze shifted to Addison, who was stirring something smelling very good in a large pot on the stove. The kitchen was homey, if a bit worn, with a breakfast nook where a round table was set for three. "I'm planning to spend all of Tuesday and Wednesday at Face Exquisite, and if Addison says it's all right, you can be my personal assistant and help me keep track of all the samples. We're going to talk a lot about makeup, advertising, and promotion. Unless that bores you to tears, of course. I'd pay you an assistant-level salary."

"Addie? Please say yes." Stacey smiled tremulously as Addison was already nodding. "Yes? Oh, cool. Thank you!" Stacey hugged her sister and then turned to Eleanor, looking like she was ready to embrace her as well. Then she caught herself and merely pushed her hands into her back pockets. "Oh, this is awesome. Thanks, Eleanor. I'll do my best. You won't regret this. I've got to tell Maureen. Call me when dinner's ready. I'll come help." She left the kitchen before anyone had a chance to say anything else.

"So that's Stacey," Eleanor said matter-of-factly. "Charming girl." She walked up to Addison and kissed her cheek. "Hello, Addison."

"Oh. Hi." Blushing faintly, Addison touched the cheek Eleanor had kissed. "You look great. Very relaxed. I don't think I've seen you quite this casual. If you don't count the sleepwear during our Skype sessions." The pink hue left her cheeks. "Oh, God. I can't believe I said that." She covered her eyes with her hand. "Don't listen to me. Can I get you anything to drink?"

"Some mineral water would be lovely, thank you." Eleanor could hardly breathe but did her best to hide it. Addison's cheek was so soft and the feeling still lingered on her lips, almost like a humming sensation. Then there was the matter of her thundering heart. How was it possible to react this way because of a simple kiss on the cheek? *Because it's her.*

"Coming right up." Addison dove into the fridge and came out with two bottles. She poured some into a tall glass after adding a few large ice cubes. "Here you go."

"Thank you."

"No. Thank *you*. You didn't have to do that for Stacey. That was very sweet of you. She was pretty upset, as I'm sure you could tell." Addison rubbed her temple. "Lately I've had to slam the brakes on practically everything Stacey loves to do. It's hard to be the one who delivers the disappointments all the time. I'm sure she feels like all I do is say 'no' nowadays, and she's right. It sucks."

"And here I swoop in and act like a fairy godmother." Eleanor wanted to kick herself. "I didn't mean to make you out to be the 'bad cop,' Addison."

"Hey, don't even think that. If I have to be 'bad cop' to keep her alive and healthy enough to sustain surgery, I will. I know Stace loves me no matter what she yells at me across the house. And for you, whom she already idolizes in many ways, to come here and show her she can be useful and that you trust her to still do a good job—that's freaking awesome." Addison's eyes shone. "I keep saying thank you but it's not enough. Not really."

"Nonsense. You don't have to thank me." Eleanor glanced around her. "If you have a corkscrew I can open the cabernet sauvignon I brought. It should breathe a little."

"Sure. Top drawer."

Eleanor pulled out the corkscrew, which turned out to have nothing in common with the high-tech version she had mounted on her kitchen wall at the penthouse. "Let's see if I can still do low-tech," Eleanor said, pursing her lips. As it turned out, the old-fashioned way worked very well and the cork came out without mishap. "Voilà."

"Great. Want to take a look at our house? It's not big, so it'll be a quick tour." Addison stood there, looking quite adorable in her blue apron with her hands clasped behind her back.

"Absolutely." In fact, she was very curious. Especially about Addison's private space in this modest house.

"Well, you know the kitchen intimately now, as you know where I keep the corkscrew. Over here is the living room, which also doubles as our family room and entertainment room." Addison began the tour through the house where she and Stacey grew up and later inherited when their parents died. "Upstairs we have the bedrooms and the room that I do the filming in. Most of the filming. Sometimes I use other rooms or even go outdoors, depending on which type of film it is." Walking up the stairs, Addison opened the door to her little home studio first. "See? Not very big."

"In your video clips it looks like it's much bigger. You do a great job, Addison, especially since you've had to fix all of this and get the equipment all on your own." She glanced at some plastic containers filling most of the far wall, which was out of the viewers' sight when Addison filmed. "What on earth is all that?"

"I told you how I felt people would think I wasn't credible if I allowed any of the brands to pay for anything, or even send me free stuff. As you can see, that still happens. When it does and I can't return it for some reason, I hold competitions or raffles and sort of pay it forward that way." Addison turned to walk out of the room, which Eleanor wasn't prepared for. Suddenly they were standing well within each other's personal space, face to face. "Oh. Sorry."

"It's all right." Eleanor greedily inhaled that special scent that was all Addison, with something spicy added to it, perhaps from the cooking. "You smell so good."

"I—I do? It's just in-shower lotion. No perfume. Well, not today." Addison then bent forward a little, inhaling as she closed her eyes. "You're wearing something soft, a little dark, but not heavy. What is it?"

"Burberry Body." Eleanor could hardly speak when Addison was this near.

"Wonderful. It suits you." She opened her eyes and seemed to realize how close she was. "Um. To the right again is my bedroom. There." Pointing, she looked confused when Eleanor didn't move.

She felt rooted in place and couldn't force her feet to budge. Only a floor lamp over by the window lit the room and also cast enticing shadows over Addison's soft features. Eleanor clenched her hands hard to make them behave and not do something completely inappropriate.

Addison's hands were under no such restraints, it would seem. Cupping Eleanor's cheek in her right hand, Addison whispered, "You're stunning, Ellie. Thank you for coming tonight." She slid her fingers along Eleanor's jawline, which nearly made her knees buckle.

"My pleasure." *God.* Eleanor cleared her voice. "I mean, I'm glad to be here."

"I'm glad you're here." Lowering her hand, Addison looked into Eleanor's eyes, as if transfixed. "I admit, I've been nervous as hell all day. I even rehearsed what to say when I opened the door, and then, as it turns out, it all went to hell anyway when you stepped right into us yelling like banshees."

"I didn't mind." Eleanor glanced down. "I like your apron. I happen to agree."

"Agree? With what?" Addison glanced down her front and then snapped her eyes back up again. "You're joking."

"I'm doing nothing of the kind. You're looking wonderfully tousled and definitely cute." She smiled as Addison became speechless for the second time this evening.

"Cute," Addison finally managed to say with a groan. "I can't believe it."

"Very cute." Eleanor pushed a wavy strand of auburn hair behind Addison's delicate ear. "Slightly messy."

"Ellie, you—you shouldn't say stuff like that. And we shouldn't touch…like that." Clearly trembling now, Addison pressed her fingers to her lips.

Pulling the hand away from Addison's full, curvy lips, Eleanor held on to it and raised it to her face. She placed it back against her cheek and then slowly slid it forward until she could press her lips to Addison's palm.

Addison in turn shook her head slowly. "Ellie…"

"Addison…" Eleanor whispered against the hand she was holding. "Please."

"Sis? You up here? Can Maureen come over too? Is there enough food?" Stacey's voice echoed throughout the house.

Eleanor let go of Addison and took a quick step back.

Her eyes huge, Addison cleared her throat. "Sure, Stace. If her parents say it's okay."

"Cool. Thanks!" Stacey yelled.

"We better go down to the kitchen and make sure I have enough garlic bread to go around." Addison moved past Eleanor and headed down the stairs. "We can finish the tour later."

Eleanor was still dizzy from the emotions infusing every part of her. Attraction. Arousal. She reeled herself in and followed Addison down the narrow stairs. Yes, they would finish the tour later. She would insist on it, as she knew very well which room was left to explore. Addison's bedroom.

CHAPTER TWELVE

It took Addison only a few moments to realize that choosing spaghetti for pasta night when she was having a special someone visit was a mistake. It was impossible to eat without making a mess. Well, unless you were Eleanor Ashcroft with perfect table manners.

Stacey and Maureen weren't being helpful either. They twirled the spaghetti around their forks but ended up slurping the last inches while giggling.

"I think the two of you need to learn the proper way to eat spaghetti from Eleanor," Addison said, and waved her fork admonishingly.

"Look who's talking," Stacey said, pointing at Addison's plate. "You're not exactly in a position to criticize too much, are you?"

Addison glanced down and saw tiny splatters of pasta sauce on the table around her plate. "Typical," she said, and sighed. "And here I was, trying to impress our guest." She glanced up just in time to see Stacey wiggle her eyebrows suggestively. "Don't even go there, sis." Addison could see Stacey was deep into one of the silly moods that she and Maureen tended to lapse into in the evenings.

"Aw, come on, Addie," Stacey said. "I'd never tell Eleanor— oops. I'm being quiet now." She could obviously comprehend that she was moving toward being in serious trouble.

"Tell me what?" Eleanor asked, dabbing delicately with her napkin at the corner of her mouth.

"Oh, you're in trouble now," Maureen said, bumping Stacey's shoulder. "You and your big mouth."

"Hey, whose side are you on?" Stacey pouted and bumped her friend back. "I'm just kidding, Eleanor. Don't mind me."

"Did I say I minded?" Eleanor tilted her head and gazed at Addison. "I assume I'll find out sooner or later if it's important."

"I thought I knew how to use a fork and spoon," Addison said, trying to get back on topic, "but I seem to do something wrong. It still splatters."

"Like this. Not too much on the fork and move your hand slowly." Eleanor performed the maneuver perfectly before tucking the forkful of pasta into her mouth. She chewed meticulously, only to start laughing once she'd swallowed. "I don't think I've had such a riveted audience, ever."

"We're trying to learn how not to have the table manners of a caveman." Stacey mimicked Eleanor's twirling of the fork pressed to a spoon. "Okay, here goes." She placed the pasta carefully in her mouth and chewed. "Whoa. I did it! Look, sis." She repeated her maneuver with equal success.

"Now me." Maureen had to try twice before she managed to avoid getting pasta sauce on her chin.

"Yay. Your turn, Addie." Stacey looked expectantly at her.

Oh, great. Addison's hands were too unsteady, too sweaty, all of a sudden. She glanced at Eleanor, who was sitting to her right at the round kitchen table.

"Not so fast," Eleanor said softly, and placed a hand on Addison's arm. "That's when it splatters."

"Guess that makes sense." Willing her hands not to tremble, Addison twirled her pasta and placed it in her mouth. And damn near choked at the hungry expression in Eleanor's eyes.

"Guess we'd know more about these things if Mom and Dad had been around longer," Stacey said, then groaned as she shoved her hands through her hair. "Sorry, Addie. I didn't mean it that way."

"Hey, Stace. It's all right." Addison smiled through the twinge of pain. Stacey had missed out on parental advice more than she had. "You're right. We got into our own habits after they died."

"Don't beat yourself up," Maureen said calmly, and stabbed a piece of mozzarella. "You guys still have better manners than most in my family. My brothers could use a few lessons."

"There you go," Eleanor said, and smiled, her eyes soft now as she looked back and forth between Addison and Stacey. "Though it may sound like I was born during the Jurassic era, trust me. I've come across some brats in my day. Neither of you resembles any of them, not even close. I can see that you miss your mother and father, but it doesn't show on the outside."

Addison could only focus on breathing in and out, very slowly, or she might have thrown her arms around Eleanor and thanked her in a way the other woman hadn't counted on.

They finished the pasta while chatting about the girls' schoolwork and their French test, which was coming up in a week. When it was time for dessert, Stacey turned to Addison, the little demons back in her eyes. "If Maureen and I do the dishes, can we take our dessert up to my room afterward? We want to watch *Vampire Diaries*. I've recorded the last two episodes since we missed them."

"Why not?" Addison answered before realizing this meant she and Eleanor would have the living room to themselves.

Addison filled two bowls with ice cream and chocolate and carried them to the coffee table, Eleanor following her.

"Am I wrong or did Stacey just wink at us and wiggle her eyebrows. Again?" Eleanor pursed her lips and Addison suspected she was being teased. Again.

"Stacey can be such a wiseass sometimes," she muttered, and then couldn't help but chuckle. "She's also very perceptive."

"Should I take that as a warning?" Eleanor sat down on the couch.

"That would be a yes. She's an unbearable tease, and she never lets you off the hook once she thinks she's on to something."

Addison stopped just as she was about to sit down on the couch. "God, where's my brain tonight—or my manners? Want some coffee to go with the ice cream? I'm sorry I can't offer anything with alcohol. You know. Teenagers often have the house to themselves while I work."

"I'm fine, thank you, as I'm driving." Eleanor regarded her dessert with something resembling surprise. "Ice cream. I can't remember the last time I had regular ice cream."

"Oh." Feeling silly and self-conscious, Addison finally sat down and fiddled with her spoon. "I hope it's not too...pedestrian."

"Not at all. I usually skip dessert altogether, but this brings back memories of my childhood. I used to adore it."

"Perhaps you still do?" Addison took a spoonful and closed her lips around it. The taste of chocolate and raspberry ice cream covered with chocolate sauce made her moan. "This is *so* good."

Eleanor's eyes narrowed into dark slits. "Are you trying deliberately to drive me crazy?" she murmured.

"What?" Addison dropped her spoon into her bowl. "I'm not—I'm—oh."

Eleanor didn't answer, but ate a spoonful of ice cream and studiously cleaned her spoon by turning it in her mouth and sucking on it. "Mmm."

Addison pressed her legs together to ward off the growing ache. Her naughty mind conjured up image after image of Eleanor using her mouth on just about any protruding part of Addison's body. It was unfathomable to have Eleanor here in her house, on her couch. People stood in line to have Eleanor lend her presence to their social circle. If any of Eleanor's business contacts knew she was here, they'd wonder what magic spell Addison had woven around her. "I'm not trying to drive you crazy," Addison murmured, a little more ready to be candid. "Honestly."

"Hmm. So it comes naturally to you, then?" Eleanor took another spoonful.

"What does?"

"The way you look at me. The way…you seem to make me forget about what I've been so sure of all my life. I never even gave my orientation a second thought." Eleanor put her bowl down on a coaster on the coffee table. "You've confused me since day one."

"I'm sorry?"

Eleanor's head snapped up. "No, don't be." She slid closer and placed a hand on Addison's shoulder. "Don't be sorry."

"Okay." Addison held her breath until she became dizzy. "I do feel this…this connection, but I've tried to hold back. I mean, I didn't want to…I didn't think you…" Sighing, Addison tugged at her ponytail. "I don't want to push you away."

"You're not. You can't." Eleanor pulled her leg up and leaned sideways against the backrest. Sitting half turned toward Addison, she rested her head in her hand.

"Really?" Addison hoped with all her heart this was true. Eleanor looked relaxed with the exception of her right foot, which she jiggled sideways, back and forth. "Good."

"You're not only important in the resurrection of Face Exquisite. I admit I've grown accustomed to your being there, on Skype, on YouTube. I'd miss you if you weren't."

It wasn't so much what Eleanor said, but how she said it. Had she sounded like her usual detached self, her statement could have come across as something unimportant, polite at best. Instead she spoke in this low, intense tone, as if each syllable was important.

"I know exactly what you mean. The nights when you've been busy, I've felt so weird. Like something was wrong when we didn't touch base." Addison fiddled with the hem of her shirt. "And as much as I care how Face Exquisite is coming along, that's not all there is to it."

"You're right. I feel like we can talk about just about anything. I've been all about business for so long." Eleanor's eyes suddenly became shiny. "I think ever since my aunt died, really. I loved spending time with her. She was only ten years older than I, and I felt she was the only one who understood me. She founded the company and loved makeup the way you do. She saw it as an artistic way of empowering women. My father never understood it. He saw it as something ridiculously frivolous. A redundant and superficial luxury…Well, I'm sure you've heard that before." Pinching the bridge of her nose, Eleanor sighed.

"I have." Addison took Eleanor's free hand in hers, shocked at how cold it felt. Warming it with both of hers, she prodded gently. "So you and your aunt were close?"

"She was something between a mother and a sister. She was the youngest child, the one with all the charm when compared to her siblings. She was so quick to love and a little on the naïve side. When the men she'd fallen for claimed to love her back, she never questioned them. She believed what they said and dived headfirst into the relationships. They broke her heart, every single time."

"Oh, God. She was all emotion, all heart, and they took advantage of her, huh?"

Eleanor nodded stiffly. "Yes. And there I was, an impressionable teenager, standing on the sidelines, watching her relationships crash and burn, over and over. My father ridiculed her for what he deemed to be her shortcomings. All of that had a profound impact on me. I grew up wary of relationships and ended up detesting my father." Eleanor smiled joylessly. "What do you think? You still sure you want to keep Skyping?"

"Yes." Addison squeezed Eleanor's hand. "Tell me. What happened to your aunt?"

"Priscilla fell in love, again, and this time the man proposed. Even my father was reluctantly optimistic. Priscilla had run Face Exquisite for about five years and it was the 'it-brand' among Hollywood's stars and supermodels. I was nineteen at the time and spent my summer after graduation from high school interning as her assistant. She and I planned the wedding and I'd never seen her happier. The man in question literally left her at the altar. In fact, he didn't show up at church at all. Via his best man he sent a note in which he told her he'd reconciled with his former fiancé."

"Oh, damn." Addison scooted closer, holding Eleanor's hand. "What happened?"

"Priscilla said she needed time to think and took her car, the one I'd driven to the church, as she'd arrived in a limousine." Swallowing visibly, Eleanor clung to Addison's hand. "She drove off the dock into the harbor. People saw the car go in and called 911. A man and a woman jumped into the water and managed to get her out. Did CPR. Saved her life. It wasn't living, though. She lived in a vegetative state until two years ago. I saw her every day for the first months. Then every week. Every other week, every month. Every other month, eventually. My father never went to see her. To him she was dead already."

"And the company became stagnant."

"Yes. My father became her legal guardian. He made all her medical decisions and ran the company into the ground, more or less. I was powerless."

"Did you try to help with the business?"

"Not during the first years, as I was an undergraduate at Wellesley College and later in graduate school at Harvard. But after that, I asked my father, pleaded with him, actually." Eleanor's face expressed how much she'd resented having to beg him. "He refused to listen and left the company to run on empty. Only the fact that some loyal customers loved the brand made it possible for Face Exquisite to survive—barely—year after year."

"And now you own it."

"Yes. When Priscilla finally was allowed peace and passed on, her will gave me all her shares. By then I'd outmaneuvered my father and anyone from the Ashcroft Group loyal to him. The fact that I now have added Face Exquisite to the conglomerate doesn't exactly thrill him."

"Why did you take over the Ashcroft Group to begin with?" Addison wondered if it was an act of vengeance only.

"Several reasons. My family had built it up for generations, and my father lacked the business sense required to bring it forward in the twenty-first century."

"That sounds like a ready-made, rehearsed explanation," Addison said carefully.

Blinking, Eleanor regarded her with darkening eyes. "That's a presumptuous point of view."

"Yes, probably, but I think there's more to it. Your father mistreated his youngest sister, a woman you idolized and really cared about. Then, you were in a position of power, with an amazing sense for business. Taking the Ashcroft Group from your father and showing him how it's really done must've been tremendously gratifying. The fact that you finally took Face Exquisite away from him as well was the last piece of the puzzle, or am I wrong?" Addison knew she was risking a lot by showing Eleanor she was ready to hear the truth instead of some prefabricated account.

Eleanor's hand jerked in Addison's grasp, but she didn't pull it free. "And if that is the truth?" Eleanor's lips tensed.

"It would prove to me that you're human and passionate. Protective."

"How about vindictive and unforgiving?"

"Yes, perhaps. I think there's more to it, and as far as I'm concerned, the person at fault here is your father."

"What?" Eleanor looked like she couldn't understand what Addison was saying. "You—what makes you say that?"

"I imagine you can be harsh when it comes to business, and I can also understand that you resent how your father treated Priscilla. What I base my opinion on is how he acted throughout the years. He never even visited her during those years she was comatose."

"No." Eleanor's jaw looked so strained now it was as if it could shatter like glass. "No, he didn't."

"And you did—all those years. I rest my case." Addison shrugged, her eyes stinging now. "And I'm sorry if I made our evening into…this. I didn't mean for you to feel like I put you on the spot."

"It's a sensitive subject," Eleanor acknowledged, the skin around her eyes tight. "You couldn't know."

"No. But I could've guessed." Concerned now that she might have ruined the evening, Addison took Eleanor's face with both hands. "I just want us to be real. You know. Authentic with each other. No hiding."

"I can't promise that. Not always, not right away, but it's something to strive for," Eleanor whispered, looking paler.

"Yes." Addison could hardly breathe, her heart was hammering so fast. Eleanor didn't hate her for pushing. Could it be that she truly understood? Perhaps Eleanor somehow saw that Addison needed whatever it was they had together to be real. But if Eleanor couldn't manage this, could Addison be just as understanding? Still, Eleanor's words also had a faint hope for more moments together, more days when they might learn to be "real."

"Addison, please," Eleanor said, her voice little more than a murmur.

"Yes?" Concerned now, Addison moved closer to be able to make out what she was saying.

"I can't stop thinking about you." Eleanor glanced over toward the hallway. "You seem to have become an integral part of my fantasies. I never used to fantasize very much, but now I do. If I don't get to talk to you, I go to your YouTube channel and all I have to do is listen to your voice and I'm…I'm…" She took a deep breath. "I'm right there with you. I close my eyes and all these scenarios play out in my mind. You're so beautiful, but that's not the only reason. It's how you are, the way you come across, and how you smell. God, I'm not making much sense."

Addison was absolutely blown away. "Oh, Ellie. It makes sense. It does. If you only knew what images my brain comes up with. And speaking of voices, yours is mind-blowing. I guess I've been worried I might make you uncomfortable. You know, since I came out to you? You're such a beautiful, charismatic woman, and I envisioned you having tons of guys wanting to escort you to functions and whatnot. I'm well aware you're out of my league. I really do get that. Just to know you find me attractive enough to…to fantasize about is more than I ever expected, or could even hope for."

"I feared you might find it a little pathetic. I mean, a woman my age." Eleanor tried to loosen the tight grip around her hand, but Addison refused to let go.

"Not by a long shot," Addison said emphatically. "Age doesn't matter to me. I'm the so-called underdog here. You're wealthy. You're powerful, famous, and worldly. I'm none of these things, but if I can overlook that, surely you can disregard the age thing?"

"When you put it like that."

"Good." Addison tried to get her breathing under control. Their conversation had become such a roller-coaster ride that she was trying to wrap her brain around what had been said. "So, no freaking out on either of our parts, all right? We're good?"

"Yes. I'd say you're better than good." Eleanor ran her thumb over the back of Addison's hand. "You're wonderful."

"Wow. I don't mind that at all. Being wonderful to you, that is." She smiled carefully, starting to feel like the ground beneath her was getting firmer.

Regaining a little color, Eleanor relaxed her hand in Addison's grip. "I'd say that's even an understatement. You're stunning."

Addison couldn't stop herself. Cupping the back of Eleanor's neck with her free hand, she dug into the depths of her soul for courage. "May I kiss you?"

CHAPTER THIRTEEN

Addison wanted to kiss her? Eleanor was sure she'd misheard. That or she was hallucinating because of all the carbs in the pasta. She still nodded, mainly because she knew she'd lost her voice.

"May I? Very softly? Like this," Addison whispered, and moved in closer. Cautiously, it seemed, she brushed her lips against Eleanor's—feathery soft caresses, no pressure at all.

Eleanor sighed and angled her head. Being cautious wasn't enough, not by far. She pressed her lips more firmly against Addison's, wanting to prolong the all-too-chaste kisses. There was so much softness, and the fragrance of Addison's skin was almost driving Eleanor insane. Having never kissed another woman, she reveled in the satiny feel, the fullness of Addison's lips, and the absence of stubble.

"Mmm." Eleanor tried to murmur against Addison's lips, but all she could think about was how badly she wanted to taste this amazing young woman's mouth. Impatient now, Eleanor parted Addison's lips. As she put her arms around Addison's neck, she ran her tongue along the inside of her upper lip.

Addison moaned, a thoroughly sexy sound that caused Eleanor to push her back against the armrest, her mouth sliding along Addison's jawline. Latching on to her neck, she pressed her lips against the velvet skin where Addison's pulse fluttered wildly.

"You…oh, God, you smell so good." Addison groaned. "And the way you touch me is…oh, Ellie…"

Eleanor could hardly comprehend how she, normally so restrained, could become so greedy and devour Addison like this. Somewhere in the hazy state she was lost in, she could tell what this did to the woman in her arms. Addison's strong hands gripped Eleanor's shoulders and held her close as she offered her neck.

"So beautiful." Eleanor ran the tip of her tongue all the way up to Addison's lips, which she covered with hers. This time they both deepened the kiss, tasting, dancing, and claiming each other. Eleanor slid her hands slowly up and down Addison's arms, feeling how this movement created goose bumps. Intrigued, she drew patterns along Addison's neck and then tangled her fingers in the long, curly ponytail.

Just then, Addison shifted angles and deepened the kiss even further. Eleanor whimpered into Addison's mouth and tugged involuntarily at the ponytail she gripped so hard now. Her fingers trembling, she undid the clasp holding Addison's hair. Addison in turn pushed her fingers into Eleanor's much-shorter hair. They both hummed now, Eleanor knowing full well she'd never responded like this to anyone. Ever.

Loud steps on the staircase outside the living room door and two voices laughing as Stacey and Maureen approached tore them apart. Their separation caused pure physical pain, and Eleanor had to bite the inside of her cheek to keep from wailing in despair.

"Mom, Maureen's dad is here to pick her up," Stacey called out as she poked her head in, along with Maureen. Eleanor saw Stacey's eyes widen as she regarded them. The girl was clearly no fool.

"Say hello to your parents, Maureen," Addison said, sounding way too out of breath to just be sitting and chatting on the couch.

"I will. See you! And it was nice to meet you, Ms. Ash—I mean, Eleanor." Maureen blushed and waved before the two girls disappeared out the door.

"Oh, God. That was painful." Addison pressed a hand against her forehead.

"What?" Eleanor wasn't sure what to think of Addison's choice of words.

"Letting go of you when I heard them on the stairs. It was painful to break the kiss. It's just that…" Addison fiddled with the hem of her shirt and then glanced at Eleanor through her eyelashes. "I wasn't done yet."

Relieved and still out of breath, Eleanor chuckled. "Yes, it was painful. And I wasn't done either."

"Oh, good." Addison tugged at her undone hair, which escaped the clasp once again.

The front door opened and closed again. Stacey was back. Eleanor patted down her hair, belatedly of course, as Stacey had already seen her looking tousled. Oddly enough she didn't really care all that much.

"Maureen and her dad on their way home?" Addison asked.

"Yup. We had a great time. How about the two of you?" Stacey grinned.

"This was a wonderful evening. Thank you. It's time for me to go home." Eleanor knew she sounded too formal, but Addison didn't seem to mind.

"Yes, it was great. More than great."

Stacey came closer, and now Eleanor could easily detect the sparkles in her eyes. "Maureen thinks you're fabulous, Eleanor. So do I." She grinned and rocked back and forth on her feet, her hands shoved deep into her back pockets. "I look forward to Tuesday."

"I'll see you at eight a.m. at Face Exquisite's executive level."

"Is it hard to find?" Stacey asked, which made Addison laugh.

"No, honey. It's the top floor."

"Ah. Of course." Stacey giggled. "That's so my thing. Going straight to the top."

"You silly goose." Addison rounded the coffee table and put her arm around Stacey. "I'm glad you and Maureen had a good time too."

"Yeah." Stacey extended her hand to Eleanor. "I'm going to head off to bed. Good night."

"Good night, Stacey. See you next week." Eleanor squeezed the girl's hand, only to be taken by complete surprise when Stacey took a quick step forward and kissed her cheek.

"I really like you," Stacey whispered in Eleanor's ear and then hurried out of the room and up the stairs.

"Oh, my goodness. That was quite the stamp of approval." Eleanor knew this evening would go down as a night of "firsts" for her.

"I'll say. Stacey isn't easily impressed. She's very outgoing, but she's also very protective."

"I can't say I blame her. You're her family. I'm relieved she likes me."

"I'm very relieved you like *me*." Addison winked and took Eleanor's hand. "Let me walk you to your car."

Genuinely charmed by an overtly flirtatious Addison, Eleanor resumed holding her hand after donning her jacket and grabbing her purse. Just as they reached the front door, Addison stopped abruptly. Tugging at her, Addison maneuvered them until Eleanor felt the wall against her back. Eleanor dropped her purse, stunned as she flung her arms around Addison's neck. Gasping at the sensation of full breasts pressing into her own, she breathed hotly against Addison's ear. "Oh, my."

"I just have to…" Addison kissed up along Eleanor's neck, following her jawline and then her lips.

Eleanor pushed one hand under Addison's shirt. Moaning, she found naked skin at the small of Addison's back and spread her fingers to feel as much of it as possible. Addison's skin was like silk, and Eleanor slid her fingers lightly, lightly over it, and again, goose bumps flared in their wake.

Addison sucked Eleanor's lower lip and ran the tip of her tongue across it until Eleanor whimpered with every breath. She dragged one of her hands to Addison's front. The increased intimacy was enough to make Addison tear her lips from Eleanor's and look unwaveringly into her eyes.

"Can't get enough." Addison drew a hot line with her tongue down Eleanor's neck and, oh God, across to her collarbone, nudging the crisp shirt to the side with her nose.

"Seems I can't keep my hands off you either," Eleanor said, out of breath. She spread her hands again, this time reaching from Addison's waist up to her ribs. "What spell have you cast on me? I'd like to know how you can wield such magic."

"No magic. Just this. Us." Addison trembled. "And you... you're so freaking gorgeous and you feel so good—ah!" She nipped at Eleanor's collarbone and then soothed the spot with more kisses.

Eleanor moaned quietly and had to force herself to remember they weren't alone in the house.

"That's right, we have to be quiet," Addison breathed against Eleanor's skin.

"Oh, God. If we don't stop, I don't think I *can* be quiet." Eleanor reluctantly moved her hands away from Addison's tantalizing skin. "I should go. I mean, I have to go. I'm going." Damn it, she was babbling. Talk about feeling like an entirely different person. Eleanor Ashcroft was normally eloquent and precise and certainly didn't babble.

"You're right. Of course you're right. I need to let you go." Addison stepped back, then bent and picked up Eleanor's purse. "Here you go." She, much like Stacey had before, shoved her hands into her back pockets. "I'll miss holding you as soon as you leave. I just want you to know that." She dragged her left foot in a small circle on the rug. Peering at Eleanor she managed to smile and bite her upper lip at the same time.

"Addison." Feeling choked up, Eleanor briefly kissed Addison's soft cheek. "Good night."

"'Night, Eleanor."

Eleanor opened the door and nearly tripped as she hurried toward her car. She was afraid to turn around and see if Addison was there. If she was, she wouldn't be able to hold herself together. As she pressed the button for the central locking system, she dared to glance back at the front door of the cozy house. Addison stood on the porch, leaning her hip against the column above the steps. The streetlight combined with the moon gave her an eerie, but beautiful, glow. She waved as Eleanor got into the driver's seat, then walked back into the house.

Driving home to Manhattan and her penthouse, Eleanor experienced their caresses and kisses over and over. How could life change within just a few minutes? Truthfully, her life had changed long before tonight. The moment she'd first had laid eyes on Addison's beautiful face and when they met that first time, something had simply fallen into place; she just didn't realize it at the time. She doubted she would ever be the same again. Now, all she could think about was how Addison had felt against her, how her scent had engulfed her and fueled her arousal even more. The physical arousal wasn't all though. She had actually talked about Priscilla, something she hadn't done for years. Addison had listened so intently it had been easy, all of a sudden, to tell the horrific details of Priscilla's suicide attempt. Just gazing into the nonjudgmental eyes and seeing nothing but compassion and understanding had loosened Eleanor's usual inhibitions.

Addison had no ulterior motives for what she said or did. She was genuine in a way that Eleanor had forgotten existed. In her cutthroat world of corporate warfare, it was always a mistake to show any weakness or bare your throat. Now, she had done just that with Addison, and something wondrous had come from it. It seemed Addison truly desired her. Then again, she was more than twenty years her junior, from a very different background, and, not to forget, a young woman who knew who she was, sexually speaking. It still astonished Eleanor to discover how her libido soared and all because of Addison. Why had she never felt this way around another woman? Had she merely stowed any such emotions in the back of her mind and refused to acknowledge them, or was this all because of Addison and the effect she had on her?

Eleanor didn't know, and right now questions like this didn't seem important. What mattered was how Addison made her feel.

Falling head over heels would likely break her heart. Eleanor had witnessed this firsthand, over and over, regarding her aunt.

The thought of Priscilla and her ever-present desire to find the right one to love gave Eleanor pause. Priscilla had believed she felt as strongly about the men she fell in love with as Eleanor felt about Addison now. And look how that had all turned out. She needed to keep this chilling thought in mind.

Gripping the steering wheel tighter, Eleanor tried to tell herself she needed to tread very carefully. She wanted to trust Addison, but witnessing her own parents' cold relationship as well as how men had treated Priscilla didn't make it easy to drop her guard. She would need a few days to regroup before they talked again.

She pulled into her garage, where a valet took care of the Maserati. Riding the elevator up to her penthouse condo, Eleanor convinced herself that Addison would have an even bigger reason to be cautious when facing so much on the home front with Stacey's upcoming surgery. Surely she wouldn't have time for any relationship drama when her sister had to come first. The more Eleanor thought about it, the more she decided it was only logical to assume Addison would feel the same way about taking a step back.

Entering her penthouse she tossed her jacket on a chair, suddenly feeling fidgety and nervous. She wasn't accustomed to ever having a case of nerves, so she walked into the kitchen and fetched a tall glass of apple juice. To be honest, she'd rather have poured herself a whiskey, but drinking alone to soothe her nerves was never a good idea.

Impulsively, she strode into her study and booted up her desktop computer. Perhaps Addison was online, and if she wasn't she might get some work done. Eleanor chuckled self-deprecatingly. That, or watch one of Addison's YouTube clips. She groaned and rested her forehead in her hand. She was a fool.

She was just about to get up when the trademark signal indicating a chat message pinged. Addison.

CHAPTER FOURTEEN

Addison saw Eleanor log on and knew her actions could be seen as needy or clingy, but she just had to make sure they were all right.

After Eleanor drove away, Addison had entertained a series of thoughts and scenarios. Of course, her mind had given her a hard time by conjuring up one pessimistic outcome after another. She'd said good night to Stacey without allowing her to ask any questions.

It was obvious Stacey was dying to ask about her and Eleanor, she could see it in Stacey's whole demeanor, but it was too soon. Too fragile and…she realized that she had too many questions herself. Taking her courage in both hands, she began to type.

Blushaddict: Hi. Glad to see you made it back in one piece.

There was a brief delay and then Eleanor answered.

Valkyrie: I did. Just got home.
Blushaddict: Thank you for coming. We loved having you over.
Valkyrie: Thank you. I had a lovely evening.

Blinking against a burning sensation behind her eyelids, Addison paused with her fingers hovering above the keyboard for a moment. That sounded awfully polite. Too polite.

Blushaddict: Are you all right? Are *we* all right?

Now it was Eleanor's turn to delay answering.

Valkyrie: I'm fine.
Blushaddict: Do you regret kissing me?

Addison's heart thundered, but she figured she better find out up front if Eleanor was seriously regretting what had gone on between them.

Valkyrie: No. Not at all.

Relieved, but only partially, Addison sighed, frustrated with this faceless, voiceless way of communicating.

Blushaddict: I wish I could see you. Can we use voice and webcam? Or do you have work waiting?

Another pause, this time so long, Addison wondered if Eleanor had left the computer or perhaps received a phone call or something. It was already past eleven o'clock, but who knew when people did business overseas?

Valkyrie: All right. Let me switch to the laptop and get ready for bed.

Bed? Oh, God. Addison's fingers trembled as she typed her reply.

Blushaddict: Okay. I'll do the same.

She rose from the kitchen chair and took the laptop with her as she made sure all the lights were off and the door locked before she headed up to her room. Once there, she remembered how she never had gotten around to showing it to Eleanor.

Addison took a quick shower, brushed her teeth, and went through her nightly makeup-removal routine. She then pulled on one of her favorite sleep T-shirts. This one was a Grateful Dead tour T-shirt that had belonged to her father. At times she could almost smell his aftershave wafting from it, no matter how many times she'd washed it. She scooted up on her bed. As if Eleanor moved at the exact same pace, the Skype logo appeared. Addison clicked on the part that said "Answer with Video" and waited for the webcam to hook up.

Eleanor came into view, and it was no surprise to see her dressed in a stylish nightgown. What did make Addison gasp and her jaw drop was how said nightgown clung to Eleanor's form and how sheer it was. It wasn't exactly see-through, but it sure wasn't covering much up either.

"You trying to kill me?" Addison managed in a husky voice.

There was something dangerous, almost reckless, about how Eleanor moved the laptop closer on the bed. She grabbed what looked like a remote from her nightstand and clicked a button. The light in the room instantly dimmed. "Not at all. Why do you ask?" Eleanor tilted her head.

"Because of that...that..." Addison motioned toward Eleanor's nightgown. "That thing."

Looking down at herself, Eleanor smiled faintly. "So, I take it you approve of my nightgown?"

"You can take it any freaking way you want. I'm just going to focus on not fainting over here."

"You're one to talk with that ghastly, barely-even-there T-shirt." Eleanor's eyes narrowed. "It's almost threadbare."

Addison mimicked Eleanor and looked down at herself. "I think it covers what it needs to cover."

"It barely covers *anything*." Eleanor waved her hand emphatically. "How can you say otherwise?"

"Again—it covers what it needs to cover."

"It does not."

"So you can tell if I'm going commando or not?" Addison smiled angelically.

Eleanor gasped and shook her head. "You're going to be the death of me. I know it."

"Likewise, if you keep showing up on Skype dressed like that."

Eleanor hesitated, looking down on something off camera, a regretful expression ghosting over her face. "I was going to suggest we, um, back off a bit," she said throatily.

Addison's heart landed in the center of her belly with a thud. The burning sensation in her eyes returned, worse than before. "Why?" she asked, her voice hardly carrying.

"I hadn't counted on...this. On how we'd end up in a virtual hurricane just from a kiss."

"And you regret it." It wasn't a question. It was obvious. Addison wanted to end the Skype session instantly, but she felt frozen. She was about to cry, but she'd be damned before she broke down and wept like a child in front of Eleanor.

"No. No!" Eleanor finally looked up, an alarmed expression in her eyes. "I said I *was*. All it took was for you to ping me, for me to see a message that 'Blush' wanted to chat with me, and I tossed the idea of backing off out the window. It's not going to work."

Confused now, Addison swallowed hard against the threatening tears. "What's not going work? Us? What?" she managed to ask.

"Backing off isn't going to work." Eleanor spoke slower, enunciating every syllable. She was pale but looked determined, if somewhat unsettled. "I'm not prepared to let this, what we've found, go. Not without exploring what it might lead to. I admit, I find it intimidating, but...you know."

Addison did know. "Yeah. Don't scare me like that. I thought you were ending what we might have before we even had a chance to fully discover it."

"I came damn close." Eleanor closed her eyes briefly and lay down against her pillows. "I'm exhausted."

"Then can we just sort of snuggle?" Addison was tired too. "I'd like us to fall asleep together, if that's all right with you?"

"Mmm. It is." Eleanor made herself comfortable and adjusted the webcam angle. "There. Now, tell me, did your feisty little sister have any comments after I left?"

Addison chuckled as she pushed the pillow in under her head. "She tried. I think only the fact that she was rather tired saved me from having to dodge more questions. I'm not ashamed and I don't mind her knowing how I feel, but this is so new."

"Yes. I understand what you mean."

"And if I feel that way, I can imagine that's why you're acting a bit shell-shocked. It's not like I'm screaming from the rooftops that I'm gay, but I'm not closeted either. You have a lot to figure out." She regarded Eleanor cautiously, not sure being out would work in her favor or scare Eleanor off. The last time she'd hoped for a loved one's acceptance, her parents had lost their lives.

"Yes, I do. I've never even considered I might not be straight. And here you blaze into my life and change every preconceived idea I have about myself." Eleanor smiled tiredly. "Like a damn force of nature."

"You've done the same for me. My work has changed, my everyday life has changed, and the way I look at myself has changed. I never thought I'd feel this way. About anyone."

"How do you mean?" Eleanor seemed to run her fingertips over the laptop screen.

"So all-overshadowing. So consuming." Addison wasn't sure she was explaining properly. "My life's been about Stacey, the YouTube videos, and going to work. Right? And it *still* is about that, it is, but it's more than that now. Everything I do…Eleanor, I think about you all the time."

"What do you think about, when I'm on your mind?" Eleanor rested her head in her hand.

"I wonder when I'm going to see you next. Right now, of course, my mind is reeling, reliving the kisses. The touching. How you smell and how you sound. Especially how you sound when I caress you. How you make me feel when you caress *me*."

Eleanor was clearly flustered now. "Oh, God. Addison."

"Yes, exactly. That's how I feel."

"Less than ten seconds ago I was tired, exhausted. Now you have me blushing from head to toe." Eleanor frowned and tugged her duvet up.

"Should I apologize?" Addison squirmed.

"You need to stop doing *that*."

Confused, Addison tried to figure out what Eleanor meant. "Doing what?"

"That. That wiggling. Honestly, it's not helping."

"I'm not wiggling."

"Yes. You. Are." Her voice a low growl now, Eleanor clasped the edge of the duvet.

The sound of Eleanor using that low register of her voice sent a flood of moisture between Addison's legs. Knowing she had never been this turned on, she also realized she was indeed squirming. How could she not? She was on fire.

"I'm sorry. You're too beautiful. Too hot," Addison said with a whimper. "You're going to make me self-combust."

Eleanor's eyes bugged out. "Addison!"

"You brought up the squirming. I was just trying to explain." Pushing a hand down between her legs, Addison closed her eyes. The pressure of her wrist against her damp cotton panties was nearly enough.

"What are you doing?" Eleanor whispered, making Addison snap her eyes open.

"Sorry. It's been such a crazy night. I don't mean to make you uncomfortable."

"You're not. But if you're doing what I think you're doing, I'm going to become very cross with you if you don't tell me the truth. If you don't share." Eleanor sounded so stern, Addison nearly came from her tone alone.

"I'll be good. We need to rest. Sleep. Yeah, that's what we need. Sleep. Tons of sleep."

"I don't think so." Eleanor looked closely at Addison. "You're trembling, perspiring, and your skin is flushed. How can you possibly relax enough to sleep if you don't bring yourself relief first?"

Her shocking words hung between them, so unexpected and so challenging at the same time.

❖

Eleanor wondered if Addison had stopped breathing completely. She ought to have realized by now that Eleanor was *always* candid. Even when it came to sex.

"Bring myself...like *now?*" Addison looked shocked, her mouth slightly agape, her eyes huge.

"Unless you'd rather do it on your own." Eleanor knew she must seem to be acting terribly out of character. The truth was, this was the first time she'd recognized some of the old unabashed streak in herself she'd thought had died when Priscilla drove her car into the water.

"No. Um, I suppose. I mean, oh God, have you ever...no? Well, me either!" Addison was adorable in the way she blushed and looked aroused at the same time.

"Addie, please. Listen. You don't have to do anything. You realize that, right?" Eleanor wondered how she could ever have thought it possible to let this young woman go. With each passing moment they were together, like this or face-to-face, she found herself more attached, more enamored than before.

"I wouldn't mind," Addison said quietly, looking through her eyelashes at Eleanor, "if it wasn't just me."

Losing her breath, Eleanor swallowed convulsively. "Oh."

"Would you, with me?"

Eleanor could barely breathe at all. "It certainly wouldn't take much. Not when you look at me like that."

"Oh, please, look who's talking. You're the one who brought it up." Addison laughed weakly and peered at Eleanor through her fingers.

"Only after you began squirming." Eleanor raised an eyebrow deliberately. The effect on Addison didn't disappoint. She shifted restlessly and pushed her long, slightly tousled hair from her face. "You're so beautiful." Eleanor traced Addison's outline on her screen, imagining just how smooth and warm her skin would feel beneath her touch.

"I—You're the beautiful one," Addison said, her voice a faint murmur.

"We could argue back and forth, but that's not what I want." Eleanor pressed her thighs together. "It's not what I want at all."

"Tell me what you want." Addison pulled a small, pink lace pillow into her arms, hugging it close.

"You're sure you want to hear it?"

"I'm sure." Addison licked her lips.

"Addison." The warning tone in Eleanor's voice only made Addison smile and repeat the maneuver, this time slower.

"Yes? You were saying?"

"Do you want to hear this or not?"

"Definitely. I do." Growing still, Addison focused on Eleanor.

"If you were here, or I there with you, no doubt you wouldn't be wearing anything," Eleanor said quietly. "I'm new at this, remember, so I would need to familiarize myself with your body," she said seriously. "I'd start peripherally and work toward the center."

"Oh, God." Addison whimpered, and Eleanor smiled inwardly at how her voice and words affected Addison.

"The question is now, how much exploration will you allow me to do?"

"I may be less new to this, but I'm not exactly experienced either." Addison's tremulous voice made Eleanor shiver. "So, I'll just have to hand myself over and trust that you'll like what you find, what you see."

"I already know I will *like* what I find." Her core was aflame now and Eleanor pulled the thigh-length nightgown up to cool down a little. Instead she felt more exposed, as if Addison could actually see her. She closed her eyes and stealthily pushed a hand down, covering herself.

"Mmm." Addison's gentle humming made Eleanor quickly open her eyes. Her back slightly arched, Addison was trembling visibly. The sight was so alluring, so unlike anything Eleanor had ever seen, she moaned out loud.

"Addison, I want you." Her fingertips were barely grazing her drenched skin, and still it was as if a flame licked along her folds. Eleanor looked longingly at the screen, desperate for any sign that she wasn't alone, that Addison was as consumed as she was.

"Ellie, Ellie." Going rigid, Addison opened her eyes and looked right at Eleanor for several moments. She then slumped back, gasping for air as she held on to the pillow in her arms as if she were drowning.

Knowing without a doubt that Addison had just come, right there in front of her, looking straight at her, Eleanor pressed the heel of her palm against her sex and that was it. She kept her gaze on Addison for as long as she could as the waves crashed in on her. Never had she felt this safe, this entitled to her own pleasure. How was it she knew she could trust Addison the way she did?

As they both regained their breath and settled against their pillows, Eleanor knew she had silenced her own doubts, at least for now. Addison deserved her trust and her honesty.

"I can't believe we just did that," Addison said, and stretched.

"You looked amazing." Eleanor smiled and shook her head. "But I know what you mean. Totally out of character."

"No kidding."

"Think you can sleep now?"

"Yeah. And you?"

"Half asleep already." Eleanor wasn't lying. She was drowsy in a wonderful way.

"Can we keep Skype on a bit?" Addison snuggled closer.

"Yes." Eleanor turned off the bedside lamp. Only the night-light from the ensuite bathroom spread a faint glow. "Good night, Addison."

"'Night, Eleanor."

She listened to Addison's breathing, and when it became even it only took moments for her to fall asleep too.

CHAPTER FIFTEEN

The subway was crammed with people as usual this time of day. Addison regarded Stacey with an indulgent smile. Her sister had been giddy and bouncing around the house for two days now.

"Can you believe I'm going to be Eleanor Ashcroft's freaking assistant for a whole day? Nobody else from my school will have that on their résumé. This is right up there with singing for the Chicory Ariose members."

Addison only smiled and watched her being thoroughly happy. She had been going in and out of a funky mood ever since she missed out on playing Elphaba, but this opportunity seemed to bring out the old, positive Stacey. She looked older than her seventeen years while dressed in one of Addison's white shirts, charcoal slacks, and a black jacket. Addison had helped her put her hair in a low bun, which accentuated Stacey's high cheekbones.

"We haven't been in Manhattan together in ages," Stacey said, and turned on the seat and smiled broadly. She was so beautiful, Addison's heart ached. "What do you say? Dinner somewhere cool before we go back to boring Newark tonight?"

"Sure. Absolutely. Why don't you think of what you're in the mood for, and we can ask Eleanor if she wants to come." Addison stopped herself. "Unless you want it to be just us. That's fine too."

"You don't have to pretend around me, sis. I know you're head over heels for Eleanor. I mean, Maureen and I practically caught you sucking face last week. What?" Stacey grinned.

"I hate that expression." Addison did her best to look stern. "We kissed," she said.

"Kissed. Made out. You had the perfect Ms. Ashcroft looking like you'd been totally working her over.

"Stacey!" Shocked, mostly because it was partially true, Addison pinched Stacey's thigh.

"Ow. Sibling abuse!" Stacey squealed and moved sideways away from Addison. Then she tilted her head and made her "adorable" face, something she'd tried to pull ever since she was four, which consisted of blinking rapidly and sucking her cheeks in. "Aw, come on, Addie. You know I'm messing with you. The two of you were totally cute. If she's into you, then I'm really happy for you."

"She seems to be. We've Skyped during the weekend."

"Oh, some hot stuff going on?" Stacey wiggled her eyebrows.

"Not really." That was true, but Addison wasn't about to share anything remotely intimate with her. In fact, both she and Eleanor had behaved, pretty much, after that Friday night, which was so clear in her mind and had such a profound effect on her. Just imagining the way Eleanor had looked while overcome by arousal made Addison completely lose track of where she was. She didn't dare think of it unless she was alone.

"Hmm. I wonder. You're totally red. Thinking about it, I don't think I want to know." She made a funny face. "Next stop's ours, right?"

"Yes." Addison stood, as did Stacey, and they elbowed their way to the doors.

Together with what felt like half of Manhattan's population, they finally reached the ground level and Addison blinked at the low sun.

"Ow. Damn." Stacey shielded her eyes. "Freaking sunlight."

"I know. Lovely day though."

"In more ways than one." Stacey donned her sunglasses. "I wonder what I'll be doing. I'm happy licking stamps, but it sounded like she had something a little more challenging in mind."

"I'm sure she has something special planned. I'm going to work with some promotion people. It's time to start figuring out how to involve The Blush Factor."

Stacey tucked her arm in under Addison's as they weaved in and out among the masses on the sidewalk. "Are you worried they'll try to switch it all around and take control?"

"Yeah, a little bit. You know how proud I am of my channel. They better not try to streamline it into something I don't even recognize."

"I don't think Eleanor would let them," Stacey said confidently.

"How can you be so sure?"

Stacey squeezed her arm. "Because she found you, among all those beauty gurus online, and she wanted you and what you represent. Why would she change a winning concept? I actually checked your stats this weekend. One of your latest videos, you know that one where you look like a Martian with the curlers in, has been watched two million times. I mean, holy fu-fudge, sis. That's awesome. Beyond awesome."

"Thank you. I can't really fathom such numbers. I mean, it's about curlers and how to look your best, to feel good. I mean, clearly I'm not the only one thinking that. Guess I'm still rather blown away by these numbers. Isn't it amazing how important that seems to be to people? To women, mainly."

"And some guys, I can tell. That or they're just happy watching a pretty girl getting herself even prettier."

"Funny." Wrinkling her nose at Stacey's laughing face, she chuckled as they entered the double glass door leading into Face Exquisite's headquarter.

"Whoa. Fancy. A little dated though?" Stacey removed her sunglasses and scanned the lobby. "Lots of gold and marble."

"Very observant," Eleanor's voice said from behind. "I knew I'd chosen you for a good reason today."

"Hi." Stacey smiled brightly. "I'm ready to dig in."

"Glad to hear that. Good morning." Eleanor smiled and placed a gentle hand on Stacey's shoulder. Her eyes went from warm to hot as she regarded Addison. "It's wonderful to see you again."

"Yes." Tongue-tied all of a sudden, Addison could only grin like an idiot. Eleanor looked amazing in a pinstripe skirt, ending just above her knees, pale-blue blouse, and a short black jacket. She carried it folded over her arm and held a Pineider briefcase.

"Oh, God." Stacey placed her hands on her hips. "Is this what it's going to be like? Changing outfits four times in the morning to make us late and then—goofy grins?"

"You were that indecisive about what to wear?" Eleanor smirked. "I'm flattered."

"Yeah. Stacie was ready to shoot me. She all but carried me here, accusing me of being, and I quote, 'a pain' this morning." Addison smiled affectionately at Stacey. "She was eager to be your assistant."

"*She* is standing right here, thank you." Stacey flicked her fingers. "Enough of the gooey glances. What's happening today, Eleanor? Oh. Should I call you Ms. Ashcroft at work, perhaps?"

"That might be best. We don't want to confuse people." Eleanor motioned toward the elevator. "I have a meeting in ten minutes. I'll need you to take notes, Stacey. Are you fast?"

"Are you kidding? I mean, yes, Ms. Ashcroft, I'm very fast. If you had Ms. Nunez in history like I do, you'd be lightning fast at taking notes too. I swear the woman sounds like she's swallowed a pair of castanets."

They entered the elevators. Addison went inside with them but pressed the button to some offices two floors below the executive floor at the top.

"Castanets? Really. Sounds painful," Eleanor said.

"Tell me about it. Half the class complains about carpal-tunnel symptoms," Stacey said, and shook her head. "I'm okay though, no hand issues. I've been told by several doctors that my issues are all in my head." She chuckled at her own joke, but Addison's nerves did a somersault.

Addison met Eleanor's eyes in the reflection of the chromed inside of the door. Noticing how carefully Eleanor was studying her in return, Addison fought to find some words, any words, to paint over Stacey's attempt at gallows humor.

"Stacey and I are having dinner somewhere around here after work. Would you like to join us?" Relieved that her voice sounded normal, Addison dared to turn to Eleanor. "Anything but pasta, I think."

"I'd love to. I have to return to my office around eight o'clock, but if we make it early enough, let's say around five, I'll be able to join you."

"Five it is then. I'll meet you guys in the lobby. If anything comes up, just text or call me." Addison smiled more easily now.

The elevator pinged and stopped at Addison's floor. She stepped outside and turned around in time to catch Stacey's brilliant smile and Eleanor's longing gaze. Walking toward her office with a new spring in her step, Addison knew dinner tonight would be great. Stacey idolized Eleanor and Eleanor seemed to really like Stacey. What a blessing.

The meeting dragged out a bit, and Eleanor turned to make sure Stacey wasn't bored to tears where she sat farther back in the room. Instead, the girl nodded subtly to her as if wanting to indicate that she was fine and handling herself professionally.

Granted, Eleanor had harbored some doubt after offering Stacey a day of internship, especially after she realized what a naughty and quick sense of humor she had. So far, those worries were uncalled for. As soon as they'd entered the conference room, Stacey had grabbed a pen and writing pad from her messenger bag, getting ready to take notes "at warp speed," whatever that meant.

Eleanor hoped the girl hadn't joked about her ability to take notes. Her next assignment would be to type them out into digital format. Normally Eleanor recorded the audio from business meetings, but this particular CEO was rather paranoid regarding such matters. In order for her to acquire the rights to his company's mascara "hardware," as in the tube and brush applicator, she needed to accommodate him. What she really wanted was to maneuver his staff over to Face Exquisite, as a long-term investment. So no audio recording, only notes.

"Mr. Tanner, I'm very pleased with our initial agreements, and I think we can now hand the fine-tuning of our contracts over to our respective associates." Eleanor stood and shook Patrick Tanner's hand. "I look forward to doing business with you."

"Likewise, Ms. Ashton." The stocky man bowed and left the room, his team remaining behind to finish the details.

Eleanor rose to do the same, signaling to Stacey to follow her. "I need some coffee. What about you? Coffee? Tea?" Eleanor walked toward the executive lounge.

"I'm more of a tea person, unlike Addison. She can drink coffee any time of day. I like herbal tea the most." Stacey hurried to hold the door open for Eleanor.

"Well, I think we have quite the variety of tea here. I'm a coffee person as well."

"Oh, wow. You've got chai tea in those little pods. I've been dying for us to get one of those machines. Maybe Addison can get one now that she's getting paid better." Stacey stopped talking abruptly. "Oops. Sorry. Not polite to talk about money. Especially other people's."

"I promise I won't tell." Eleanor made herself a double espresso, using one of the Keurigs. She walked over the far end of the lounge and took a seat by the window as she watched Stacey make some chai tea. "So was this morning what you expected?" Eleanor asked as Stacey approached. Sipping her espresso, she thought of how using Addison as a consultant must be changing Stacey's life in some ways. She made a mental note to surprise Stacey with a coffee machine and a variety of flavors.

"Yes. And no." Stacey blew at her tea and then sipped it carefully. "It was about as demanding to take notes as it is in school, but then I started to sort of listen at the same time. You know, to try and figure out if I could understand what was being discussed. I was totally floored when I realized I got it. I mean, most of it. I'd expected it to be all this legal and business babble, but it was actually kind of neat."

"How so?" Intrigued by Stacey's reasoning, Eleanor leaned back and listened.

"Addie says she's learning about business from the bottom up. By listening. I figured if she can do it, I can too. I mean, math and social science are my strongest subjects, if you don't count music, and that's got to be a good base for business, right?" Stacey looked expectantly at Eleanor.

"Yes, I'd say so. Is that something you've thought about? Going into the world of business?"

"Yes. I thought about it. I'd like to work with Addie. She's great at what she does, but I think my head for business might be better than hers. She's too sweet." Stacey looked serious. "I did a whole lot of research about you when she decided to give you a chance. And we're just talking the business side for now."

For now? Eleanor blinked. The girl looked very serious, and Eleanor acknowledged a slight onset of nerves. "And what did you find out?" she asked noncommittally.

"Your business reputation's pretty interesting," Stacy said, and nodded thoughtfully. "I liked what I found. You're called the Boardroom Barracuda, but I think that's because you make everyone else look stupid. And when it comes to guys, they usually think they rule…just because they're born with…you know." Stacey blushed and shifted her tea mug back and forth between her hands.

"Oh, I know. Trust me." Smiling broadly, Eleanor found herself utterly charmed by the perceptive but refreshingly non-precocious girl. "Have you thought about your senior year yet, what subjects you're interested in?"

"I have." Stacey rested her elbows on the small table, her eyes sparkling. "Math, of course, being the big deal. I'm okay there. I'm also thinking about the m-macroeconomics pre-coll—collage, no, college c-course—oh! Damn, Addie's going t-to shoot me…it's her shirt." Stuttering, Stacey began to slur and tea flowed over the table as she tried to grab the mug she'd just dropped. Her hand seemed limp, as if it wasn't working.

"Stacey?" Alarmed, Eleanor pushed back, away from the river of chai tea. "Did you burn yourself?" she asked sharply.

"N-no? The mug. I can't get—the mug." Stacey was fumbling over the table still but couldn't seem to grab the mug. "Ow. Oh, fuck it hurts. My eye…Elea—Ellie?"

Eleanor stared for a few moments that seemed endless, unable at first to understand what was going on. One moment Stacey was reaching for the mug, practically chasing it over the table with her trembling hand, and the next, she was pressing the same hand over her eye, reaching for Eleanor with the other.

"Ellie." Stacey slurred her name.

"Oh, God. Stacey." Eleanor rounded the table and hugged the girl as she sank to the floor with her. "Call 911!" She gazed around her and saw one of the receptionists pull out her cell phone. "Emma? Make sure they realize this is a young woman with a known aneurysm that's collapsed. Alert security to show the paramedics where we are."

"Yes, Ms. Ashcroft." Emma hurried out the door.

Eleanor zoomed in on the closest individual, a woman she vaguely recognized. "You, get my cell phone out of my briefcase. Then go get a blanket and some pillows from the couch in my office." Eleanor thought she remembered some decorative pillows and a throw on the leather couch in the corner office.

The woman turned out to be quick and efficient as she handed Eleanor the cell phone. Sitting on the floor with a whimpering Stacy curled up in her arms, Eleanor quickly moved her thumb over her contact list. A. Addison.

"Paramedics on their way, ma'am," Emma's voice said just as Addison picked up.

"Hello there." Addison sounded as if she was walking. "I was just—"

"Addison, listen. Stacey collapsed in the executive lounge. Paramedics are on—"

"Stacey?" Addison's voice rose an octave. "Oh, God. What happened?"

Eleanor heard Addison begin to run. "I have her. We're taking care of her until the paramedics get here. I'm not hanging up on you. I just have to check on her, all right? Stay connected until you get here."

"Yes. Yes. Oh, my God. Stacey. Tell her I'm on my way."

Eleanor put the phone on the floor and placed Stacey, who was eerily quiet, on her side on the floor. Someone passed pillows and blankets to her, which she tucked around the still form. Eleanor tried to think logically. If the aneurysm was bursting or leaking, should any part of Stacey be elevated? She kept her fingers on Stacey's wrist, where the pulsations fluttered a bit too fast. Stacey's skin was clammy and cold, and Eleanor could tell she was going into shock. Tugging the blankets closer around the girl, Eleanor bent over her, speaking into her ear.

"Addison is on her way. She'll be here any minute. Just relax, Stacey. I've got you until Addison comes." She picked up the phone. "Addie?"

"Yes?" Addison's voice echoed in a strange way.

"She's breathing. Her pulse is fast, but even. Are you in the staircase?"

"I'm almost at the executive...floor..." Gasping, Addison sobbed. "Tell her again that I'm almost there."

"I will."

Eleanor bent over, placing her lips against Stacey's ear. "That was Addie. She's running as fast as she can up the stairs to get to you. She'll be here any moment and we'll take you to the hospital, all right?"

"Mom." Stacey whimpered and opened one eye. The other remained shut, which Eleanor realized was a very bad sign. Looking closely, she could see that the corner of Stacey's mouth on the same side wasn't moving.

Almost like an answer to Stacey's moans, the sound of running feet announced Addison's presence.

"Baby-girl." She sobbed and threw herself down next to Eleanor, who had to stop Addison from falling over Stacey. "I'm here. I'm here." Addison was trembling all over, her teeth clattering. "The doctors said the risk of a rupture was minimal. What's happening to her, Ellie?"

"I don't know, but the paramedics are on their way. She'll be taken to the ER and they'll help her."

"Mom." Stacey moaned.

"I've got you. I'm here." Addison kissed her sister's forehead. "Easy now."

"H-hurts." Wailing, a low, heartbreaking sound that chilled Eleanor, Stacey raised her arm and pressed it against her eye. "So bad. So bad."

"We have you. Don't we, Ellie?" Addison looked up at Eleanor with swollen, mascara-smudged eyes.

"Absolutely. We do." Eleanor hugged Addison close and wrapped one arm protectively around Stacey. She refused to let it show but admitted to herself she hadn't been this afraid since she was nineteen years old.

"She's so cold." Addison held onto Stacey's listless hand, massaging it as if she could wake it up by her mere touch.

"Let us through, please," a calm female voice said from behind.

Eleanor glanced up. The paramedics had arrived.

CHAPTER SIXTEEN

L et us help her now. What's her name?"
"Stacey. Stacey Garr. She's my—my sister." Addison
had to let go of Stacey, but it hurt her worse than anything ever
had. Tears flooded her eyes but defied gravity and refused to fall,
making the flurry of activity around Stacey into a dreamy blur.
Fumbling around her for something, or someone, she felt strong
arms wrap around her from behind.

"They're going to take care of her, Addison," Eleanor
murmured in her ear. "Stacey's going to be all right."

"You don't know that," Addison whispered. "Look at her.
Something's very, very wrong."

"Yes. I see that, but they're going to do everything they can. I
know it's difficult...just allow them do their job." Eleanor cupped
the back of Addison's head and held her close.

Burying her face into the warmth of Eleanor's neck, Addison
inhaled deeply. After a few breaths she felt calmer. "Thank you."
She looked over at Stacey, where the paramedics had placed her
on a stretcher. The female paramedic had inserted an IV cannula,
and the male had wrapped Stacey in blankets and was strapping
her in.

The man turned to Addison, his expression kind and
sympathetic. "We need to get her to the hospital. Presbyterian is
the closest and we can't afford to lose any time."

"We're coming too." Eleanor helped Addison to her feet. Her voice left no room for argument.

"All right. One of you has to ride up front, then."

Addison barely remembered the elevator ride afterward. She clung to Stacey's hand, wanting to make sure her sister knew she was there. Suddenly they were in the ambulance. Eleanor took the front passenger seat while Addison still held on to Stacey.

"I'm calling it in, Mike," the female paramedic told her colleague. "You need to push it."

"Gotcha." Mike drove the ambulance into traffic and soon they were tearing through Manhattan, sirens blaring, each of their high-pitched wails coming together like a pained choir in Addison's head.

"Can you look up at me, Stacey?" the paramedic said after she talked to the staff at the Presbyterian, and Addison watched as Stacey's right eyelid fluttered, but not the left. "That's it. Good job. Your sister is here. We're taking care of you and of her too." She gazed with professional sympathy up at Addison. "How are you holding up?" She inflated a blood-pressure cuff as she spoke.

"I'm okay." Swallowing with difficulty, Addison stroked Stacey's hand. "Everything's going to be okay, Stace. I promise."

"I have to cut your shirt off, Stacey." The paramedic pushed some strange-looking scissors against the fabric. "We're going to place some electrodes on your chest and check your heart."

"No. No, it's Addie's. She'll be upschet." Stacey tried to push them away with her listless hand, which obviously wasn't successful. "It's a Cal—Callie. No, fuck. A Calvin *Klein* shirt."

"Keep still, please, Stacey." The paramedic smiled gently as she cut through the front. "I can promise you, your sister won't be upset."

"'Kay."

The paramedic pushed the shirt off and attached the electrodes.

"I'll buy you all the shirts you want, baby-girl. Just let her do her job." Addison forced her voice not to tremble. Stacey was slurring badly and seemed to have very little control of her left arm.

The paramedic nodded at her with approval. "We'll be there soon." She glanced out the narrow window above them. "Traffic's not so bad. I'd say another minute."

"Hurts, Addie." Stacy moaned. "My eye. Will I...loosche my eye?"

"No, you won't. You'll be okay." Addison wiped at the occasional errant tear as she tried to not break apart. Flashbacks from another hospital, another accident made her nauseous. "We're nearly at the hospital, baby-girl." She saw tears run from Stacey's closed eye and brushed them gently from her pale cheek. "I'm not leaving your side. I promise."

"Just as a tip—keep out of the neuro-team's way and they might let you stay in the room. If it gets crowded, just wait right outside." The paramedic nodded toward the front of the ambulance. "Let your friend help you with the paperwork. You'll have enough on your hands."

"Yeah. Thanks." Addison kissed the back of Stacey's hand.

"Here we are," the paramedic said, and tucked her report into a folder. "Stacey, we're at the hospital. We're going to be in the ER in no time, all right? When you get inside, tons of people are going to flock around you. Don't be alarmed. They're all there to help you."

"Mmm, 'kay." Stacey's left eye opened a fraction. "Addie..."

"Here, Stace. Right here. Got to let go of your hand while they pull the stretcher out, but then you'll feel me again."

"Pwomisch."

"I promise." *Oh, God.* Addison jumped out of the ambulance and found Eleanor already there, carrying both their briefcases and Stacey's bag. Not even thinking about it, Addison grabbed Eleanor's hand and more or less clung to her arm as they unloaded Stacey.

"How is she?" Eleanor's voice was thick and she sounded almost angry, which was oddly comforting.

"Same. I think. Left side is affected. She slurs, but at least she's conscious."

"I had my assistant call ahead, and she found some of the information the hospital needs to start a chart for Stacey. Am I right to assume she's never been to this hospital?"

"Yes. Her neurologist did mention the aneurysm center here and that it might be one way to go if we had complications." Shuddering, Addison sobbed once. "Guess this qualifies. Oh, God, where's my purse?"

"Right here. I took care of it." Eleanor held it up. "Do you need it?"

"No. I mean, yes. Stacey's documents are in there. I always carry them. Can you—?"

Looking confident and like a woman on a mission, Eleanor nodded. "I'll take care of everything. Just focus on Stacey and I'll come find you when I'm done. All right?"

"Thank you." Addison squeezed Eleanor's arm and then let go and took Stacey's hand in a gentle grip. "I'm back."

"Ellie?" Stacey's voice was thick and raspy.

"Eleanor is helping us. She's right over there taking care of paperwork, and she'll join us later. Thank God you were with her."

"Mmm."

Addison lengthened her stride as the paramedics hurried through the corridor toward a team that stood waiting for them. A tall, confident man stood in the doorway to a large examination room.

"Hello. I'm Dr. Stromberg. So this is Stacey Garr. Let's see what we can help you with, young lady." He turned to Addison. "Are you feeling strong enough to stay by her side? I like to involve the closest next of kin if possible. It soothes the patient."

Pleasantly surprised, Addison kept a firm but gentle grip of Stacey's hand. "I'm doing fine. Thank you."

"Good." He turned to a young woman to his left. "A stool for Ms. Garr." He cocked his head. "You her sister?"

"Yes. Her sister and legal guardian." Narrowing her eyes, Addison dared him to question this fact. It had happened before, especially when they were younger.

"Very well. Let's see what's going on."

After that, the flurry of activity became too much for Addison to keep up with. They drew blood, asked questions, and then Dr. Stromberg placed a gentle hand on Addison's shoulder.

"We're going to take Stacey up for an MRI. Depending on what we find there, we'll choose the best method for dealing with it. We'll then ask you to sign a consent form that allows us to do whatever surgery necessary to provide your sister with her best chances to recover."

"So I can't come?"

"You can't go with her, no. You can accompany us over to the radiology unit, or you can wait here."

"I'm coming for as long as you'll let me." Pushing back her onset of fatigue and nausea, Addison held on to Stacey's hand as they moved through the corridor toward the elevators. As they were waiting for the elevator to arrive, Addison thought of something. "A friend of ours, Eleanor Ashcroft, is helping with the forms. When she asks for Stacey, please treat her as next of kin. She's a very close friend."

"I'll make sure." a young nurse said, and patted Addison's arm before hurrying along the corridor toward the nurses' station.

❖

Eleanor raised her eyebrows at the woman behind the counter. "I believe you have everything you need in these papers."

"I still need Ms. Garr's legal guardian to sign the forms." The secretary pinched her lips. "There's a matter or insurance and—"

"Are you saying you're delaying me here because you're worried the hospital won't get paid?" Tapping her foot, Eleanor was ready to reach over the counter and throttle the annoying woman.

"We've been in contact with the insurance company, and since Ms. Garr's guardian is no longer employed by Starbucks, there seems to be a—"

"Oh, for God's sake. Here." Eleanor placed her Platinum card on the counter. "I will cover the cost for Stacey Garr. Bill this card for any tests, procedures, and rehabilitation the girl needs." She looked sternly at the now-gaping woman. "And do not bother Ms. Garr's sister with any of these details or I will involve my very good friend Monica Beyer. Yes, *that* Monica Beyer, a member of the board for this fine hospital."

"Of course, Ms. Ashcroft. I'll make sure you're billed." The woman took the card and registered it. "If you sign here, then Ms. Garr can focus on her sister's recovery."

"We have consensus. Perfect." Eleanor signed the financial agreement and left to find Addison and Stacey.

Walking through the corridors, asking a few people who clearly knew nothing, Eleanor could feel the tremors reverberating through her. She had kept her mask in place for Stacey and Addison, but truth be told, she'd been terrified. For a frightening moment, she'd pictured Stacey dying in her arms before Addison reached them. Then when Addison was kneeling next to Stacey, she feared it was still too late for the young woman she already cared about. Not just because Stacey was Addison's sister, but because the teenager was amazing and showed such promise in her own right.

Eventually Eleanor found a young nurse who lit up when she asked about Stacey.

"Miss Ashcroft, right? They just took Stacey up to do an MRI. Her sister told me that you're to be considered next of kin as well, when it comes to Stacey." She described the way to reach radiology.

Eleanor thanked her and chose the stairs instead of the elevator. She just wanted to be by Addison's side before Stacey was done with the MRI. She was pretty sure Stacey would need some sort of procedure and suspected Addison would feel the weight of such news even if she had to know this. After all, Stacey had already been scheduled for surgery before this happened, so it was likely to assume it would happen sooner rather than later.

When she reached the waiting-room area, she spotted Addison immediately. For the first time since she'd met her, Addison looked small, fragile, and very young. The room was full of waiting people, and Eleanor wanted Addison to have more privacy than that. She spotted a smaller area with only a few chairs that were all vacant.

"Addison?"

Addison's head snapped up. "Oh, thank God. Eleanor." She rose unsteadily and walked over to Eleanor, who merely took her by the hand and guided her over to the vacant area.

Not feeling the least bit guilty, Eleanor took their coats and arranged them in the other chairs, together with their purses and her briefcase, to make them seem occupied by temporarily absent individuals.

"Stacey's having an MRI," Addison said, trembling. "The doctor thinks the aneurysm is leaking, but it hasn't burst. Not yet. Not…oh God, tell me it's not going to, Ellie. Please, please, please."

Eleanor's heart broke at Addison's frantic words, whispered with such frenzy. "Listen, darling, she's in the best place possible for her. Presbyterian has a renowned aneurysm clinic and stroke unit. They'll take care of her and see her through this. You'll be there for her and so will I."

"Her neurologist said the risk of this was minimal and she was due for surgery next week. Next *week*! How could he say that? How could he be so sure and gamble with her life like this? Why didn't he schedule her sooner? Why didn't I push harder?"

"Shh. Addie, please. You're making yourself sick. Calm down. Listen to me." Eleanor took Addison in her arms where they sat on the small settee. "This is not your fault. You did what you thought was best for Stacey and you've taken the best care of her, even keeping her from fun things she wanted to participate in, in order to keep her safe. Don't you dare think you're not the best parent for her, because you are. I heard her call you Mom."

"She—she does that when she's truly upset or afraid. She did it more often when she was little, right after our parents died. She made a conscious decision that I was her mom now." Wiping at more tears, Addison clung to Eleanor. "When we learned of her aneurysm, she was the strong one at first. She consoled me and reassured *me*. So, that's why I can't help but feel I failed her somewhere along the line."

So much guilt. So much unnecessary pain. Eleanor knew she couldn't wipe those erratic feelings away for Addison, but hopefully, just by being there, she could be of some comfort.

"Ms. Garr?" A young man strode up to them. "Hello, I'm Dr. Walker. Stacey's condition is status quo, since she came here to radiology. From what we can see, the aneurysm is seeping and the bleeding is pressing on her brain. She's on her way to surgery so if you would like—"

"I want to be there." Addison stood. "She needs to see me before you...you sedate her."

"You can see her very briefly, but she's barely conscious, Ms. Garr." He motioned for them to follow him down the corridor and into another.

"You said her condition was status quo." Eleanor glared at the physician.

"Yes," Addison said. "She was communicating earlier, if a bit slurry."

"I'm sorry. She isn't communicating now." He lengthened his stride and his whole demeanor suggested great urgency. Eleanor was a good judge of character, used to reading the opposition's body language and facial expression.

Everything about this young doctor told her Stacey was getting worse.

CHAPTER SEVENTEEN

Addison kissed Stacey's forehead several times, but she could tell her sister was too out of it to reciprocate. She could only hope Stacey could feel her presence. Eleanor surprised her by leaning down and whispering something in Stacey's ear. Then the staff rolled Stacey into the operating room.

"We have a private room for you where you can stay while waiting for updates." A young woman guided them down the corridor. "I hope you'll find it comfortable. If you need something to eat, you'll find a room-service menu on the desk. The room also has wireless Internet access and cable."

"Like a freaking hotel," Addison muttered as they entered the room. It did look like a hotel room, in fact. She stood there, in the middle of it, looking around the tasteful décor and the flat-screen television. Her entire body ached and she couldn't remember ever being this cold. The world seemed fuzzy at the edges. Was she about to pass out?

Strong arms folded around her and pulled her toward the couch. "Come on, Addison. Sit down and I'll order us some soup and coffee. You need to eat."

"I don't feel like eating." Addison wasn't sure why she resisted Eleanor when she was guiding her toward the couch, but she somehow felt safer standing there in the middle of the floor, being cold. If she gave in to Eleanor's embrace, she would start to cry and most likely never stop.

"Darling, come here. We can hold off on the food. Just sit with me." Eleanor's voice was low, soothing, and still very authoritative. It was oddly comforting, as it was how she'd come to perceive this woman.

"All right." Her legs wobbly, Addison walked over to the leather couch and sat down. Eleanor wrapped a blanket around herself and then extended it around Addison.

"You're so cold. Here. Lean against me." Eleanor's hands pulled her close. "Let's just sit here and collect ourselves."

"Thank you." Addison spoke in spite of the lump in her throat. "Thank you. I know you must have things you need to do. I mean, other places you need to be."

"Don't even think that. I had planned to spend the entire day with Stacey. We were off to a really good start. I'm not backing away from that commitment." Hugging Addison closer, Eleanor stroked her back. "Besides, I want to be here. For her. For you. Absolutely for you."

"Don't get me wrong. I'm thrilled that you're here. I—I really need you." It wasn't easy to say. Somehow it felt presumptuous and too demanding, to need Eleanor in this so very basic way.

"If the situation were the other way around, if what happened to Priscilla had happened now, I would have needed you just as much." Eleanor pressed her lips to Addison's temple. "See?"

"Yeah. You're right." Knowing without a doubt that she would've dropped everything to be there for Eleanor if their roles had been reversed, Addison allowed herself to relax into the embrace.

They sat in silence for the first half hour. It was way too soon for an update, but Addison flinched every time footsteps passed their door, hoping, and fearing, someone would stop and knock. She closed her eyes and thought of Stacey. "Until lately, she was always healthy," Addison said in low voice. "I remember when our mother came home from the hospital after having this little dark-haired bundle. I was nine years old and not into dolls at all, but I loved my baby sister more than anything else. I learned to change diapers, mix the formula, and check the temperature of her bathwater."

"No wonder you're so close." Eleanor caressed her cheek.

"Yeah. As she got older, I taught her to ride a bike, spell her name, make a peanut-butter-and-jelly sandwich, and operate the remote control to the TV." Addison snorted softly but then grew serious and shuddered. Eleanor held her even closer. "When our parents died, the thing Stacey needed from me, not counting providing food on the table and a roof over our heads, was to debate the concepts of life and death. Where were Mom and Dad? How long would they be there? Could they hear her? Years later we had The Talk, where I tried to explain about sex. Not very easy when your own experience is limited. That was also when I told her about how I was different from most girls Stacey knew. When I broke the news to her that I was attracted to women only, Stacey took that as something entirely natural. I was floored. In fact, she demanded to meet my girlfriend. I felt pretty mortified but had to confess that I wasn't in a relationship at the moment—the truth was, I was having issues when it came to letting someone in—but I promised Stacey that I'd introduce her as soon as I started dating someone."

Curling up against Eleanor, Addison sighed. Immediately, Eleanor pressed her lips to her temple again.

"Two years later, I thought it might be okay to let Stacey meet my then girlfriend, my first serious one. Her name was Julianne, and it turned out to be a catastrophe. Stacey was so full of expectations. I think in her mind she believed we would become a family, something she yearned for. When I introduced Julianne to Stacey, it didn't take me long to know that this relationship was over—less than an hour, I think. Julianne went from being seductive and fun to overbearing and demonstratively exasperated, which made Stacey defensive and angry. I could see how hurt and disappointed Stacey was. I simply apologized for making such a mistake and asked Julianne to leave."

"Oh, darling. The two of you had such hopes, didn't you?"

"Yeah. Afterward I held Stacey, like you're holding me now, and comforted her. She, being typically Stacey, blamed herself for 'ruining my life.' It took some persuading, weeks actually, before I could convince her she was the only person who mattered to me." Turning her face into Eleanor's neck, Addison murmured, "I never did bring another date home."

"What?" Eleanor jumped. "So when you asked me to come over…?"

"It was a bit of a nerve-wracking moment." Addison tipped her head back. "Stacey already knew how attracted I was to you. God, it only took her *minutes* to figure that out."

"And you still wanted me to come to dinner."

"Yes. I had plan B figured out." Addison trembled but tried to smile anyway.

"Plan B?"

"Yes. If you and Stacey didn't hit it off, I wouldn't be able to fool her, I knew that, but I would still be able to let you believe we were strictly about business. Luckily, we kissed."

"Which of course your sister figured out." Eleanor chuckled wryly. "I've *never* been caught necking on the couch. Never."

"Me either. And when Maureen…Maureen!" Addison sat up so fast, she nearly tipped Eleanor over. "I have to call Maureen. She has to know. They've been best friends for ages. She has to—"

"Calm down, Addison." Eleanor tugged at her gently. "Let's wait until we have the first update from the surgeons. As of now, we don't really have anything to tell her. Also, she's on that outing Stacey couldn't attend, isn't she? In Connecticut?"

"Oh. Oh, yes, she is. Damn, I forgot. She won't be home until late this evening." Sagging back against Eleanor, Addison hid her face against her neck. "I feel like I'm losing my mind. You must be totally unimpressed." She sighed.

❖

Eleanor shook her head. "You're anything but." In fact, she admired how Addison managed to keep it together as well as she did, considering this was her only next of kin, her beloved little sister, on that operating table.

If it had been Addison on that table, she would even have been dangerous to be around. No doubt she would have lashed out and fired half her staff.

As it were, only the fact that she needed to be there for Addison kept Eleanor strong. She'd spent only a few hours with Stacey, if you added them up, but the girl had quickly grown on her. She had none of the traits she found annoying in some other teenagers she'd come across but wasn't a precocious mini-adult either, which could be just as exasperating. Her sweetness, combined with a wicked sense of humor, made Stacey Garr irresistible and impossible not to like. She glanced down at Addison, who now had closed her eyes as she rested her head on the back of the couch.

Eleanor wanted to shield Addison, and Stacey, from any heartache or misery. Not a very protective person normally, Eleanor wondered where this ferociousness came from on her part. But she did know that she didn't intend to back down. Addison needed her and so did Stacey. Eleanor could imagine exactly which people around her would have a problem with this. Stockholders and associates be damned. So she was attracted to a woman. She couldn't care less what others thought.

A door slammed farther down the corridor and Addison jumped. "Ellie?" She tried to stand, but Eleanor held her back.

"Shh. Let's see if it's anything that concerns Stacey. They'll come here if it is."

Rigid, Addison sat on the edge of the seat. Taut, her body shivered in a barely noticeable way, as if she might shatter even if you just looked at her. Pain constricted Eleanor's heart and she kept her arms around Addison.

"Please. Lean back again, darling." Tugging gently, Eleanor managed to coax Addison into reclining sideways across her lap, her head resting on Eleanor's shoulder. Addison inhaled and exhaled deeply, clearly trying to regain her calm.

"That's it. You're doing fine. I have you."

"I feel like I'm falling to pieces. What the hell? What kind of help am I to Stace when I'm acting like a total wimp?" Addison made a wry face. "She's going to need me to be strong, and it feels like I'm about to rip apart at the seams all over."

"Then rip right here with me. Just let yourself go now, and then you can be strong for Stacey later." Eleanor ran her hand in a circle on Addison's back. "It's all right."

"But what if I can't put myself back together again? What then?" Turning her head, Addison looked up at Eleanor, her eyes swollen and her face pale.

"You will. You're strong, and once it's time to go to Stacey, you'll have let some of this steam out. Just hold on to me." Eleanor made sure she sounded equal parts firm and understanding. "When the doctor comes to talk to us, I'll help piece you back into Stacey's strong sister again."

At this, Addison flung an arm around Eleanor and wept quietly. As Eleanor's blouse soaked up her tears, she tried to find the perfect words to make Addison believe everything would turn out all right, but such words didn't exist. Instead, the only thing she could do that had any such effect was to hold Addison tight. Hiding her own tear-filled eyes by pressing her face into Addison's hair, Eleanor knew that when it came to making Addie feel wanted and safe, she couldn't imagine ever wanting to let her go.

CHAPTER EIGHTEEN

At the knock on the door, Addison stood on legs so unstable she was sure she'd topple headlong into the opposite wall. Fortunately, Eleanor stood with her and steadied her.

"Let me get that." Eleanor walked over to the door and opened it.

"Ms. Garr?" A tall man gazed over Eleanor's shoulders at Addison.

"Stacey? Is Stacey all right?"

"Come inside, Dr. Stromberg." Eleanor looked up from his nametag. "I'm Eleanor, a friend of the family." They shook hands before Dr. Stromberg turned to Addison.

"It's only been a few hours. How is she?" Addison felt herself go pale.

"Stacey is resting comfortably after the procedure," the doctor said quickly. "Why don't we sit down and I'll give you a rundown on the surgery."

Holding blindly to Eleanor's hand, Addison sat on the couch again. "Resting comfortably? It's over?"

"The procedure went very well, Ms. Garr. After reviewing the results of the MRI my team and I were in complete consensus as to the method. Coiling was the only alternative, as Stacey's aneurysm is located in a place where we wouldn't have been able to reach it surgically without risking vital functions."

"Dr. Reimer said coiling was the way he meant to operate as well," Addison murmured, fighting back nausea.

"Stephen Reimer? I know him well. I'll get in touch with him when I've looked in on Stacey, to update him on the fact that we sort of beat him to it."

"What does coiling entail?" Eleanor asked.

"As Stacey's aneurysm was located close to her speech centers and had begun a slow, but obvious seepage, we couldn't surgically clip it without endangering the surrounding brain tissue. Instead we used coiling, an endovascular treatment. I inserted a catheter into a blood vessel at Stacey's hip, and, with the help of that, my team and I packed coils into the aneurysm until the blood flow couldn't reach it anymore. It went extremely well, and Stacey's condition remained stable throughout the procedure."

"Can we see her?" Addison clasped her hands, tugging hard at her fingers.

"Yes, as soon as she's settled in the ICU. We'll monitor her closely until we're sure there's no further swelling of the brain. So far, we see only minimal signs of it. The seepage was also slight, and we hope to see a full reversal of the symptoms she had when she was admitted."

"Oh, God." Addison was trembling hard enough for her teeth to clatter. She felt Eleanor's hand take her own, gently unclasping them and pulling them apart.

"You're hurting yourself, darling." Eleanor massaged Addison's hands.

"Oh." Taking a deep breath, Addison returned her focus to the doctor. "So the bleeding has stopped completely?"

"Yes. As Dr. Reimer might have explained to you, Stacey will need regular checkups, as the risk of the problem recurring is greater than with open-brain surgery."

"I want to see her. How long before she's in ICU?"

Dr. Stromberg checked the clock on the wall. "Oh, I'd say we could start walking over there now."

"Oh, yes. Let's go see her. Right away." Bouncing up from the couch like it was electrocuting her, Addison looked pleadingly at Eleanor. "You're coming too, right?"

"Try to stop me," Eleanor murmured.

"This is still your private waiting room, which you can keep for as long as Stacey is a patient in the ICU. I don't expect she'll need more than a few days, unless she has complications. She should be able to go on to the rehabilitation clinic after that." Dr. Stromberg politely held open the door for them.

"Oh, the keycard?" Addison stopped outside the door, turning too fast and running back into the room. Inside she looked and looked, but everything was spinning and she couldn't find the little pamphlet with the keys. "No, no, no. Where is it? I can't...I can't..."

Strong arms wrapped around her. "I have them, darling," Eleanor whispered in her ear. "You're panicking. It's all right. We're going to see Stacey and she's going to be all right too."

"Yes." Addison leaned against Eleanor for a few moments. "Yes. Thank you. Let's go." Calmer now, she passed Dr. Stromberg, her hand safely in Eleanor's.

❖

Stacey was pale, but not the way she'd been when the aneurysm started leaking. Eleanor stood behind Addison, who sat on a chair at the side of Stacey's bed. Holding Stacey's hand carefully, Addison murmured terms of endearment. Eleanor kept her hands on Addison's shoulders as she studied the unmoving form in the bed.

Stacey's long hair lay in a brown river of curls above her head. Her face, now void of makeup and so very young looking, appeared serene, and Eleanor didn't want to think about how contorted in pain it had been only hours ago. The way Stacey had clung to her as they both went down in the lounge, looking at her in sheer terror and agony…Eleanor prayed she would never have to witness that again.

A nurse came up to the bed and checked Stacey's vital signs. She smiled encouragingly at Addison. "Everything checks out. Her blood pressure is fine and so are her pulse and respiration."

"What does that mean?" Addison pointed at a monitor. "I get the pulse and respiration part of it, but that one, that says 98?"

"That's her oxygen level. 98 is normal so she doesn't need oxygen." The nurse checked the IV fluids. "I'm responsible for Stacey until my shift ends. Just holler if you have a question, Ms. Garr."

Eleanor grabbed another chair, as her feet were beginning to object to standing in her high heels. She sat down next to Addison and placed a hand on Stacey's lower leg.

"I'm glad I could persuade you to eat earlier." Eleanor caressed Addison's shoulder. "Not to mention that you actually nodded off for half an hour."

"I could do that only because you were there. Really." Addison tilted her head until her cheek touched the back of Eleanor's hand.

Around them, nurses carried out their jobs, efficient and kind. Dr. Stromberg seemed pleased with Stacey's condition and had come and gone twice since they took up their vigil.

"Addison? I have to go make a few phone calls." Eleanor bent down and spoke quietly to not disturb Stacey. "I'll be right back."

Her head snapping up, Addison nodded solemnly. "It's all right. I've kept you from your appointments and meetings all day."

Eleanor realized Addison had misunderstood. "I'm coming right back. I'll just be gone for half an hour or so. As we're spending the night here, I figured I'd save time if I worked from here. We also need a change of clothes."

Blinking rapidly, Addison mouthed "Oh" and then smiled. "Thank goodness. I really need you here. I have so much to do tomorrow with all the paperwork. I'm surprised nobody has come to push a bill under my nose yet."

"Hmm. Yes. Well. I'll order us some food for tonight." Eleanor checked her watch. "It's almost eight. What would you like to eat?"

"Anything. Something light. Chicken?"

"I'll figure it out." Eleanor made a mental note about what to have them bring Addison. She rounded the bed and pressed her lips softly to Stacey's forehead. "See you soon." She turned as if to leave and then pivoted, took two quick steps toward Addison, and kissed her gently on the lips. "Hang in there. I have my cell phone if you need me."

"Good to know."

Eleanor stepped into the corridor, her cell phone already at her ear. "Susan, hello."

"Eleanor? How's the girl doing?" Susan sounded relieved to hear from her, and Eleanor guessed she had been more or less sitting with her phone in hand, ready to answer.

"She's doing well considering she just had surgery. Addison is with her and we're staying here tonight. We have a private room, which means we're going to need clothes. Messenger over one business outfit for me, the charcoal one with the ivory shirt. Black Manolo Blahnik pumps. I will also need some sleepwear. Any of the flannels. Two sets of lingerie. Something comfortable for my feet. My Nikes. When it comes to Addison, buy her two leisure outfits. Two sets of camisoles, socks, and underwear. She's a size eight. Oh, and some Nikes for her as well. Size 8½. We also need two servings of chicken salad, mineral water, and orange juice. Did you get all that?"

"Yes, Eleanor. I'll have it delivered to your room."

"Good. Now, make sure all the documents I need for tomorrow are available on the server. I have my laptop here with me, and I want you to set up teleconferences for all my meetings as I will be here." Eleanor gave Susan the number of Addison's and her room. Disconnecting the call, Eleanor closed her eyes briefly. She trusted Susan implicitly after having worked with her for years, but she was also certain her assistant was curious and wondering why Eleanor was taking such a personal interest in Addison and Stacey Garr. Eleanor also knew Susan was too professional, and also too nice, to ask questions or gossip about something that didn't concern her.

Returning to Stacey's room, she stopped in the doorway, taking in the sight of the two sisters. Addison was bent over resting her upper body on the bed with her head next to Stacey's, her eyes closed. Stacey's eyes, however, were open.

Eleanor walked as quietly as she could, despite her heels, up to the bed. "Hello, Stacey," she said in a low voice. "How are you feeling?"

"Th-thirschty." Stacey's voice was slurry, but it sounded like it was more because her mouth was dry. Her eyes appeared a little swollen, but other than that, she looked remarkably good. "Addie's sleeping."

"She's tired. She's been very worried about you." Eleanor moved her chair to the other side of the bed. "We should call the nurse." She pressed the button on the panel next to the bed. "Addison?" Placing her hand on the top of Addison's head, she scratched her scalp gently. "Addie?"

"Mmm? What?" Looking pale and drowsy, Addison blinked toward them and then her eyes grew huge. "Stace? Stacey!" She took a firmer grip of Stacey's hand. "You're awake."

"And looking great," the nurse from earlier said from the foot of the bed. "I'll page Dr. Stromberg."

"Can she have anything to drink? She's thirsty." Eleanor blinked tears from her lashes at the sight of Addison's expression of total relief.

"I'll bring some ice chips until Dr. Stromberg okays something else. I'm sure fluids will be fine shortly." The nurse made a note on the chart and left.

"How are you feeling, baby-girl?" Addison patted Stacey's arm.

"Foggy. What happened?"

"How much do you remember?" Eleanor asked.

"Taking notes. The tea…P-pain." Her brow furrowed. "Bad headache."

"And now? Are you in pain now?" Addison sat up, looking alarmed.

"No." Stacey shifted toward her. "Oops. Oh. Yeah. My hip? Ow?"

A male voice interrupted. "Hello there. Easy. You'll be a little sore for a few days. We poked around just above your thigh quite a bit with a catheter. I'm Dr. Stromberg. I performed the procedure with my team." The doctor held out a mug with a spoon tucked into it. "Here. Start with some ice chips, and if you're not nauseous from that, we can move onto water, apple juice, and so on."

"Juice…" Stacey said in a longing voice.

Eleanor took the mug and scooped up a few chips with the spoon. Placing it at Stacey's lips, she watched the girl suck on them with what had to be described as a blissful look.

"Do you know why you're in the hospital?" Dr. Stromberg smiled gently, but his steel-gray eyes were focused like lasers on Stacey's face.

"I don't remember, you know, exactly what happened, but I suppose my aneurysm blew or something." Stacey was regaining her voice and motioned for Eleanor to give her more ice.

"Not quite that dramatic, but it did begin to leak. What do you remember?"

"As I told Eleanor and Addie, not a lot. Just moments. And pain. And people speaking in my ear and poking me."

"I apologize. We do poke and prod a lot around here." Leaning against the foot of the bed, the doctor smiled crookedly. "Can you tell me the names of these two lovely ladies and your relationship to them?"

Eleanor wanted to roll her eyes, but she guessed Stromberg had adopted this light and flirty tone for Stacey's benefit.

"Of course." Stacey actually looked quite affronted. "This is my sister Addison Meredith Garr. And that's her girlfriend, Eleanor Maryanne Ashcroft."

Eleanor never, *never* dropped her jaw. Nothing surprised her very much these days, but now, this fragile-looking teenage girl had managed to shock and surprise her with just a few words. Girlfriend, indeed. And how the hell did Stacey know her middle name? Oh, that was right. She'd confessed earlier that day about researching her on the Internet.

"Stacey." Addison covered her eyes and cautiously peered at her between her fingers. This gave Eleanor a flashback from when they'd Skyped only four nights ago. *Oh, God.* She forced those images out of her mind instantly.

"Well, that settles that, then." Dr. Stromberg smiled even more broadly. "Now, I want to perform some basic neurological tests to see how you're doing. Squeeze my hands as hard as you can, please." He moved up next to Stacey and took her hands.

Eleanor tried to determine if Stacey was stronger in the hand that had been affected before, but it was hard to judge from just observing.

"Good," Dr. Stromberg said noncommittally. "Close your eyes and point at your nose like this." He demonstrated with wide gestures.

Stacey did as told, and this time it was obvious that she missed her nose by a few inches with her left hand. "Damn," Stacey said, and tried again, but with the same result. Her chin began to tremble.

"Don't worry about it. It's early days yet and you will get better. Try this." The doctor wiggled his hands back and forth.

Stacy did better with that movement, which made her look a little less stressed. After several other tests, Dr. Stromberg smiled encouragingly. "Well, first, I'll let the nurses know you can have water and juice. If that goes well, you can have some yogurt or ice cream."

"Oh. Ice cream." Stacey lit up.

"Then I want you to have a good night's sleep. It's late." He checked his watch. "Almost midnight. The staff will be checking you several times during the night, but in between that, I hope you'll be able to sleep."

"Okay. Thanks, Doc."

"Stacey." Addison looked at her sister with tender admonishment.

"Sorry. Thanks, Dr. Stromberg."

"You're very welcome. And if I'm not overstepping any boundaries, I suggest that you ladies get some rest too. We promise to call your room if Stacey needs you." He nodded and strode out of the room.

"I'm not leaving you!" Addison looked shocked.

"Sis, honestly. I'm fine. I'm going to drink some juice and hopefully have some ice cream and then sleep. I'm so tired."

"But I can sit here and—" Her voice catching, Addison gripped the bedding as if she thought they'd drag her out of there.

"No, sis. Please." Stacey tugged weakly at Addison's shirtsleeve. "Give me a big hug and then go get some sleep. I promise if I need you, I'll have them call you."

Addison sucked her lower lip in between her teeth and blinked rapidly. "You sure?"

"Very. I'm going to need you tomorrow when some perky PT forces me out of bed."

Eleanor knew that in ICU, they didn't allow you to stay inside the room but didn't see the need to inform Addison just yet. She hoped Addison would listen to Stacey and feel reassured enough to leave, but if she didn't, she'd have to let the stubborn and worried woman know.

Addison glanced between them, her chin lifting as if to challenge anyone, but then her shoulders sagged and she pushed her hair behind her ears with a defeated expression. "All right. Just promise me, Stace. Okay?"

"Are you kidding? You think I'd suffer anything without you here?" Stacey was also paler now and seemed happy just to rest against the pillows up in the hospital bed and close her eyes. "I'll just stay awake enough to persuade them about the ice cream."

"Anything for ice cream. That's my girl." Addison kissed Stacey's forehead. "Rest, and I'll see you tomorrow morning, first thing."

"Sleep well. I'm fine, remember? Freshly coiled and hardwired."

"God," Addison muttered.

Eleanor bent and kissed Stacey's cheek. "I'll take care of her," she whispered in her ear.

Stacey nodded. "Good night. Thanks for being here for Addie and for me."

"I'm glad I could help. Get some sleep, Stacey." Eleanor rounded the bed and wrapped her arm around Addison's waist. "See you tomorrow."

"'Night." Stacey closed her eyes and looked as if she fell asleep instantly.

Eleanor guided Addison back to their room. Inside, she noticed that Susan had fulfilled her assignment as two overnight suitcases sat just inside. Two wardrobe bags hung against the closet door.

"Who—? Oh, you arranged this?" Addison looked at the bags with surprise written across her face. "But how?"

"Susan. I had to guess what you might like to wear while you sit here with Stacey, but I'm sure you'll be comfortable."

"And here I was dreading having to wear the same underwear one more day. Or going commando." Addison gave half a laugh but seemed ill at ease. "I don't think my insurance covers this room, Eleanor."

"Don't worry. It's included. I checked." She crossed her fingers, hoping Addison wouldn't ask more in-depth questions tonight. Addison needed rest, they both did.

"Yeah?" Frowning, Addison rubbed her temple. "Well, if you're sure." She seemed too fatigued to remain focused. "I'm dying for a shower. Can I go first?"

"Of course. When you're done, there's a chicken salad with your name on it over on the table."

"Really? Wow. I'd forgotten about that."

"That's why you have me here. To make sure you rest and eat, so you can focus on Stacey."

Addison's expression altered immediately. Her eyes glowed a soft amber, and then she threw her arms around Eleanor's neck. "God, Ellie. I don't know what I would've done without you here. You're amazing. Absolutely amazing."

"I'm no saint," Eleanor said, cautiously. "I have a vested interest in both of you."

"You do?" Leaning back to gaze into Eleanor's eyes, Addison looked questioningly at her. "How so?"

"I care about you, and to quote you, I can't imagine what I would do without you."

"Ellie…" Addison caressed her cheek and moved in for a soft kiss. "Why don't you eat while I'm in the shower, and I can do the same? I'm so tired, and all I can think of right now is sleeping next to you."

CHAPTER NINETEEN

Addison dried herself after a quick, hot shower. Her stomach was growling, and even if it was very late, she was ready to dig into the chicken salad. She pulled on a pair of white panties and the blue-and-white-striped flannels Eleanor's assistant had brought. Browsing the toiletry bag sitting on the counter, she discovered new toothbrushes and toothpaste. She would have to brush her teeth again after eating the salad, but she was dying to feel fresh all over.

She found Eleanor on the couch, focusing on her laptop with a half-empty plate next to her.

"Did you fall behind a lot after today?" Addison walked over to the table and lifted the lid of the second plate. After pouring herself some mineral water, she grabbed a fork and carried it all to the couch. "Ellie?"

"Mmm? Oh, sorry. What did you say?"

"Did you miss a lot of important stuff today?"

"Some, but nothing that even comes close to how important it was for me to be here."

The small flame in her stomach that was always lit when she was around Eleanor erupted into a bonfire. Addison ate in silence as she observed Eleanor working. It was fascinating to watch how the woman focused as she flicked at the touchpad while browsing her densely written documents and charts. Every now and then she frowned, but eventually she smiled, sighed, and snapped the laptop closed. "There. Now I'm going to shower."

"Mind if I just brush my teeth first so I can crawl into bed?"

"Go ahead."

Addison put her empty plate back on the table and walked into the bathroom. Brushing her teeth, she jumped as Eleanor walked in behind her and began to undress. Addison wanted to hurry up, give Eleanor her privacy, but then again, Eleanor knew she was in here. She didn't have to undress right here while Addison was brushing her teeth. Could it be that Eleanor was already this comfortable around her? She didn't seem like a casual, free-spirited person who undressed easily in front of just anybody. And since Addison was hardly anybody…

"I can hear the wheels turning from here," Eleanor said quietly, a faint smile on her lips. "No, I'm not trying to embarrass either of us, or flaunt anything, or even tease. I'm just eager to take that shower so we can finally settle down and get some sleep."

"Of course. Got it." Addison could confirm her blush in the mirror as she rinsed her mouth before hurrying out of there. Of all the immature, idiotic ways to act. Ogling Eleanor through the mirror like a complete moron.

Addison rounded the queen-size bed on the left side, and, for some reason, it dawned on her that they would be actually sharing a bed. "Not exactly how I fantasized about it." Muttering, she pushed at two of the pillows until they were positioned to her liking. As she curled up, her arms wrapped around her midsection, she closed her eyes and tried to will herself to instant sleep. Of course the faint sound of water running in the bathroom didn't help. It seemed as if the images flickering through her overtired brain were either that of an unconscious Stacey or a half-dressed Eleanor. "Ah!" She shoved her fist into one of the pillows.

"Oh, my. What did the pillow do?"

Addison turned onto her back. Eleanor stood at the opposite side of the bed, also dressed in flannels. She was placing her watch and cell phone on the shelf doubling as a nightstand.

"The pillow's innocent," Addison said glumly. "I'm just—I feel like I'm about to go nuts."

"No wonder. This day has been horrible for you."

"Yeah, but not only that. It started out great, then slammed right into horrible, and slowly became pretty okay again when Stacey came to after the surgery. What was great about it was how wonderful and caring you've been to us. Then we're showering and sleeping together…well, I'm torn."

"Torn about who you were really giving a sucker punch?"

"I wasn't hitting a person!" Aghast, Addison stared at Eleanor, until she realized she was being teased. "Oh. Hmm." She covered her face with both hands. "I'm all messed up. A total idiot. Don't listen to me."

The bed dipped as Eleanor settled in on her side. "Yes, I agree, you're messed up after today, but that's not your fault. As for being an idiot, I beg to differ." She rolled Addison gently until they ended up right next to each other. "And I want to listen, but how about we talk tomorrow when we've had time to sleep and recharge?"

"Sounds terrific. That'll keep me from planting more feet in my mouth." Addison inhaled the luxurious scent of Eleanor's body wash.

Eleanor chuckled. "Understood. No more foot-plants."

The fact that Eleanor could make light of the situation and seemed at ease just relaxing next to her made it possible for Addison to breathe. "Stacey started sounding like herself."

"Yes, I'd say so, if you mean when she introduced me as your girlfriend."

"I know. I can't believe she did that. No doubt she's going to blame coming out of the anesthesia." Addison moaned.

"That makes sense. She comes out of the anesthesia thinking it's a bright idea that we come out to her neurologist."

It was harder now to know if Eleanor was teasing or not. "Um. Yeah. Hopefully that lies within doctor-patient confidentiality."

"We're not the patients."

"We weren't the ones doing the outing."

"True." Eleanor turned fully on her side and placed a hand lightly on Addison's shoulder. "Time to go to sleep."

"Okay. Good night."

"Good night."

Addison was sure it would be impossible to sleep, but hoped for some quality rest at least. To her surprise, it took her only three or four minutes to become drowsy. Next to her, Eleanor's breathing already indicated she was fast asleep. Some light shone through the curtains and illuminated the ice-blond highlights in her hair and outlined her face. Addison let herself absorb Eleanor's heart-wrenching beauty until she couldn't keep her eyes open any longer.

❖

Eleanor woke up from a dull pain in her side. She moaned and tried to shift to find a more comfortable position. A moan startled her and then something hard hit her shin.

"What the hell?" Turning cautiously toward Addison, she just barely caught a long, swinging arm before it hit her again. "Addie? Addison!" Now wide-awake, Eleanor quickly realized that Addison was caught in the throes of a nightmare. "Darling, wake up. Please."

Addison was shaking, and as Eleanor tried to push the long hair from Addison's sweaty temples, she could hear soft whimpers with each breath. She couldn't bear to see Addison in such torment. Capturing the other flailing arm with her free hand, she put her lips to Addison's ear.

"Wake up. Addison!" She spoke sternly, hoping to break through, but it was clear the nightmare had dug its claws deep into Addison, frightening her badly.

"St-Stacey." Addison tugged to free herself. "No, no, no…"

"Stacey's all right. Everything's fine. It's me. It's Eleanor. Please, wake up, darling."

Addison kicked out with her legs and hit Eleanor's shin again. Groaning in pain, she hooked her leg over both of Addison's to try to subdue her.

"Addie, open your eyes. It's just a dream. It's not real. Whatever you're dreaming, it's not real."

"Ellie. Eleanor!" Addison's eyes snapped open, tears pouring from them. "They're gone. They were here and then they were gone and I can't find them. I was holding on to them and then they disappeared and they left me behind—" Her voice shook so much, it was hard to understand what she was saying.

"Stop it, please. Please, Addie. You're safe. I'm not gone and neither is Stacey. You're not alone. You're not. I promise."

"Ellie?" Addison blinked and slowly stopped fighting. "What—oh. Oh."

"A nightmare. A bad one." So relieved that Addison was finally awake, Eleanor let go of her and sank down on her pillow. She kept an arm protectively around Addison's waist, not about to let her feel abandoned. "I'm here."

"Oh, thank God. You are. You are." Addison hid her face in Eleanor's neck. "I was so scared and it was so real. I was running along some tracks and there were car wrecks everywhere, but no sign of the train. And I saw your car. The Maserati. And you were gone. And Stacey too."

"Sounds very frightening. Your mind seems to have mixed your parents' accident with what it fears the most right now. No wonder you were so distraught after seeing Stacey so sick yesterday."

"It was horrible. I was all alone." Pushing her hair from her face, Addison took a deep breath. "Thank you for waking me up. I'm sorry I woke you though."

"No need to be sorry." Eleanor kissed Addison's forehead before checking the time. "We can still get another two-and-a-half hours' sleep if we're lucky."

"Yeah." Addison didn't sound sure.

"Are you afraid to go back to sleep?" She cupped Addison's cheek. "I'm here. I'll wake you if it happens again. I promise."

"I don't know. I'm jittery all over, as if all my nerve endings are on alert. You know, like you can get when a thunderstorm is about to hit?" Addison hugged herself and rubbed her arms. "It's the weirdest thing."

"What if you lie down facing away from me? I can hold you, and if you wake up, I'll feel it."

"You're so great for not losing patience with my being so freaking needy." Addison shifted until she was on her side, and Eleanor snuggled up with her from behind.

"You'd do the same for me, wouldn't you?"

"Yes, of course. In a heartbeat."

"Well then." Eleanor wrapped her right arm around Addison. Faint tremors reverberated from her to Eleanor. "Shh. Just relax."

Eleanor closed her eyes and held Addison tight to her. When she was still as tense after several long minutes, Eleanor began rubbing her belly slowly to try to relax her. Oddly, this seemed to make Addison even more rigid and even move away from body contact with her.

"Darling? What's wrong? You still upset?"

"No. No, I'm just not tired. Well, I am, but I can't relax and go to sleep." Addison was babbling, which showed how nervous she was.

"Want me to let go of you?"

"No!" Addison reached for Eleanor's hand and pulled her arm back around her. "I need you. I really need you."

"Tell me what you need. Please, will you share with me why you're still so on edge?" Eleanor began caressing Addison's stomach again, occasionally sliding her hand down her hip and up and down her thigh. "Just relax, darling. I have you."

"Without your touch, I'm cold and trembling, and with you holding me, I'm on fire and shaking all over. I'm totally screwed up."

Burying her face in the hair at the nape of Addison's neck, Eleanor inhaled deeply. "What do you need? I can think of something that will help you unwind." She slid her hand up and cupped Addison's right breast on the outside of her pajama jacket.

"Ellie!" Arching, Addison placed her hand on top of Eleanor's, holding it more firmly against her breast. "Please."

"I have you. Trust in me, Addie. Let me help you."

"Oh, God. I'm so worked up. Fuck." Her voice a mere whimper, Addison squirmed against Eleanor.

"Shh. There. How's that?" Eleanor felt the hard protrusion of Addison's nipple against her palm and massaged it gently. Kissing Addison's neck, she pressed her right leg forward, in between Addison's. Addison's center was hot against her thigh, like she was on fire.

"Oh, God, Ellie. Please, please, please." Addison's feverish whispers went straight to Eleanor's core, but she wasn't about to let this be about her, not for a moment. This was about being there for Addison.

"I want you to come for me, darling," Eleanor said, clenching her own thighs as her words made Addison moan. She hadn't quite counted on Addison's needing her touch this much. Nor had she expected herself to respond the way she did.

"Touch me, please?" Addison whispered.

For a moment, Eleanor didn't get what Addison meant, but then her cheeks burned and she slid her hand downward. She wasn't going to touch Addison's skin, as that somehow seemed taking it too far, too soon, and at the wrong time. Pushing her fingers in between Addison's legs, she was amazed at how hot and damp Addison was. She maneuvered her leg to part Addison's a bit more, for better access. Addison was trembling and gasping for air now. Pushing forward, she clearly tried to make firmer contact with Eleanor's hand.

"Like this?" Eleanor murmured, circling her fingers against where the seam of the flannel pajama pants rubbed against Addison.

"Yes, oh, yes, like that. Ellie, don't let go."

"Never."

"I'm burning up. So hot. So—oh! Oh!" Addison grew so rigid Eleanor almost feared she might hurt herself. Then she slumped back against Eleanor, gasping for air in long breaths that sounded painful. "Ellie, Ellie…"

Curling up behind Addison while holding her close, Eleanor hummed soothingly as she moved her hand to stroke her hip. "Mmm. That's it. That's better."

"What—what about you?" Addison tried to move her head around to look at Eleanor.

"I'm fine," she lied. "I'm quite tired and there'll be other times."

"You sure?"

"Absolutely." Eleanor hid her face in Addison's hair again. Truth be told, she was on fire too, but this wasn't the right time for a mutual encounter. She tried to think past the heat radiating from Addison. Right now she shouldn't allow any suddenly awoken libido to roam freely. Addison needed every minute of sleep she could get to face a new day at Stacey's side. She certainly didn't need Eleanor lusting after her.

"I have wanted you since day one." Addison spoke quietly. "It's not right that it's this one-sided. Making love, I mean."

"You need *sleep*, and if I find myself…affected by your presence, then it's for me to deal with." Groaning inwardly, Eleanor closed her eyes hard, as if that would help with her lack of self-control.

"Affected by my pres—what—as in turned on?" Addison's expression went from surprised to affectionate. "Ellie." She pressed her lips against Eleanor's in a gentle kiss. "Why would that be embarrassing or inappropriate? I agree that I have pictured our first real time together in another setting and definitely when I wasn't so messed up—"

"Even so, I'm not as vulnerable as you are, no matter how much I've come to care for Stacey. I should be able to control myself." Eleanor wiped her damp palms on her pajama jacket.

"I don't think you can control when arousal hits. Surely you felt how bad off I was just now? Do you honestly think I don't realize being tossed into closeness after such trauma might make us fire on all four cylinders?"

How could Addison be so understanding, so strong, after having gone through hell and then woken up after a horrible nightmare? No wonder she loved her so much. Eleanor's thoughts stopped so fast, she could have sworn they left tire marks in her brain. *Love her?* But of course. Of course she loved this wondrous young woman. Eleanor knew of Addison's capacity for love as well, but that didn't mean Addison would ever return her feelings in the same, all-overshadowing way. Still, admitting to herself how much she loved Addison, and how much she honestly cared for Stacey, made it possible for her to harness her arousal and settle down.

"You're totally right, darling," Eleanor said, snuggling closer again. "But please, let's save it for when we're rested and in a better frame of mind."

"If you insist." Addison seemed to want to say something more but then sighed and settled in against her.

"Go to sleep, Addie. Tomorrow will be better."

"I hope so. I can't bear to think otherwise."

Eleanor didn't know why she suddenly wondered if Addison was talking only about Stacey.

CHAPTER TWENTY

Stacey was sitting up in bed having her breakfast when Addison and Eleanor arrived. She looked up at them, smiling broadly, and to Addison's relief, the smile wasn't lopsided and both her eyes crinkled in the same manner, making them sparkle.

"Look who's doing so much better," Eleanor said, sounding just as relieved. "Good job, Stacey."

"Hey, you should praise Doc Stromberg. He's the one who filled my head with junk. In a manner of speaking. No doubt I'll set off the metal detectors." Stacey finished her yogurt and picked up a mug. "And I called Maureen."

"Oh, God! Maureen!" Addison slapped her forehead. "I knew there was something I forgot yesterday. I'm so sorry, Stace."

"No worries. It was kind of cool that I got to call her, sis. Less time to worry, and now she knew right away that I was doing much better. New and improved, so to speak. She's going to visit this afternoon when I'm at that other ward."

"What other ward?" Addison wondered if her brain was malfunctioning too, as her thought processes seemed to have slowed to unmovable.

"Doc said it was fine for me to move to a regular neurological ward. The PT person is supposed to show up any moment to help me get started with my exercises, and then if she's happy with how I'm doing, I don't have to stay here in the ICU. Cool, huh?" Stacey sipped her tea. "And how are the two of you? I remember you both reaching zombie stage yesterday. You look a little more... um, less pale. More like flushed." She raised an eyebrow. "Aha."

"Don't you aha me, you little brat." Addison knew she was blushing, she could feel it, and now she hugged Stacey and hid her face at the shoulder of her far-too-perceptive sister. "I'm thrilled that you're doing so well, but please be careful and listen to the staff."

"I'm doing fine. I'll be running circles around them soon enough."

"Stacey, please." Addison pulled up a chair and sat down next to her. "Listen to me. Don't be too cocky and overconfident. I realize you're relieved that the procedure's over and done with, but you have to pace yourself."

"Okay, okay. I'm only kidding. You should've seen me when I had to go to the bathroom this morning. I had two nurses holding on to me, but I was like totally wobbly."

"See?" Addison caressed Stacey's cheek.

"But what about the two of you? You must have stuff to do at work. You don't have to sit around here to hold my hand or anything." Stacey turned her focus to Eleanor. "And no offense, guys, but you look like you didn't sleep a wink, either of you."

"Charming," Eleanor said, placing a hand on her hip as she gave Stacey a mock glare. "And I have to be at a meeting with the members of the board and able to wow them. Now you tell me I look horrible." She shook her head at Stacey.

"Ah, don't listen to me. You still look awesome. You're rocking that skirt suit, and I bet Addie couldn't take her eyes off you when you put on that blouse. Ow! You can't pinch someone in a weakened state." She swatted playfully at Addison.

"God, Stacey. You seem hell-bent on embarrassing me. Brat!" Addison wished for a sinkhole to open. She glanced at Eleanor, and at first she thought the other woman was annoyed, but then Addison realized Eleanor was only trying not to laugh.

"As a matter of fact, I chose this blouse for that very purpose," Eleanor deadpanned, which nearly made Addison choke. "And now I need to head back to my office. You both have my number, right?"

"We do." Addison stood and kissed her cheek. "Thank you. I'll talk to you later?"

"I'm counting on it. I'll see you back at the room, right?" Eleanor returned the kiss and then turned to Stacey. "Take care, Stacey. Say hello to Maureen." She kissed Stacey's forehead and then strode out of the room, her heels echoing down the corridor.

"Wow. She's so awesome. She really is." Stacey pushed the tray aside and lay down against the pillows. "And she's crazy about you, sis."

"I wouldn't go that far, but she does seem...interested." Addison didn't know how to phrase how she and Eleanor felt for each other. Of course it was more than interest. Words like mind-blowing passion came to mind, but there was a limit to what she could share with Stacey. A small voice insisted that it wasn't so much the wording as the conflicting emotions after their night together that made it difficult. Why was she feeling so uneasy and on guard? Was it because of yesterday's anguish while waiting for news about Stacey—or did it have to do with what she and Eleanor had together?

"And you're way past just being interested, aren't you?" Stacey smiled gently. "I know I'm an unbearable tease, but it's so obvious to me how you both feel. I can't help myself."

"What do you mean, obvious?" Addison folded her arms over her chest.

"You're totally gone on her." Stacey enunciated the words as if Addison were in the habit of reading lips. "Eleanor can't take her eyes off you and you keep touching each other. Typical signs."

"And you know this how?"

"*Cosmopolitan.* You read that magazine too. Come on, Addie. Everybody knows this."

Addison didn't know whether to hug her or choke her. Of course her little oracle of a sister was right. She loved Eleanor Ashcroft so much it was almost beyond comprehension.

"Addie? You look like you're about to fall off the chair. I didn't mean to upset you." Her eyes huge, Stacey plucked at her blanket.

"You didn't, baby-girl. I just have a lot on my mind. I'm going to talk to the billing office and try to straighten out all the documents. You know, that sort of thing." Addison smiled faintly, knowing she wasn't fooling Stacey. "Why don't you rest up until they come and start messing with you? You can just text me when they do so I can go with you to the new digs, okay?"

"Mmm-hmm. I'm pretty wiped out, so crashing for a while sounds like a plan."

"Good." Addison hugged Stacey. "See you later, baby-girl."

"Later."

Stacey closed her eyes immediately and she did look exhausted. Addison reminded herself that Stacey would need time to recuperate and this was only the first day after the surgery. No wonder she was tired.

Addison went back to the room to call the billing administration and pulled out the information regarding the new insurance she'd arranged for when she started working with Face Exquisite.

A woman picked up at the other end, rattling off her title and name. Addison only caught the name Colleen but figured it was enough.

"Hi, Colleen." She introduced herself, explained why Stacey was in the hospital first, and then asked about how the billing process worked as they had never been to Presbyterian before.

"I'm looking at your sister's information here, and I'm afraid I don't understand your concern. We gave you all this information when your sister was admitted."

"No, you didn't. I was with my sister. A friend of mine handed over Stacey's details and documentation. Our insurance papers were among them. I have the envelope right here."

"I see. Well, everything's been taken care of already, so your sister can just focus on recuperating. I hope you find her stay at Presbyterian satisfactory."

"Hey. There is the small matter of the bill. What do you mean, all taken care of? I haven't signed anything except a consent form for the surgery."

"The bill is being paid continuously through a credit card."

Addison flinched, missing a beat. "What?"

"Everything, including the guest room, is set to be billed automatically to a credit card belonging to—oh, it's not yours. The card belongs to an Eleanor—"

"Ashcroft."

"Yes. That'd be your friend then? Wish I had a friend like that." Colleen giggled but then probably realized Addison wasn't thrilled. "Um, is there a problem, Ms. Garr?"

"Yes, there is. I want an itemized bill for my sister's care and procedures this far. I have a new insurance company, and I'll send it to them. You can also get in touch with them. Here's the information." Addison read the information from the insurance company.

"Ms. Garr, all of the expenses to date have been billed to Ms. Ashcroft's credit card."

"Then refund them."

"I'm not sure how to do that. I'll have to talk to my manager." Colleen definitely sounded stressed now.

"You do that. I expect you to pay Ms. Ashcroft back ASAP and send a letter or e-mail to me confirming your transaction. I'll call my insurance company and tell them to expect your call. I also expect you to not bill Ms. Ashcroft a single dollar more. I hope I make myself clear?"

"Crystal clear, Ms. Garr."

"Good. I'll be in touch. Good-bye." Addison disconnected the call and looked around the room. A luxurious room, worthy of a four-star hotel. She was ready to strangle Eleanor for lying, for going behind her back, and—no shit—for adding this no doubt super-expensive room to her bill.

Why hadn't Eleanor told her about the billing arrangement? Why had she paid for Stacey's care in the first place? Addison had given her everything she needed to get things started, including the envelope with the insurance information. Why would Eleanor use her own money? It didn't make sense. A thought struck her. She'd asked Eleanor about this room. Clearly remembering how Eleanor had claimed it was included in the *insurance* and for her not to worry about it, she moaned and covered her face with her hands. What kind of weird lie was that? This was crazy. She needed to talk to Eleanor.

She dialed Eleanor's cell phone, but the call went straight to voice mail. She waited five minutes while pacing the room, not quite sure why she was so worried. Eleanor had surely just been trying to help. Right? She redialed; the call was sent to voice mail again.

"Hi. Eleanor. It's Addison. I need to talk to you as soon as you have a moment." She thought of something and added, "Oh, by the way, don't worry about Stacey. She's doing fine. This is about…something else."

She disconnected the call and sat down. Gazing around the room, she realized she had to pack up really fast to avoid being charged for yet another night. Gazing at the two overnight bags and the garment bags, she sighed. It was going to be a pain to get all that on the train if Eleanor didn't show up before she had to go home.

❖

Eleanor stepped out of the conference room, her head aching after having had to listen to one windbag after another ramble on and on about which direction to take one of the sister companies. Most of the opinions presented had been in direct opposition to each other, which made Eleanor bless the fact that she owned fifty-five percent of the shares in the Ashcroft Group. She still had to listen to the board of directors, but she had the last word.

Pulling up her phone, she saw she had several voice mails, two of them from Addison. Instantly worried, she stepped aside and dialed. Eleanor listened to Addison's message and took a deep breath. Stacey was all right. Still, something in Addison's voice sounded off. She had somehow spoken in a more precise way than usual. Eleanor glanced at her watch. The meeting had dragged on, but if she hurried she might be able to run over to Presbyterian and take lunch.

Eleanor dialed Addison and continued walking down the corridor.

Addison picked up right away. "Hi, Eleanor. Meeting over?" Her voice was tight and hollow.

Eleanor frowned. She could hear from the sounds around Addison that she was outdoors. "Yes, finally. Where are you?"

"I'm home. Just paid the cab."

Eleanor stopped walking so abruptly she had to steady herself against the wall. "Home in Newark? Why?"

"I checked out of the room. I have your stuff here, and I'll give it to you when we see each other next time."

Something painfully cold ran in a zigzag pattern along Eleanor's back. "I see." But she really didn't.

"You didn't tell me the truth, Eleanor."

The noise of the wind disappeared over the phone, and she heard the sound of a door closing. Or being slammed shut, rather.

"You needed to focus on Stacey," Eleanor said. Glancing around her, she saw one of the smaller conference rooms and entered it. She placed her briefcase on the table and locked the door behind her. "I was trying to help."

"We have insurance. You didn't need to use your credit card."

"They said your insurance wasn't enough to cover it."

"I have new insurance with extra stuff added to it for Stacey's sake. I do *not* need your money." Addison sounded so angry now, and hurt, Eleanor couldn't remain standing still.

Pacing back and forth she tried to explain. "I wanted to be with you and Stacey as quickly as possible. I didn't want to bother with that person behind the counter who was clearly not doing her job properly, as she never found anything about a new insurance policy in your documents."

"So you just wielded your credit card and poof, like magic, you paid for everything, including the room, which isn't covered, by the way. It costs a fortune. Not to mention the clothes you bought, the high-end toiletries, and the food. You intended to pay for all of that, since you figured I couldn't take care of anything."

"You're berating me for buying you a damn chicken salad?" Getting angry at Addison's reasoning, Eleanor stopped pacing and rested her hip against the back of a chair. "Isn't the most important part the fact that Stacey is getting better?"

"Don't you dare suggest that I don't have my priorities straight when it comes to my sister. You don't get to do that. Not ever. Enough people tried to take her from me by declaring me too young, too naïve, and, oh yes, too 'without prospects' over the years." Addison's voice sank to a low growl.

"I'm not them. I would never do that."

"So why didn't you just tell this incompetent person behind the counter that Stacey Garr's legal guardian would stop by and straighten it up later?"

"Because you needed to be with her and I can easily afford—"

"No. Wrong answer." Addison took a deep breath. "I don't really think we should talk anymore about this. I'm so angry I might say something I'll regret."

"I don't understand why you're angry. I really don't." Eleanor couldn't bear it if Addison hung up on her when she was in this frame of mind. "It's only money, Addison. Means to a goal."

Addison laughed mirthlessly. "Only someone like you would say that."

"Like me?"

"Born to old money. Born with that proverbial silver spoon, or in your case, I'm sure it was gold or platinum, tucked firmly into your mouth. Only money."

"Addison. You're being unreasonable. If you think about it clearly—"

"I'm clear. I'm more clear about how I feel than I've been the last few weeks."

"So what we have isn't worth fighting for?" Her chest ached now and Eleanor leaned against the table, supporting herself with her free hand.

"What we have? I'd be willing to fight for what I *thought* we had. Right now I'm so confused and pissed off I shouldn't be making any decisions. I've got to go. I promised Stacey I'd come right back."

"Wait." Eleanor swallowed hard, her mind rushing in all directions as she tried to solve this situation with her usually dependable logic. "I was going to join you—"

"No. Please. Let's—let's wait a bit. I need time to think."

"But—" Panicking now, Eleanor fought to keep her tears at bay. She just didn't understand where all of Addison's anger and resentment stemmed from. How could trying to help be so wrong? She guessed they'd reached a fork in the road and she could only give in, or she might lose any chance to salvage this relationship. "Very well. Tell Stacey I'm thinking of her. I'll give you time and await your call." Eleanor wondered if she sounded as defeated as she felt. She hoped not.

"Thank you." Addison's voice sounded distant, as if she'd put her phone down and moved away from it. "I need to go. Bye."

The call disconnected and Eleanor's knees buckled. She sat down heavily on one of the chairs, tipping her head back as if this position would make the errant tears run back into her tear ducts. What the hell had just happened?

CHAPTER TWENTY-ONE

Addison held the door open for Stacey. Maureen was right there, her arm wrapped around Stacey's waist as she guided her up the garden path.

"Honestly. I'm perfectly able to walk, you guys. Really." Stacey huffed good-naturedly at their fawning over her.

"I know," Maureen said, smiling brightly. She still kept her arm in place around Stacey as they moved inside.

The Russian-speaking cabdriver came with their bags, and Addison tipped him generously, which rendered her a heartfelt "*Spasibo*."

Inside, the girls curled up under blankets on the couch to watch some old movie, and Addison went upstairs to her bedroom. She was happy Stacey was home after nine days in the hospital. Ecstatic. She'd spent half her days at Stacey's side, half at Face Exquisite—and the nights tossing and turning. Having her at home and back at school in a week or two would bring some normalcy to her life—finally.

Eleanor had called her every day, but just seeing her name on the phone's display hurt. She knew she was taking the coward's way out by dodging the calls, but it was too confusing and painful to hear Eleanor's voice. That said, she'd listened to the two voice mails Eleanor had left over and over, like some masochistic rite at night.

As if her thoughts had been broadcast through cyberspace, her cell phone rang, making her jump. Eleanor. Perhaps she figured calling in the early afternoon would make Addison more likely to pick up. All right. Why not? She touched the green button.

"Hello, Eleanor." Relieved that her voice wasn't trembling, Addison sat down on her bed, clasping her fingers around her grandmother's crocheted throw.

"Addison." Eleanor sounded taken aback; perhaps she hadn't counted on Addison's answering. "I've been trying to reach you."

"I've been busy. You know. Stacey. The launch of the makeup. Everything." God, why did her throat hurt so much just from talking?

"Yes, of course, but let's not kid ourselves. If you hadn't been so upset with me, you would have taken the time."

"Yes, who knows?" Now Addison tried to sound flippant, but she failed and had to slam her hand over her mouth to suffocate the sobs threatening to break free. "What can I do for you?"

"You could say you want to see me. Preferably tonight."

"This is Stacey's first night home. I can't go anywhere."

"Stacey's been discharged?" The catch in Eleanor's voice made Addison fall to her side on the bed and pull her legs up. "And you—you didn't tell me? Surely you must've known how much I worried about her?"

"I—"

"And you wouldn't answer your damn phone!" Eleanor raised her voice now. "Never in my wildest dreams did I ever think you could be cruel."

Cruel? "Now wait just a goddamn minute! You're painting me out to be the bad guy here? You lie to me and act like I'm a complete idiot and incapable of doing anything for my sister, and—"

"I did nothing of the sort. You know very well I had only good intentions."

"Yeah. Sure. Good intentions with *you* calling the shots, *you* being the hero, and *you*...you acting like you were the decision maker not only in one of your fucking boardrooms, but in my home...my family."

"Is that how you see me? Like some...some tyrant that tries to take over your family?"

"I didn't say that!" Addison raised her voice to match Eleanor's. "Don't put words in my mouth."

"Oh, I think that's exactly what you meant. You've been Stacey's mother for the last eight years, and you'd see any attempt from anyone as a threat. You said so yourself. People doubted your ability to care for her from day one. So when I try to help—"

"You did help. You helped wonderfully when you were there for Stacey, when the aneurysm started leaking. That and by giving her the chance to be your assistant for the day. *Not* by taking on my responsibilities and flashing that platinum card of yours. Then you rack up more costs without consulting me and lie about it. And you think it's strange that I get upset?"

"I do. You know I have more money than I know what to do with. I give as much as I can to charity anyway, so why wouldn't I—"

"Charity?" Aghast, Addison sat up, wiping furiously at her tears. "Can you hear yourself, Eleanor? Can you? So Stacey is a charity case now?"

"God, you're infuriating. You don't hear what I say—you hear what you think I say!" Eleanor's voice was like an icicle piercing Addison's skin and going straight into her heart.

"So you're saying you didn't lie about paying, about adding the guest room?"

The silence from the other end lasted for a few beats. "No. I don't deny withholding that information from you." Eleanor's voice quivered now, and Addison realized to her shock that Eleanor was crying. "I was trying to be there for you, ease your burden so you could focus on Stacy. I don't understand why you can't see this."

"Look, obviously I can't make you understand what it feels like to be something or someone that needs fixing. Like that night in the hospital. You made love to me, or should I say, you helped me orgasm to relax me. You used sex as a way to calm me down and wouldn't let me reciprocate. Because I needed *fixing*." Crying openly now, Addison knocked over the box of Kleenex sitting on her nightstand. She reached for it and then suddenly found herself sitting on the floor.

"You couldn't be more wrong. You've misconstrued and misunderstood everything I've said and done since that day Stacey became ill. I think you're afraid of letting me in, or perhaps you don't care for me as much as you thought. A passing fancy, as it were. Well, at least we know where we stand. Perhaps it was just as well we figured it out before we let this go too far." Eleanor swallowed audibly. "I guess there's nothing left to say on a personal note. We'll have to see each other regarding the makeup brand, but I'll make sure that's kept to a minimum. I wouldn't want you to feel uncomfortable at work." She paused briefly and Addison tried to picture Eleanor, which was far too easy. No doubt she was standing with one hand on her hip, the other one holding the phone, staring out through a window as she tried to keep her anger at bay. "Good-bye, Addison."

"Bye."

She disconnected the call and curled up on the floor just as her door opened.

"Addie? Addie? What's wrong? We heard the yelling all the way downstairs despite all the explosions in the movie. What's going on?" Stacey knelt next to Addison and soon Maureen did the same.

"I'll be okay." The two girls sat there wide-eyed and she had no desire to explain. She just wanted to lie there and let the pain subside on its own.

"Don't even try," Stacey said, her eyes stormy. "You were yelling at someone at the top of your voice, and I bet that someone was Eleanor."

"What—what makes you say that?" Addison blinked the tears away and sat up.

"Because you love her. It's the only thing that makes sense. I'm home, doing tons better, your job is fabulous and pays well. The only missing piece is Eleanor. I haven't seen her since the day after the surgery. You've had so many excuses when I've asked about her that it would've been funny if it wasn't so damn sad. You two had a fight, didn't you?" Cupping Addison's cheek, Stacey ran her thumb over her cheekbone, wiping away more tears.

"I—yes, we had a falling out, you could say."

"But you love her?" Stacy frowned. "You don't see what I'm looking at right now, but sis, you look like you've lost *everything*."

"Of course I haven't. You're here. That's what's most important."

"I don't think so. Yeah, well, of course it's important that I'm alive and kicking, but right now, right here, I don't think I'm all that matters. You need to fix this with Eleanor. She loves you back. The way she looks at you, it's obvious. Didn't we say so already when she was here that Friday evening, Maureen?"

"We did. She looked at you like she was trying to figure you out and like she adored you." Maureen smiled carefully. "That's worth fighting for, isn't it?"

"She lied to me."

"What?" Stacey looked startled. "What about?"

"Doesn't matter. She made me feel like someone less…less capable, like I was someone you can't count on. Like she assumed I couldn't be trusted. Oh, damn, I can't explain."

"I don't get it. Did she do something without you knowing about it? What?"

"Pretty much."

"That's bullshit. She admires you. She's said so—many times. Eleanor thinks the world of you for being a single mother, practically, all these years. For you to raise a teenager and have your own company on top of that. She came to *you* because of your expertise, remember? You bring something to Face Exquisite that nobody else can. Or at least, not the exact way you can. Eleanor's smart. She wouldn't hand over the future of the company that means so much to her to someone she felt she had to hold by the hand the entire time."

"But you don't know all of it." Addison refused to talk about their last night. "You just don't."

"And you won't tell me, so how could I? I just know that when two people love each other against all odds, like you and Ellie do, you need to figure things out." Stacey moved to sit to Addison's left, leaning her back against the side of the bed. Maureen took up the spot on the right. "If you're thinking about those days when that idiot from Children's Protective Services kept harassing us, well, you just have to let that go. Eleanor isn't out to prove that you're incompetent. Why would she?" Stacy squeezed Addison's arm. "You've got to get a grip here, sis, or you'll lose the best thing that's ever happened to you—if you don't count me, of course." She crinkled her nose, but her eyes were serious as she held Addison's gaze. "You won't forgive yourself if you don't, Addie. I know you. You carry so much guilt around, and you sort of wear it like a shield."

"I don't know what you're talking about," Addison said, running her hands over her face.

"Yeah, you do. In some twisted way, you've always been weird about how Mom and Dad died. Like you take the blame for it or something. You've talked circles around it for years and never quite let me in."

Stacey was right, of course. It was time. Nauseous, she forced her voice to not shake. "Because—because it was my fault they crashed." The pain in Addison's stomach erupted again, exacerbated by the agony already there because of Eleanor.

"That doesn't make sense. You were here with me. You were on the phone—uh-oh. Don't tell me they were yelling at each other again about something and you overheard. They did that all the time."

"How can you possibly know what they did all the time?"

"Because I was *nine*, not *two*. I remember tons. I remember them yelling at you in particular, even if I didn't understand why at the time. They were serious homophobes, especially Dad. I didn't get that then, but I remember some of the words he threw around. I know what they mean now, and he was wrong."

"Dad was shouting at me over the phone, Mom was nagging him for being on the cell while driving, and they were arguing, and then they screamed…and, and…" Addison relaxed against the bed and just surrendered to the truth of how she'd felt all these years. The relief of telling Stacey the truth was immense.

"And they found themselves on a stupid train track." Stacey sobbed. "They had an accident because they were careless. Not only with their own lives, but they were careless with you. With your feelings. With your self-esteem. They made you feel *less*—"

Stacey stopped talking and looked back and forth between Addison and Maureen. "That's it. That's exactly it. Goddamn it, Addie, I get it now. Don't you see? Whatever Eleanor did made you feel like before. Like Mom and Dad made you feel. Like you were less of a person. Tons of fools did the same thing when you were fighting the system to keep us together. Can't you see what's happened? Even if Eleanor was wrong or whatever, that's not what she was trying to do." Stacey hugged Addison hard, sniffling against her shoulder.

"I don't think Eleanor really meant that." Maureen spoke quietly, her pale-blue eyes pensive. "I don't think that at all. You have to make sure, Addie. If you don't, you'll always wonder."

"Yeah, that's my brilliant Maureen—and she's damn near always right. Her IQ is freaking off the chart, did you know that?" Stacey grinned affectionately at her friend. "So, you need to talk to Eleanor again and make sure."

"I think there's no going back even if I wanted to. We said some pretty bad things to each other. She won't ever want to talk to me again."

"Not true. She loves you. If you give it a shot and just tell her the truth without yelling and stuff, you'll at least know you gave it your best, your all. If it still doesn't work, then you can heal and move on. You're gutsy, sis. You can do it."

"God, Stacey," Addison whispered, and rested her head on her shoulder. "Who's the mature guardian here?"

"I'd say I am, but we both know I'm very good at screwing up half the time. Listen, Eleanor made me believe I can really be something—some*one*—when we were on our break. She's a great mentor. When it comes to you, she's just figured out she's all hot for a girl, I mean, a woman, and this in itself must be pretty big. Then the woman she has the hots for needs her help and support, and she only does what she knows best, takes over and overcompensates. Basically she doesn't know any better." Stacey shrugged. "Please give her a chance to get it right. I've never seen you so consumed by another person, Addie."

Addison nodded slowly. It was excruciating to envision her life without Eleanor in it. Her pain when she felt disqualified as a guardian, as a person, was nothing compared to the torment at the idea of losing her completely. Eleanor had tried to reach out and make things right, but she had shot her down mercilessly.

What chance could she possibly stand now?

CHAPTER TWENTY-TWO

Eleanor stepped inside her penthouse and just stood there in the hallway. She had never felt as cold, or as lonely, nor had her home seemed as desolate as it did now. Determined not to think about the cozy, unassuming house on that tree-lined street in Newark, she of course ended up doing just that. She certainly wasn't going to think about the two young women living there.

Tossing her coat on the chair next to the dresser, she walked into her living room and over to the windows. She could see a huge part of Manhattan from here, and it glittered like the metropolitan jewel it was. The crisp, cold air made it possible to see even farther than usual, but not far enough. Not over to that house where her happiness had seemed to live. Oh, who was she kidding? Her happiness? She should have known such foolish hopes of love and something lasting a lifetime weren't for her. Hadn't enough employees and business associates cursed her enough times, not to mention her competition in the business world, to know that at least a few of those curses would have to take hold and stick to her like pins in a voodoo doll? Surely a few of those spell-casters had sold their souls to the devil and thus were well connected.

Eleanor snorted unhappily and continued into her bedroom and from there to her ensuite. She pushed off her clothes and let them lie where they dropped. More or less falling into the shower, she let the scorching-hot water hammer at her shoulders, but it didn't help. Soon she was pressing her forehead to the Italian ceramic tiles, crying in deep, painful sobs. Images of Addison flickered through her mind—how she looked across the dinner table when kidding around with her sister. But mostly the haunting images showed how Addison looked when Eleanor had kissed her lips swollen.

Stumbling out of the shower, she tugged her silk robe on, not bothering to dry herself. She rubbed a towel against her hair, getting off enough water so it wouldn't drip down her back. Untangling it with her hands, she didn't take the time to comb it. She merely wanted to pop two of her sleeping pills and crawl into bed, forget about anything else, and preferably sleep the weekend away.

The last phone call sat in her brain much like a threatening aneurysm, ready to burst and make her crumble at any given time. The words they'd yelled at each other—accusing, horrible words—haunted her. Soon, of that she had no doubt, she wouldn't be able to run from them any longer. They would pierce her everywhere and she would bleed out emotionally. There would never be another Addison in her life. Nobody would ever make her feel like that again. Addison had brought out the best in her, and yet she'd failed when it mattered. Her actions had turned Addison into a stranger—someone who clearly hated her. It was hopeless.

Eleanor opened the medicine cabinet and grabbed the pill bottle. She was just about to open it when the intercom by the front door buzzed. Sighing impatiently, she hurried to the foyer and answered.

"Ms. Ashcroft, this is Matt." Matt was the one of the doormen. "I have a young lady here to see you. Addison Garr."

What? Clutching at the lapel of her robe, Eleanor closed her eyes. What could Addison possibly have to add after their screaming match earlier?

"Ma'am? You there?"

"I'm here, Matt."

"I think you need to take care of this girl," Matt said in a low, kind voice. "She's clearly upset."

Oh, God. Eleanor wasn't sure she could handle more "upset." Closing her eyes briefly, she breathed evenly through her nose. "Very well. Send her up." She pressed the button again to close the call.

A minute later the doorbell rang. Tiptoeing back out into the foyer, Eleanor checked the peephole. It was Addison. Eleanor didn't want to let her in, and she certainly wasn't ready for another round. In so much pain she could hardly breathe, she flung the door open.

"Yes?" She was rigid enough to shatter if anyone even breathed on her.

"May I come inside?" Addison asked in a low, shaking voice. She looked pale, but had her chin courageously raised. "I promise I haven't come to fight or even argue."

"I don't know what purpose this could possibly serve. I'm on my way to bed, and I'm sure you're as tired as I am." Speaking curtly, Eleanor allowed the Boardroom Barracuda to take the lead.

"I'm very tired, yes, but this can't wait."

"Well, it's going to have to!" Suddenly raising her voice, Eleanor made them both flinch. This was a mistake. She wouldn't be able to handle Addison being in her home after all.

"Please. Eleanor, I'm *begging* you." Addison was shaking harder now, her face, void of makeup, as pale as it had been when Stacey was having her surgery. "Stacey went over to Maureen's for a sleepover because this is so important. It'll only take a few minutes, and if you still want nothing to do with me after that... I'll go. I promise."

A few torturous minutes. Her last minutes ever with Addison and then she'd be back to normal. Alone. Eleanor nodded stiffly and stepped aside. "Very well."

Addison placed her tote bag on the floor and began unzipping her jacket. When she had it halfway off her arms, she stopped and looked at Eleanor with huge eyes. "Okay if I—"

"For God's sake, take your jacket off." Flinging her hands in the air, Eleanor padded into the living room. "I'm going to have a bourbon. What about you?"

"Nothing, thank you." Addison sat down on the armchair angled next to the couch. She waited while Eleanor poured herself a drink and then sat down before opening her mouth to speak, but nothing came out.

When Addison had attempted to speak twice without being able to make a sound, Eleanor was becoming concerned. Addison was plucking at the armrests, her eyes looking wild, her lips so tense they were whitening at the corners of her mouth.

"What did you want to say? Or need to say?" Eleanor kept her voice even. Sipping her drink, she felt it burn.

"Ellie." Addison corrected herself. "Eleanor. I want to ask you for forgiveness. No matter whether you forgive me, I want you to know that I'm sorry. I'm so very, very sorry." Fat tears ran down her cheeks, but it was as if Addison didn't notice them. "I spoke to you in an unforgiveable way. I shouldn't have second-guessed you that way or let my insecurities get the better of me. All I could think about was how brushed aside I felt in so many ways, and it all just took me back to when…when Stacey was little and the authorities kept trying to take her from me. When you sort of took over—or seemed to, at least—I…I couldn't handle it. Not from you. It shattered me." Addison laced and unlaced her fingers repeatedly. "Stacey and Maureen overheard me yelling at you over the phone. I guess you could say they talked some sense into me." She smiled weakly.

"So you're here because Stacey overheard?"

"No. Yes, but—"

"Well, you can go home to your sister and tell her you apologized." Knocking back the last of the bourbon, Eleanor put the glass down on the coffee table. "Was that all?"

"I thought you'd decided I wasn't good enough," Addison whispered.

"What?" Eleanor was halfway standing up but now sat down again.

"I let the past rule me, and I thought you couldn't feel remotely what I feel for you. It was as if you took over so easily, disregarding my concerns and showing your superiority so clearly. I felt so small. So unqualified, in a sense." Wiping at her wet cheeks, Addison hiccupped.

"What are you talking about? Unqualified to do what?"

"To lead my life. To be the best for Stacey. To provide the best for her. It scared me that it was so easy for you to lie to me. When you wouldn't let me reciprocate in—in bed, I felt you used sex to fix me, to relax me, because it was good for me, not because you couldn't wait to touch me. Don't get me wrong, I loved your touch, I really did, but I struggled with this weird feeling of humiliation afterward."

"I'm trying to follow this. You felt I took over at the hospital and thus made you feel outmaneuvered? Not once could you take a step back and see I was only trying to help?" Eleanor shook her head. This was so complex and hard to understand.

"I might have been able to if you'd told me right away. You had plenty of opportunities to let me know. Or did you think I'd crumble because there was an administrative issue?" Addison tugged at her hair. "And then that room we stayed in. I might just have gratefully accepted so I could be close to Stacey, if you'd just told me."

"I see." Eleanor finally began to understand where she'd misjudged Addison's reaction. "I apologize for lying. I did it for a reason, but even so, I was wrong." She pulled up her legs and made sure the robe covered her, suddenly remembering she was naked underneath. "I would never want you to feel unqualified or inferior in any way. I happen to admire how you lead your life on all levels. You should remember I find you amazing."

"I believe you," Addison said quietly.

"You practically called me a tyrant, said I was trying to take over your family, had ulterior motives for my transgression." Eleanor's throat hurt as she swallowed.

"I know. I shouldn't have said all that because it's not true. I know I screwed up everything during our phone conversation, and I'll be paying for it every single day of my life. I'm so sorry for hurting you. I'm here to ask if you could please not abandon Stacey." Standing up, Addison held up her hands, palms toward Eleanor. "Please. She loves you. She thinks the world of you as a person, as a mentor. A family member." She whispered the last words and they skewered Eleanor's heart.

"And you? How do you regard me?" Eleanor rose and stopped in front of the shaking Addison, having to forcibly restrain herself from wrapping her arms around her. She just couldn't risk it.

"I love you." The words came with such honesty and without any drama. "I should apologize for telling you this way, but you asked, and I'd promised both Stacy and myself no more lies, no screaming, no more accusations. No more protecting myself, because, really, it's too late for that."

"Tell me again."

"I love you."

"You love me, but you don't have any faith in me?"

"I love you and I have very little faith in myself. I don't deserve you. Even from the beginning I knew I didn't. Or, rather, I thought you deserved better than me. And I thought, if I could understand that, it's clear that you, being so much more worldly and experienced, had to see that too. When you used your money in the manner you did, it made some sort of cruel sense."

"And when I tried to protect you in bed by taking a step back, I ended up hurting you instead." Eleanor spoke slowly as her mind began finally to focus again. Her heart picked up speed as well, when things started to make sense. "You, who took the blame for your parents' accident, who assumed blame for Stacey not having the surgery sooner...you assumed I saw all these perceived flaws and thought I needed to take over and that you weren't—what did Stacey call it—'girlfriend material'?"

"Yes."

"You seem to have forgotten something here. You haven't even asked." Trying to keep her voice stern now was almost impossible.

"What?" Addison's swollen eyelids blinked slowly as she clearly couldn't keep up. She looked exhausted.

"You haven't once taken into consideration how deeply I love you."

Addison's knees buckled and she began to topple sideways.

"Fuck." Eleanor barely caught her but then held Addison close.

"Oh, why did you tell me that? You shouldn't have. I may have screwed up so badly, but telling me that is just cruel. Too cruel. You should've let me just go and think you might have cared for me a little bit for a while, but…you *can't* tell me that and expect me to just be able to go on without—"

"If you for one second think I can let you go one more time, you're sorely mistaken, Addison." Eleanor held onto her, though she was struggling. "We both made mistakes. I wasn't forthcoming but was overly protective. I'm so very sorry. I really am." Eleanor hoped her words got through to Addison. "Now listen to me, darling. I love you, and now that I know you love me back, you're not leaving. Stacey is safely in Maureen's home with her parents present, right?"

"Yes?" A surprised, tiny smile appeared on Addison's face.

"And you will text her in just a little bit and tell her you're staying here with me this weekend, and then we'll figure out how to proceed with who stays where, but you are *not* going anywhere. Do you understand?"

"Yes." Addison flung her arms around Eleanor's neck. "Yes. Oh, yes, I do."

Eleanor could barely fathom that Addison was now in her arms, clinging to her as if her life depended on it. Heat erupted in her belly and spread throughout her system. "You'd better text her. Now."

"Oh. Okay."

"Or there might not be time for quite a while."

Eleanor could see exactly when Addison realized what she meant. "Let me get my phone."

"Tell Stacey I said hello." She wanted to talk to her and assure her how much she cared for her, but she'd do that in person, not via Addison's cell phone. Instead, she enjoyed watching Addison punch in letters with trembling fingers. She looked flustered and her swollen eyes sparkled. She'd never been more beautiful.

CHAPTER TWENTY-THREE

A ddison tapped the screen of her phone with unsteady fingers.

At Ellie's house. Communicating. Took your advice. Staying the weekend.

Stacey's reply came within seconds.

GREAT! Did she forgive you? And have you forgiven her? Are you happy?

Addison thought for a moment before responding.

It seems so. I have. Yes, happy and nervous. Will text you tomorrow.

Answering with a simple "OK," Stacey seemed satisfied at her end. Addison wished she felt as confident. Riding these emotions like a bucking horse was nerve-wracking, but Eleanor was worth every effort, even the ones that intimidated and frightened her.

"Is Stacey all right?" Eleanor murmured from behind her.

"She wanted to know if we'd forgiven each other." Addison turned after placing her phone back in her tote bag.

"I have," Eleanor spoke slowly. "What about you? Have you forgiven me for using my wealth the way I did?"

"Yes. Once I realized why and that you were acting the only way you knew how, because you wanted to protect us, I forgave you."

"Thank you." Eleanor smoothed Addison's hair back from her face. "God, you're so lovely. Even when you're exhausted with dark circles under your eyes."

"Guess the concealer I'm in the process of evaluating doesn't do the trick for very long."

"No, I guess not." Lowering her head, Eleanor pressed her lips gently to Addison's. "I don't care." She drew a line along Addison's jawline with her fingertips. "Hungry? Thirsty?"

"Cold."

"I'd suggest a hot bath then."

"All right."

Eleanor shivered. "Let me draw one for you. Or would you prefer a hot shower? I just had one."

"As you can tell, I'm a bit wobbly. Perhaps a bath is better?"

"Bath it is then."

Addison followed Eleanor through the large rooms, all of them perfectly designed but a little lifeless, somehow. The fact that it was very late and she was exhausted might be changing her perception. In the bathroom, Addison stood watching as Eleanor opened the faucet in the oval soaking tub. As it quickly filled with water, she turned to Addison and began undressing her with gentle hands.

"The bath will have you nice and warm in no time." She peeled back Addison's shirt, tugging it from her arms. Addison wore only a spaghetti-strap camisole underneath. Leaving that for now, Eleanor unfastened the button and unzipped the fly of Addison's jeans. Pushing them down Addison's legs, Eleanor pulled her sneakers off, together with her socks, and then helped her take off her jeans. She frowned as she cupped Addison's knees.

"You're very cold. Better get you in that hot tub right away." Unceremoniously, Eleanor removed Addison's camisole and boy-briefs. Then she seemed to falter, her eyes raking up and down Addison's body, which kick-started the heating process quite nicely. She was pretty sure she didn't imagine the hunger in Eleanor's eyes.

Addison tried to get into the tub, but it wasn't easy to move; her legs felt like they were about to give in. Standing naked in front of Eleanor made her tremble, and she had to forcibly try to not imagine those hands exploring her more thoroughly. She made another attempt to get into the tub, which proved more successful. The water was hot, but not scalding. She sat down with a groan. "Thank God. Oh, this is so nice."

"Here. Let me help you keep all that hair dry. Once you're out of there I have other plans for you that don't include blow-drying that mane of yours for hours." Eleanor used a large hair clip to keep the long auburn curls out of the water. "Not too bad. A good look for you."

Addison smiled and sank into the tub, water up to her chin. "Heavenly."

"Can you manage not to fall asleep and drown as I take care of a few things?" Eleanor raised a questioning eyebrow.

"I think so. You have me way too curious about your 'other plans.'" She teasingly raised her eyebrow.

"Good." Eleanor rose and left the bathroom.

Addison could hear Eleanor walking in and out of the rooms of her penthouse. What was she doing? Afraid she might become sleepy after all, Addison perused the long row of body washes and bubble baths sitting on shelves along the inner rim of the tub. Choosing one based on ginger, she rubbed it all over herself. Only when she was massaging the body wash into her legs did she realize just how close to the surface her arousal was. What if she'd misunderstood Eleanor and her "other plans"?

Jittery now, she stood as the bathwater began to drain and rinsed herself off with the handheld shower. Stepping out of the tub, she took a towel from a cabinet with glass doors over by the sinks. As she wrapped it around her she noticed absentmindedly that her clothes were missing from the bathroom floor. She padded back into the bedroom and met Eleanor carrying a tray of what looked like juice and fruit.

"Already done?" Eleanor put the tray down on one of the nightstands and came up to her. Stroking her arm and neck with the back of her curled fingers, Eleanor nodded. "You're warmer. Good."

"You're standing this close to me in what has to be the sheerest looking robe known to mankind. I'm amazed I'm not bursting into flames."

"Oh, give it time, darling." Eleanor tugged her closer. "That might still happen."

"Wow." Swallowing against the sudden dryness of the back of her throat, Addison let go of her towel and held on to Eleanor's shoulders for balance. The towel began to slip and only their closely pressed bodies kept it in place.

Eleanor wasn't having any issues with being cold. Addison registered the massive amount of heat radiating from her silk-clad body, and it proved Eleanor right. It was setting her aflame.

"I can't seem to keep my hands off you." Eleanor ran her hands over Addison's back. "I have no defense against this... against you."

"You don't need any defenses." Addison pulled back enough to lose the towel. Standing there naked, she held out her arms. "I'm yours."

"Oh, damn," Eleanor whispered. "You're so beautiful. I— I..."

"All right if we get rid of this?" Addison tugged at the belt at the front of Eleanor's robe. "I want to see you, feel you, so badly."

"By all means." Eleanor stood very still as Addison untied the belt and pushed the robe off her shoulders.

"Holy smokes." Addison slid her hands up and reverently cupped Eleanor's breasts, unable to wait a second longer. She'd dreamed of holding her, of touching and caressing her like this for so long. She kissed a trail down Eleanor's neck, took a detour around her shoulder, and followed her collarbone to her sternum. Tracing it down between Eleanor's breasts, she flicked her thumbs over the rock-hard pink nipples.

"Addie." Moaning, Eleanor gripped her shoulders, holding on so tight Addison could feel her blunt nails make indentations in her skin.

Addison straightened and pulled Eleanor into a firm embrace as she kissed her thoroughly, probing her mouth with her tongue, inviting its counterpart to play.

"Bed, Addison. Now." Eleanor was clearly trying to issue orders, but they came out sounding more like begging.

Addison didn't want Eleanor to beg, or to believe she needed to resort to giving orders, so she kept kissing her, changing angles as she explored the sweetness of those lethal lips. Moving toward the bed, Addison wasn't sure how, she found herself straddling Eleanor's thighs, their lips still fused. Even more interested in what other places of Eleanor's body there were to explore, Addison let her lips slide down Eleanor's neck.

"Mmm. Addie...yes." Eleanor pushed her hands into Addison's hair, fisting them at her scalp and tugging gently. "Like that. Your mouth, darling."

"Here? Like this?" Addison kissed down the gentle slope to a hard, puckered nipple. Running the tip of her tongue around it, she made Eleanor whimper, a sound she already was addicted to. As she closed her mouth around the nipple and sucked it in against the roof of her mouth, Eleanor's whimper turned to a faint wail. She could easily get hooked on that sound too.

Addison worked Eleanor's left breast until weak hands pushed at her, as she begged for mercy.

"Sensitive."

"I can see that." Addison looked with glowing eyes at the now bright-red nipple. "Let's see if the other one can become just as sensitive."

"Oh, God."

❖

Eleanor arched, moaning loudly, encouraging Addison to just barely sink her teeth into her right nipple. So aroused now, she was perspiring enough for the bed sheet to stick to her back, Eleanor knew it was her time to act. Addison had feasted on her enough to nearly send her hurtling into an orgasm. Not yet. She needed more.

Taking a fortifying breath, Eleanor pushed her fingers into Addison's hair again and cupped the back of her head. She pressed down with her left leg hard enough to roll them, which probably only worked because Addison was preoccupied with devouring her.

"Ellie!" Addison was on her back, hair spread over the pillow and looking up at Eleanor with her mouth half open.

"My turn." Eleanor kissed that surprised mouth and ran her tongue over Addison's lower lip. "My turn now to be the one in charge."

"But you're always in charge." Addison pouted, her eyes glittering.

"Yes, I know," Eleanor said casually, "and there's a reason why I'm always in charge."

"Oh, there is, is there?" Addison crinkled her nose at her. "And why might that be?"

Leaning down, Eleanor kissed the soft spot just behind Addison's earlobe, smiling against the skin as she did so. "Because," she murmured into the nearly transparent shell of Addison's ear, "I'm *that* good."

"Oh, yikes. At everything?"

"Sooner or later I make sure I master whatever I decide I want to do."

"And now?" Addison was gasping for air.

"And now I want to do…you." Eleanor chuckled at how her words made Addison squeak.

As it turned out, Eleanor was barely able to get past Addison's breasts. Those perfect globes with the dark, maroon tips were simply too delicious, too wonderful. When she finally let them go—and by now, Addison was actually purring—she kissed her way down a slightly rounded stomach. She saw the pierced belly button up close for the first time, and somehow, as it was Addison's pierced belly button, it was the most adorable and the sexiest thing she'd come across. She tugged at it gently with her teeth, making Addison yelp before this act of nibbling eventually made her spread her legs and make room for Eleanor.

Eleanor hadn't been sure how she'd feel when she was in close contact with Addison's sex. As it turned out—and this she hadn't expected—she had the urge to touch and taste every inch of the drenched folds; in other words, she wanted to devour Addison right back. Still, she was wary of doing something that might hurt Addison, which to her was unthinkable, so she approached her lover slowly. Starting with the supple thighs, she wasn't very surprised to find them slick halfway down to Addison's knees, as she was just as wet herself. Eleanor licked and kissed her way along Addison's thighs up to the junction of her legs.

"Ellie, oh, God, Ellie, you're driving me crazy. You know that, right? Absolutely insane. I can't...oh, fuck..." Addison parted her legs farther and pulled her knees up. "Your lips, your mouth...oh, God, your *mouth*!"

"Where do you want my lips? My tongue? Here?" Eleanor tried flattening her tongue against the hard clit. Pressing it in little circles seemed to work well, as Addison cried out and pushed her fingers into Eleanor's hair.

"Yes. Yes!" Her hips undulating beneath Eleanor's mouth, Addison wailed louder with each caress. "Yes, like that. Like that. Oh, you're going to make me come. Please. Please!" After that, Addison's words became unintelligible as she dug her heels into the mattress and pushed up against Eleanor's mouth.

Eleanor could feel the flutters begin against her lips and knew Addison's orgasm was happening. Carefully, she pushed first one finger and then two into her lover, wanting to experience Addison's pleasure with her as much as humanly possible.

"Ellie!" Addison cried out and squeezed Eleanor's fingers in a passionate rhythm that pulled her farther in.

Eleanor moved slowly up Addison's body, kissing her way, trying to show with each kiss that she had forgiven her, that she hoped Addison had done the same in return. She was quivering with unbridled arousal, but she was prepared to wait for Addison to regain enough strength to touch her. She wanted her lover to enjoy every second of the blissful, overwhelming pleasure, and she didn't want to miss a second of how Addison looked and sounded and *felt* as she trembled in her arms.

Eventually, and startlingly quickly, Addison pushed herself up on her elbow as they now were lying side by side. "Wow."

"That's it? Wow?" Eleanor pressed a hand to her chest. "And here I thought I'd rocked your world."

"You did more than that. You rocked it, turned it upside down, flung it around, and crashed it, pulverized it, and then…" Addison kissed her tenderly. "Then you put it back together again. You set everything in my world back in its place, but you also made it brand new. And you made it better."

Nearly sobbing at the sudden onslaught of emotions that Addison's words caused, Eleanor wiped at her wet lashes.

"Hey, no tears. That was a compliment." Addison slid her hand down along Eleanor's body.

Shivering in its wake, Eleanor placed her own hand on top of Addison's and pushed it down between her legs. "I'm so ready for you, darling. I *ache* for you. Please, put my world back in a new and better way too."

Addison's eyes softened and yet a new fire seemed to ignite at the same time. "My pleasure." She pushed two fingers inside Eleanor, who couldn't take her eyes off the determined woman hovering above her. "Yes. Mine." Addison started a slowly escalating thrusting movement, the heel of her palm pressing and caressing her swollen, sensitive clitoris.

Eleanor wrapped her arms around Addison's neck, needing to hold on as her entire universe spun out of control.

"Breathe, Ellie. You can't keep holding your breath."

Right. Breathing was good. Eleanor took a deep breath and then her world exploded, starting in the middle of her belly, piercing down her legs, up through her chest, and into her brain where it sizzled for long, wonderful moments. Clinging to Addison, she wailed, simply because she'd forgotten how to use words.

"Addie, Addie," she whimpered when her brain finally allowed her to form syllables again. "Oh, please."

"I have you. I have you right here and, oh, my God, it was amazing."

"You think it was amazing? Imagine...how I felt." To be honest, sex had never been that good. It had rarely even been okay.

"I love you, Addie. I love you." She tugged Addison close. "No matter what, no matter how crazy our upcoming weeks get, don't ever doubt it. I love you, and it's the most selfish and unselfish emotion I've ever had."

"That makes the strangest sense." Addison laughed and pressed quick kisses across Eleanor's forehead and down her temples. "And I love and adore you. No matter what."

Eleanor held on to Addison, not about to let her move. She needed the sensation of this full body contact. Instead she slid her hand down and pulled at Addison's leg, coaxing it over her hip. "I'm not finished with you. Not yet. Not ever."

"What? Oh!" Addison arched as Eleanor drew one of her nipples into her mouth. She sucked in long, slow movements, making Addison whimper and moan before she let it go.

"You have the most gorgeous breasts. So stunning." Her mouth greedy for the other one, she latched on to it, tugging with her teeth and reveling in the puckered, velvety texture.

Addison pushed her fingers into Eleanor's hair, pulling gently at it, clearly wanting her even closer. "This...is fucking unbelievable," Addison said, moaning louder with each pull of her nipple. "You sure you haven't done this before?"

"Positive." Eleanor said against the supple breast, licking at the nipple. "I guess I'm a natural."

"Oh, God."

"Turn over, darling." Eleanor nudged Addison and guided her on to her stomach. "That's it. Very good." Wanting to explore every square inch of Addison, she ran her fingertips, occasionally her blunt nails only, up and down Addison's back. Flawless, satin-smooth skin, so enticing to touch, made Eleanor's hands tingle. She rose and straddled the back of Addison's thighs, cupping her bottom with greedy hands. Eleanor could hardly breathe, her arousal spiking again at the mere sight of Addison's curves. She couldn't comprehend the fact that she was allowed to touch, to taste, this gorgeous creature.

She squeezed the firm globes and then nudged Addison's legs apart with her knees. She could tell how turned on Addison was. She was shivering, and her body seemed to undulate by its own volition. Eleanor spread her knees, opening Addison's legs farther. Trembling with a need to be one with Addison again, to feel her trust Eleanor with her pleasure, she bent down so she could place her lips at Addison's ear.

"So sexy, so beautiful," she whispered hotly. "So wet that it will be so easy to fill you. Is that what you want too, darling?"

"Oh, damn, yes."

"Yes?" She circled Addison's entrance with her fingertips, lightly, lightly.

"Yes! Oh, please. Go inside. Please."

Her own sex clenching in anticipation, Eleanor slowly entered Addison with two fingers.

"More."

"More? Oh." Carefully, Eleanor added a third finger, and this was clearly just what Addison needed. Pushing her bottom up toward Eleanor, she impaled herself completely and then rocked back and forth in the most beautifully flowing movement Eleanor had ever seen. Mesmerized by the vision of how Addison moved with abandon, Eleanor bent forward again, straddled Addison's left thigh, and ground her swollen folds against her.

Addison got up on hands and knees and pushed back at Eleanor. "Ellie, oh, Ellie," she sobbed. "I love you. I love—what you—do."

Eleanor increased the pace and wrapped her arm around Addison's waist. She tugged her up against her, holding Addison in place as she moved them in unison. "Reach down and touch yourself," she murmured huskily. "Like you did that time we Skyped. You made me so horny just by squirming in front of your webcam, and I couldn't get enough of you, watching your flushed skin and the way you looked when you came."

Addison whimpered and pushed her fingers in between her legs. "Oh, fuck." She started shaking instantly. "I'm…I'm going t-to…ah! Ellie…" Bucking against the double onslaught of fingers, Addison cried out and came, flooding Eleanor's hand.

This made Eleanor push harder against Addison's hip, and she couldn't hold back the all-overpowering surge of pleasure that flooded her senses. Flames erupted, licked along her legs, up along her hips, and she convulsed over and over.

Eleanor managed to hold on to Addison and gently remove her fingers before they tumbled down against the pillows, spent and trying to catch their breath. Settling, they tugged the covers up and created a cocoon of sorts where Addison curled up on Eleanor's shoulder.

"I'm not too heavy, am I?" Addison peered up at her, still looking dazed.

"You're fine. Stay right where you are." Eleanor was finally relaxing, and she didn't think she could've moved even if a fire engulfed the building.

"Mmm-hmm. I was hoping you'd say that." Addison wrapped her arm around Eleanor. "I love you."

"I love you too, Addie. I hope I'll never ever give you any reason to doubt that."

"Same here."

They just lay there, holding each other, their breathing almost synchronized and, Eleanor had no doubt, their hearts in tandem as well. As passionate and filled with arousal as she'd been only moments ago, she now felt just as relaxed and safe in Addison's arms. Closing her eyes, Eleanor knew she would finally be able to sleep—at least until her love and desire for Addison roused her again.

❖

"The trick is to add some ice-cold mineral water to the batter." Addison held up a bottle of Pellegrino as evidence and Eleanor looked duly impressed, at least until she started chuckling where she sat perched on a stool on the other side of the kitchen island. "I don't think I'll be baking waffles in the morning any time soon, darling."

"Why do you keep a fully stocked kitchen with all these food items, not to mention all these machines? I mean, I'm expecting a robot to show up that's a high-end back-scratcher or something."

"Oh, you mean Sean the Butler 3.0? He turned out to be too frisky so I had to return him to the robot store."

Addison burst out laughing. Leaning against the counter, she howled at this unexpected joke. And there might just be more of this now that Eleanor was starting to be more relaxed around her. "Well, good thing you have me now, then. To scratch your back, I mean."

"Yes." The mischievous sparkle in Eleanor's eyes morphed into tenderness. "It's a very good thing."

Smiling at the woman she loved, Addison removed the waffles from the iron and placed them on a plate before pouring more batter on the hot surface. "Stacey can totally eat five or six of these. My limit is two or three, max."

"Where on earth does it go? She's so slender."

"All that freaking energy. You've only known her since the aneurysm made itself known. No doubt you'll get to see the full-speed-ahead Stacey once she's fully recuperated." Addison grinned happily. "That's just such an awesome thing to look forward to, even if the kid can talk your ears off."

"So I need to prepare myself for a chatty, energetic teenager to keep me on my toes?" Eleanor didn't look worried.

"That sounds like a logical conclusion. Stacey adores you. She isn't the reason I wanted to come here last night, but she helped me find the courage to face you."

Eleanor jumped off the stool and rounded the kitchen island. Pushing some errant tresses of hair from Addison's face, she kissed her lightly. "About that. I shouldn't have left it this long. I should've come to see you and sorted this out much sooner."

"I was a total ass about it though."

"And I wasn't very forthcoming. No wonder you were suspicious."

"But we're fine now?" The tiniest uncertainty lurked in Addison's voice.

"We're fine. I feel very safe, and quite wonderful, here with you. When I came home, this penthouse felt like a cold, luxurious prison. I wanted to go to your house in Newark and forget about this place."

"Is that your way of saying we're going to live our lives together in Newark? That might disappoint Stacey. I think she and Maureen are looking forward to life in the fast lane in Manhattan."

Eleanor had to laugh. "Oh, goodness. I can only imagine. Well, if they work hard at their respective college educations, I might be able to assist somehow regarding the Manhattan part, for instance helping with appropriate internships. I also have this strong need to be there for you and Stacey when it comes to her health situation. Now, as for life in the fast lane, I don't know about that. I plan to spend a lot of time in Newark in this cozy little house where the love of my life resides."

"You—you would stay there with me? With us?" Addison knew she was gaping, but that was unexpected.

"If you'd have me there with you, yes, absolutely. I really like your home, darling. And when we wanted, what was it? The fast lane? We would have this penthouse, or perhaps a townhouse on the Upper East Side or something. As long as we're together, I'm happy. When it comes to us I can't wish for anything else than that."

Hugging Eleanor, Addison buried her face at her neck. She understood exactly what Eleanor meant. As far as wishes went, she had what she desired right here in her arms.

EPILOGUE

Seven months later

"Welcome, everybody!" Eleanor stood by the microphone and, next to her, arm in arm, Addison was smiling broadly at the gathered guests and members of the press. She could barely believe that the day she'd worked so hard for the last eight months was finally here. When Eleanor had suggested she create her own brand, more affordable and geared toward the drugstores and supermarkets, she'd jumped at the chance.

"We are here to launch a new line for Face Exquisite and to launch a new makeup brand, The Blush Factor. Nothing about this would have been possible without the woman standing next to me, Addison Garr." Eleanor kissed Addison's cheek. "Help yourself to the gift baskets and, by all means, the buffet over there by the far wall."

They stepped away from the microphone while everybody applauded and walked toward Stacey and Maureen. "She looks fantastic," Eleanor murmured in Addison's ear, nodding toward Stacey. "Nobody can believe how sick she was only a few months ago."

"Thanks to you. Thanks to Dr. Stromberg and the staff at the PT clinic I could afford because I have you as a client." Addison refused to shed any tears on such a happy day, but she was close.

"She did far more for us, for *me*, than I'll ever be able to do for her." Eleanor's smile wobbled some as well. "Your sister is our very own angel, isn't she? She got us communicating again."

"She is and she did." Addison wrapped her arm around Eleanor's waist. "On the other hand, this, her first success, must've gone to her head. She seems to think she's got a future in matchmaking."

"Any chance we can steer her toward Broadway instead, now that she impressed the women from Chicory Ariose so much?"

"There's hope, I suppose. I'll never be able to thank her music teacher enough for making it possible to do half the glee-club shows as Elphaba after all. The other girl as well, who didn't mind giving up half the part, so to speak, when Stacey made such a fast recovery."

"I know. She's so talented, but I have a feeling she's after my job rather than Broadway. Maybe that at least can keep her away from matchmaking." Eleanor looked hopeful.

"Or maybe not."

"Oh, God." Eleanor chuckled. "Heaven help anyone single in sight. She's going to make everyone at Face Exquisite and The Blush Factor one happy family."

"You're laughing. You should know better by now. Stacey is a fighter. If she feels someone is acting against their own best interests, not to mention their heart, she'll move in on them…like this love missile or something."

"Well, she has my blessing. Might keep people focused on her and keep them off our backs a little bit."

Addison grew serious and stopped walking. "Has it been too horrible? I mean, have people meddled or been total jerks?" Worried, Addison focused only on the woman next to her.

"They wouldn't *dare*." Showing her teeth in a feral grin, Eleanor managed to scare off one of the board members who was on his way over with a congratulatory smile on his face. "I think by our conduct, by not apologizing or trying to hide, we've stumped those who rely on the shadows to dare to attack."

"Speaking of that," Addison murmured, lowering her voice.

"Of what? Attacking in the shadows?" Eleanor tilted her head.

"Mmm-hmm. Yes."

"You know what you do to me when you purr like that." Eleanor did her best to look stern.

Addison smiled as she lowered her voice another few pitches. "Oh, but you love when you make me purr...in the shadows, or in daylight. Just about any time of day, when I think about it."

"You're in for a world of trouble, darling," Eleanor said with a growl, maintaining her polite smile as she nodded to some new guests entering the foyer.

"Oh, babe, you say the sweetest things."

"And don't—call—me—babe."

"If you don't like it, I won't do it, sugarplum."

"Addison."

Laughing now, Addison offered Eleanor her arm. "Oh, okay, I'll be good. For now. Let's mingle and do our jobs. If we let Stacey have the entire playing field, she'll have them all married to each other before this year's over."

"God forbid." Eleanor glanced at Addison in a way that could only be described as adoring. "Then again, she's a clever girl with a lot of brilliant ideas."

"What?" Addison asked. "Stace? About what?"

"You said it yourself." Eleanor squeezed Addison's arm as they resumed walking. "Marriage."

About the Author

Gun Brooke resides in the countryside in Sweden with her very patient family. A retired neonatal intensive care nurse, she now writes full time, only rarely taking a break to create web sites for herself or others and to do computer graphics. Gun writes both romances and sci-fi.

Web site: www.gbrooke-fiction.com
Facebook: facebook.com/gunbach
Twitter: twitter.com/redheadgrrl1960
Tumblr: gunbrooke.tumblr.com/
Live Journal: redheadgrrl1960.livejournal.com/

Books Available from Bold Strokes Books

Wingspan by Karis Walsh. Wildlife biologist Bailey Chase is content to live at the wild bird sanctuary she has created on Washington's Olympic Peninsula until she is lured beyond the safety of isolation by architect Kendall Pearson. (978-1-60282-983-1)

Night Bound by Winter Pennington. Kass struggles to keep her head, her heart, and her relationships in order. She's still having a difficult time accepting being an Alpha female. But her wolf is certain of what she wants and she's intent on securing her power. (978-1-60282-984-8)

Slash and Burn by Valerie Bronwyn. The murder of a roundly despised author at a LGBT writer's conference in New Orleans turns Winter Lovelace's relaxing weekend hobnobbing with her peers into a nightmare of suspense—especially when her ex turns up. (978-1-60282-986-2)

The Blush Factor by Gun Brooke. Ice-cold business tycoon Eleanor Ashcroft only cares about the three P's—Power, Profit, and Prosperity—until young Addison Garr makes her doubt both that and the state of her frostbitten heart. (978-1-60282-985-5)

The Quickening: A Sisters of Spirits Novel by Yvonne Heidt. Ghosts, visions, and demons are all in a day's work for Tiffany. But when Kat asks for help on a serial killer case, life takes on another dimension altogether. (978-1-60282-975-6)

Windigo Thrall by Cate Culpepper. Six women trapped in a mountain cabin by a blizzard, stalked by an ancient cannibal demon bent on stealing their sanity—and their lives. (978-1-60282-950-3)

Smoke and Fire by Julie Cannon. Oil and water, passion and desire, a combustible combination. Can two women fight the fire that draws them together and threatens to keep them apart? (978-1-60282-977-0)

Asher's Fault by Elizabeth Wheeler. Fourteen-year-old Asher Price sees the world in black and white, much like the photos he takes, but when his little brother drowns at the same moment Asher experiences his first same-sex kiss, he can no longer hide behind the lens of his camera and eventually discovers he isn't the only one with a secret. (978-1-60282-982-4)

Love and Devotion by Jove Belle. KC Hall trips her way through life, stumbling into an affair with a married bombshell twice her age. Thankfully, her best friend, Emma Reynolds, is there to show her the true meaning of Love and Devotion. (978-1-60282-965-7)

Rush by Carsen Taite. Murder, secrets, and romance combine to create the ultimate rush. (978-1-60282-966-4)

The Shoal of Time by J.M. Redmann. It sounded too easy. Micky Knight is reluctant to take the case because the easy ones often turn into the hard ones, and the hard ones turn into the dangerous ones. In this one, easy turns hard without warning. (978-1-60282-967-1)

In Between by Jane Hoppen. At the age of 14, Sophie Schmidt discovers that she was born an intersexual baby and sets off on a journey to find her place in a world that denies her true existence. (978-1-60282-968-8)

Secret Lies by Amy Dunne. While fleeing from her abuser, Nicola Jackson bumps into Jenny O'Connor, and their unlikely friendship quickly develops into a blossoming romance—but when it comes down to a matter of life or death, are they both willing to face their fears? (978-1-60282-970-1)

Under Her Spell by Maggie Morton. The magic of love brought Terra and Athene together, but now a magical quest stands between them—a quest for Athene's hand in marriage. Will their passion keep them together, or will stronger magic tear them apart? (978-1-60282-973-2)

Homestead by Radclyffe. R. Clayton Sutter figures getting NorthAm Fuel's newest refinery operational on a rolling tract of land in Upstate New York should take a month or two, but then, she hadn't counted on local resistance in the form of vandalism, petitions, and one furious farmer named Tess Rogers. (978-1-60282-956-5)

Battle of Forces: Sera Toujours by Ali Vali. Kendal and Piper return to New Orleans to start the rest of eternity together, but the return of an old enemy makes their peaceful reunion short-lived, especially when they join forces with the new queen of the vampires. (978-1-60282-957-2)

How Sweet It Is by Melissa Brayden. Some things are better than chocolate. Molly O'Brien enjoys her quiet life running the bakeshop in a small town. When the beautiful Jordan Tuscana returns home, Molly can't deny the attraction—or the stirrings of something more. (978-1-60282-958-9)

The Missing Juliet: A Fisher Key Adventure by Sam Cameron. A teenage detective and her friends search for a kidnapped Hollywood star in the Florida Keys. (978-1-60282-959-6)

Amor and More: Love Everafter edited by Radclyffe and Stacia Seaman. Rediscover favorite couples as Bold Strokes Books authors reveal glimpses of life and love beyond the honeymoon in short stories featuring main characters from favorite BSB novels. (978-1-60282-963-3)

First Love by CJ Harte. Finding true love is hard enough, but for Jordan Thompson, daughter of a conservative president, it's challenging, especially when that love is a female rodeo cowgirl. (978-1-60282-949-7)

Pale Wings Protecting by Lesley Davis. Posing as a couple to investigate the abduction of infants, Special Agent Blythe Kent and Detective Daryl Chandler find themselves drawn into a battle over the innocents, with demons on one side and the unlikeliest of protectors on the other. (978-1-60282-964-0)

Mounting Danger by Karis Walsh. Sergeant Rachel Bryce, an outcast on the police force, is put in charge of the department's newly formed mounted division. Can she and polo champion Callan Lanford resist their growing attraction as they struggle to safeguard the disaster-prone unit? (978-1-60282-951-0)

Meeting Chance by Jennifer Lavoie. When man's best friend turns on Aaron Cassidy, the teen keeps his distance until fate puts Chance in his hands. (978-1-60282-952-7)

At Her Feet by Rebekah Weatherspoon. Digital marketing producer Suzanne Kim knows she has found the perfect love in her new mistress Pilar, but before they can make the ultimate commitment, Suzanne's professional life threatens to disrupt their perfectly balanced bliss. (978-1-60282-948-0)

Show of Force by AJ Quinn. A chance meeting between navy pilot Evan Kane and correspondent Tate McKenna takes them on a roller-coaster ride where the stakes are high, but the reward is higher: a chance at love. (978-1-60282-942-8)

Clean Slate by Andrea Bramhall. Can Erin and Morgan work through their individual demons to rediscover their love for each other, or are the unexplainable wounds too deep to heal? (978-1-60282-943-5)

Hold Me Forever by D. Jackson Leigh. An investigation into illegal cloning in the quarter horse racing industry threatens to destroy the growing attraction between Georgia debutante Mae St. John and Louisiana horse trainer Whit Casey. (978-1-60282-944-2)

Trusting Tomorrow by PJ Trebelhorn. Funeral director Logan Swift thinks she's perfectly happy with her solitary life devoted to helping others cope with loss until Brooke Collier moves in next door to care for her elderly grandparents. (978-1-60282-891-9)

Forsaking All Others by Kathleen Knowles. What if what you think you want is the opposite of what makes you happy? (978-1-60282-892-6)

Exit Wounds by VK Powell. When Officer Loane Landry falls in love with ATF informant Abigail Mancuso, she realizes that nothing is as it seems—not the case, not her lover, not even the dead. (978-1-60282-893-3)

Dirty Power by Ashley Bartlett. Cooper's been through hell and back, and she's still broke and on the run. But at least she found the twins. They'll keep her alive. Right? (978-1-60282-896-4)

The Rarest Rose by I. Beacham. After a decade of living in her beloved house, Ele disturbs its past and finds her life being haunted by the presence of a ghost who will show her that true love never dies. (978-1-60282-884-1)

Code of Honor by Radclyffe. The face of terror is hard to recognize—especially when it's homegrown. The next book in the Honor series. (978-1-60282-885-8)

Does She Love You? by Rachel Spangler. When Annabelle and Davis find out they are both in a relationship with the same woman, it leaves them facing life-altering questions about trust, redemption, and the possibility of finding love in the wake of betrayal. (978-1-60282-886-5)

The Road to Her by KE Payne. Sparks fly when actress Holly Croft, star of UK soap Portobello Road, meets her new on-screen love interest, the enigmatic and sexy Elise Manford. (978-1-60282-887-2)

Shadows of Something Real by Sophia Kell Hagin. Trying to escape flashbacks and nightmares, ex-POW Jamie Gwynmorgan stumbles into the heart of former Red Cross worker Adele Sabellius and uncovers a deadly conspiracy against everything and everyone she loves. (978-1-60282-889-6)

Date with Destiny by Mason Dixon. When sophisticated bank executive Rashida Ivey meets unemployed blue collar worker Destiny Jackson, will her life ever be the same? (978-1-60282-878-0)

The Devil's Orchard by Ali Vali. Cain and Emma plan a wedding before the birth of their third child while Juan Luis is still lurking, and as Cain plans for his death, an unexpected visitor arrives and challenges her belief in her father, Dalton Casey. (978-1-60282-879-7)